THE COURT OF A THOUSAND SUNS

ALLAN COLE and CHRIS BUNCH

A Del Rey Book

BALLANTINE BOOKS • NEW YORK

A Del Rey Book
Published by Ballantine Books

Library of Congress Catalog Card Number: 85-91154

ISBN 0-345-31681-9

Manufactured in the United States of America

First Edition: January 1986
Second Printing: February 1989

Cover Art by David B. Mattingly

AFTER-DINNER MINCE

"It's a gurion!"

The thing was closing on the skiff so quickly it seemed to be walking on the water.

Alex desperately tried to turn the clumsy boat, but it just whirled freely on its axis as if on ice. Sten grabbed for a pole and, as the creature rose to its full height and hurled a huge stomach-mouth at them, he heard the sound of another one approaching from behind.

He rammed the pole straight into the first gurion's maw. The tip of the pole splintered and gave as it speared past the concentric rows of teeth into soft flesh. The gurion howled but continued its rush, lifting the skiff upward and slamming it over.

Then a thick arm clasped Alex's body and dragged him under...

By Allan Cole and Chris Bunch
Published by Ballantine Books:

The STEN Adventures:
   STEN
   THE WOLF WORLDS
   THE COURT OF A THOUSAND SUNS
   FLEET OF THE DAMNED
   REVENGE OF THE DAMNED

A RECKONING FOR KINGS

To
Elizabeth R. & Leo L. Bunch
And
The brothers four: Charles, Phillip, Drew,
and David

Note

The titles of Books 1, 2, 3, and 4 are Parisian slang for various parts of the guillotine. The "bascule" is the board on which the condemned man is laid; the "lunette" is the circular clamp fitted around the man's neck; the "mouton" is the cutting blade, plus its eighty-pound weight; and the "declic" is the lever the executioner hits to drop the blade.

The title of Book 5, "The Red Mass," comes from a phrase used by a French deputy during the Terror of the A.D. 1790s, one Monsieur Amar, in a letter inviting his fellow deputies to witness an execution "to see the Red Mass celebrated..."

—AC and CRB

BOOK ONE

BASCULE

CHAPTER ONE

THE BANTH PURRED at the quillpig, which, unimpressed, had firmly stuffed itself as far as it could into the hollow stump.

The banth's instinct said that the porcupine was edible, but the six-legged cat's training told it otherwise. Meat was presented by two-legs at dawn and dusk, and came with gentle words. The quillpig may have smelled right, but it was not behaving like meat. The banth sat back on its haunches and used a forepaw to pry two needles from its nasal carapace.

Then the animal flattened. It heard the noise again, a whine from the forest. The banth looked worriedly up the mountain, then back again in the direction of the sound before deciding.

Against instinct, it broke out of the last fringe of the tree line and bounded up the bare, rock-strewn mountain. Two hundred meters vertically up the talus cliff, it went to cover behind a mass of boulders.

The whine grew louder as a gravsled lifted over the scrubby treetops, pirouetted, searching, and then grounded near the hollow stump.

Terence Kreuger, chief of Prime World's police tactical force, checked the homing panel mounted over the grav-sled's controls. The needle pointed straight up the mountain, and the proximity director indicated the banth was barely half a kilometer away.

Kreuger unslung a projectile weapon from its clips behind his seat and checked it once again: projectile chambered; safe off; ranging scope preset for one meter, the approximate dimensions of the banth's chest area.

He checked the slope with a pair of binocs and after a few seconds saw a flicker of movement. Kreuger grunted to himself and lifted the gravsled up the mountain. He'd already missed the banth once that day; he was less than pleased with himself.

Kreuger fancied himself a hunter in the grand tradition. Time not required for his police duties was spent hunting or preparing himself for a hunt, an expensive hobby, especially on Prime World. The Imperial capital had no native game, and both hunting preserves there charged far more than even a tactical group chief could afford—until recently.

Kreuger's previous hunts had been restricted to offworld, and mostly for minor edible or nuisance game. That was well and good, but provided Kreuger with little in the way of trophies, especially trophies of the kind that the gamebooks chronicled. But things had suddenly become different. His friends had seen to that. After thirty years as a cop, Kreuger still prized his honesty. He just rationalized that what his new friends wanted wasn't dishonest: look at the benefits! Three weeks away from Empire Day madness. Three weeks on a hunting reservation, expenses paid. Tags for four dangerous animals— an Earth rhino, a banth, a male cervi, and a giant ot.

He had already planned on which wall each head would be mounted. Of course, Kreuger did not intend to mention to his soon-to-be-admiring friends *where* those trophies had been taken.

The gravsled's bumper caromed him away from a boulder, bringing Kreuger back to the present. Concentrate, man, concentrate. Remember every bit of this day. The clearness of the air. The smell of the trees below. The spray of dust around the gravsled.

Kreuger guided the gravsled up the slope, following the homing needle toward the sensor implanted in the banth.

Below, a second, one-man sled coasted through the

trees. Clyff Tarpy did not need binocs to follow Kreuger's sled. Contour-following, he lifted his sled after Kreuger.

The banth was cornered.

Ahead of him to the right, the ground fell away steeply, too steeply for even his clawed legs to descend. To the left was a sheer cliff. The banth huddled behind a boulder, puzzling.

Kreuger's gravsled landed just outside the nest. Weapon ready, Kreuger moved forward.

Again, the banth was perplexed. The whine had been the cause of a loud explosion and searing pain earlier, the pain that sent the banth fleeing through the forest toward the mountains.

But the smell was two-legs. Two-legs, but not familiar. Had the banth done something wrong? The two-legs would tell him, feed him, and then return him to the warmth of his pen.

The banth stood and walked forward.

Kreuger's projectile weapon came up as the banth walked into view. No errors now. Safety off, he aimed.

The banth mewed. This was not his two-legs.

"Bastard!"

Kreuger spun, the banth momentarily forgotten. He had not heard the second gravsled land behind him.

From five meters, the barrel of the weapon was enormous. Tarpy allowed just enough time to pass for terror to replace the bewilderment on Kreuger's face. And then he fingered the stud. The soft metal round expanded nicely as it penetrated Kreuger's sternum, then pinwheeled through the tac chief's rib cage into his heart. Kreuger, instantly dead, sat down on a small boulder before slowly toppling forward onto his face.

Tarpy smiled as he took a thick chunk of soyasteak from his beltpak and tossed it to the banth. "Eight lives to go, pussycat."

Tarpy took a small aerosol can from his pak, and, backing up, erased his footsteps from the dusty rock. He paused by Kreuger's gravsled long enough to shut the power off and disconnect the beacon. The longer it took to find the body, the better. Tarpy mounted his own sled and nudged it back down the hill.

The banth's tail whipped back and forth once. He did not like the smell from the strange two-legs. He picked up the slab of soyasteak, sprang over the rock wall, and went back down the mountain. He would eat on the ground he was familiar with, and then perhaps unravel the puzzle of the other soyasteak, the one with needles that walked.

CHAPTER TWO

THE MAN IN the blue boiler suit had his long knife against the throat of Admiral Mik Ledoh. With his other hand, he forced the Eternal Emperor's Grand Chamberlain closer to the edge of the battlements.

"Either our demands are met immediately, or this man dies!" His amplified voice echoed across the castle's stonework, down the 700 meters of emptiness and across the parade ground.

One hundred meters below and to the right, Sten checked his foot/handholds. His clawed fingers were barely clinging to mortar notches in the stone. One foot dangled over emptiness, the other was firmly braced on the face of Havildar-Major Lalbahadur Thapa. Sten's willygun was slung from a clip-strap on his dark brown combat suit. Snapped to one arm was a can of climbing thread. At its end was a grapnel.

From above them the terrorist's voice came again: "You have only seconds left to reach your decision and save this man's life!"

Sten's left hand went up and out, stretching for a new hold. At first he thought he had it, then the mortar crumbled and he almost came off. Sten forced his body away from its instinctive clutch at the wall, then inhaled deeply.

"Kaphar hunnu bhanda marnu ramro," came the pained mutter from Lalbahadur below him.

"But cowards live longer, dammit!" Sten managed as he one-handed out, lifting both feet clear. Then his climbing boots found a hold, and Sten was momentarily secure. Breath . . . breath . . . and he once again became a climbing machine. Below him, Lalbahadur and the rest of the Gurkha platoon moved steadily up the vertical granite wall toward the two men above them.

Five meters below the parapet. Sten found a stance—a protruding knob of rock. He touched the second can of climbing thread attached to the swiss seat around his waist, and a spidery white line spat out, touched the rock facing, and bonded to it.

Sten motioned outward then toward his waist, signaling that he was secure and could belay the rest of the troops below him. From a third can, on the rear of his harness, a thread descended to the Gurkhas below.

Lalbahadur came up into position, on a single line to Sten's immediate right.

Sten pain no attention. He touched the nozzle of the thread can on his arm, and allowed about fifteen meters of thread, the grapnel at the end, to reel out. He freed one hand from the wall and weaseled it into the thread glove clipped to a carabinier sling, then began rhythmically swinging the grapnel back and forth. Suddenly he cast upward.

The twenty-gram-weight grapnel flickered upward and then caught, spinning twice around the muzzle of an archaic cannon which protruded from the crenellation above him.

Sten clipped his special jumars on the thread and snaked upward while the man in the boiler suit was staring out, into the lights. He never saw Sten lizard up, past the cannon and onto the battlement.

"We have waited for enough time," the voice boomed, on cue. The knife arm came back for the fatal stroke, and Sten came out of the shadows low, coming straight up, one clawed hand slamming into the man's face and a blocking hand snapping into the knife.

The man in the boiler suit staggered away, and the Chamberlain tottered for a minute on the edge of emptiness, then caught his footing. The man with the knife recovered, long blade ready.

But Sten was already inside his attack, double-fisted hands swinging. The strike caught the terrorist on the side of his head, and he dropped limply.

Behind the battlements, the other terrorists spun toward the threat. But they were far too late. The Gurkhas swarmed up from the darkness and came in, 30-cm kukri blades glittering in the spots. And, once again, the cry "Ayo Gurkhali" rang around the castle, a battle cry that had made thousands of generations of violent men reconsider their intentions.

To a man, the terrorists were down.

Lalbahadur checked the downed men to ensure they were, indeed, out. Naik Thaman Gurung unslung the rocket mortar from his back and positioned it. Sten nodded, and the mortar bloomed fire as the round lofted up, out into blackness, and then curvetted down to thud onto the parade ground far below.

Gurung bonded the line that ran back from the mortar, impacted far below in the parade ground to a battlement, then grinned at Sten. "We barang now, Captain."

"Platoon up," Sten shouted. "By numbers—*move!*"

The first to go was Thaman. He attached jumar clamps to the thread that reached more than 700 meters down to the parade ground, swung his feet up, and was off, whistling down the near-invisible thread to safety.

Sten saluted the Chamberlain. "Sir."

Admiral Ledoh grimaced, shoved the ceremonial cocked hat more firmly on his head, took the pair of jumars Sten handed him, and then he, too, disappeared down the thread.

Sten was the next to go, freewheeling off the tiny clamps toward the solid concrete ground. He braked at the last minute, took his hands from the jumar handles, hit, and rolled twice.

Behind him, Lalbahadur and the others descended the thread, hit, recovered, and doubled into platoon formation. Admiral Ledoh, a bit breathless, took two steps forward and saluted. Above him, the Eternal Emperor applauded. Following his cue, the half a million spectators filling the grandstands that lined the five-kilometer-long parade ground broke into cheers—applauding as much for the "terrorists," who were taking *their* bows high above, as the Gurkhas, Ledoh, and Sten.

Ledoh broke his salute and puffed toward the steps that led to the Imperial stand. By the time he'd made it into the stand itself, the Emperor had a drink waiting for him. After Ledoh shuddered the alcohol down, the Emperor asked with a grin, "Who had the idea of that stupid hat?"

"I did, Your Majesty."

"Uh-huh," the Emperor snickered. "Howinhell'd you hold it on down that Slide for Life?"

"A superior, water soluble glue."

"It had better be. No way am I going to live with that—that—bedpan attached to the head of someone I must see every day." Without waiting for a response, he added, "Have another drink Mik, for godsakes! It isn't every day you play Tarzan."

The second order was followed quickly and thankfully.

The Emperor was celebrating an invention of his own. Empire Day.

He'd begun the ceremony more than 500 years earlier to celebrate winning a war that he'd since forgotten.

The premise was simple: Once a year, every year, all Imperial Forces put on a display, on whatever world they happened to be assigned to, with everyone welcome.

There was, of course, more purpose to Empire Day than just a parade. There was a second or tertiary purpose to almost everything the Eternal Emperor did. Not only did the display of armed might reassure the citizens of the Empire that they were Protected and Defended, but also, Empire Day served to discourage potential Bad Guys from developing Evil Schemes, at least toward Imperial Interests.

The most massive display on Empire Day occurred on Prime World. Over the years, Empire Day had become the culmination of a two-week-long celebration of athletics and the arts as well as of military might. It was a cross between Saturnalia, Oktoberfest, the Olympics, and May Day. For that one night, the Imperial palace was thrown open to everyone, which by itself was a major encouragement.

The Emperor's main residence and command center on Prime World, the palace, was set in a fifty-five-kilometer-diameter circle of gardens. The fifty-five-kilometer measure was significant, since that was the line-of-sight horizon limit on Prime. The Emperor was not fond of stumbling across people whose presence he had not planned on.

At the center of the circle of manicured and wildly varying parklands was the main palace itself, possibly the ultimate motte-and-bailey design, occupying an area six by two kilometers.

The "bailey" consisted of high, fifty-degree-banked walls that vauban-vee-ed back and forth, from the main entrance gate toward the palace itself. The walls were 200 meters high, and buried within was a high percentage of the Emperor's bureaucracy. They were not entirely nuke-proof, but it would take direct hits to wipe out the structure, and the Emperor could continue operations even if his palace was completely sealed off; decades worth of food, air, and water were tanked below the walls for his staff.

The palace itself, a large-scale copy of Earth's Arundel Castle, stood at the far end of the five-kilometer-long parade ground that made up the center of the bailey.

Even more so than the bailey walls, the castle had been built on the iceberg principal. Imperial command barracks/living quarters tunneled underground below the castle itself for more than 2,000 meters.

The castle was faced with huge stone blocks behind which were nuclear-blast shielding, and meters of insulation. The Emperor liked the look of Earth-medieval, but preferred the safety and comfort provided by science.

The palace was open to the general public on Empire Day, when huge Imperial Guard gravlighters carried the tourists in. During the remainder of the year, only palace employees boarded a high-speed pneumosubway thirty-four kilometers away in Fowler, and were blasted to their duty stations.

Since attendance at Empire Day on Prime World was roughly akin to being presented at Court, the Emperor had figured out long ago that many more millions of his people would want to go than there was space for. So he'd set up attendance much like what he'd described to an uncomprehending official as a "three-ring circus." Nearest to the castle were the most desirable seats. These the Emperor allowed to be assigned to Court Favorites, Current Heroes, Social Elitists, and so forth.

The second "ring," and there was no easy way to tell where the dividing line was, went to the social climbers. Those seats could be sold, scalped, threatened for, and otherwise acquired by those people who knew that seeing Empire Day on Prime World was the culmination of their entire life.

The third area, farthest from the Imperial reviewing stand itself, was carefully allotted to Prime World residents. Of course, many of these tickets ended up in the hands of outworlders rather than in those of the Prime Worlders they'd been assigned to, but the Emperor felt that if "local folks" wanted to make a credit or two, he certainly had no objections.

Seating was on bleachers that were installed weeks before the ceremony, on the banked walls of the bailey that surrounded the parade ground.

Technically, it didn't matter where the attendees sat; huge holographic screens rose at regular intervals atop the walls, giving the spectators access to instant close-ups as well as to occasional cut-arounds to those people in the "first circle" who were somehow Noteworthy.

Some events, such as Sten's "rescue," were only held at the far end of the parade ground, next to the castle itself. But most were set up to run continuously, down each area to an eventual exit at the far end of the parade ground.

Empire Day was the most spectacular staged event of the year. The Court still proclaimed itself the Court of a Thousand Suns, even though the Empire numbered far more systems than that, and Empire Day was when those suns shone most brightly.

It was also a night on which anything might happen...

Wheezing, Sten leaned against the wall of the concrete tunnel—a tunnel normally sealed by heavy collapsed-steel blast doors. Now the doors were raised to permit the Empire Day participants entry onto the parade ground.

Beside him, panting more sedately, was Havildar-Major Lalbahadur Thapa. The other Gurkhas had been praised and dismissed, to spend, for them, a far more enjoyable evening devoted to gambling and massive consciousness-alteration by whatever substances they chose.

"That was a famous display," Lalbahadur grunted.

"Yuh," Sten said.

"I am sure that, should any evil man desire to hold our Chamberlain for ransom, he will never do it on the edge of this castle."

Sten grinned. In the three months he'd commanded the Emperor's Own Gurkha Bodyguard, he'd learned that the Nepalese sense of humor matched his own, most especially in its total lack of respect toward superior officers. "You're cynical. This has given us much honor."

"That is true. But what puzzles me is that one time I made my ablution in one hand, and waited for the other hand to fill up with honor." Lalbahadur mocked sadness. "There was no balance.

"At least there is one thing," Lalbahadur brightened. "Our heroism will be shown to the parbitayas back home, and we shall have no trouble finding new fools who want to climb walls for the glory of the Emperor."

Sten's comeback was broken off as a band crashed into noise behind him. The officer and the noncom straightened as the Honor Guard of the Emperor's Own Prae-

torians thundered forward. Sten and Lalbahadur saluted
the colors, then shrank back against the wall as the
600-plus men of the palace guard, all polished leather,
gleaming metal, and automata, slammed past.

At the head of the formation the Praetorian's commanding officer, Colonel Den Fohlee, ramrodded a salute
back at Sten, then snapped his eyes forward as the honor
unit wheeled out onto the parade ground, to be met with
cheers.

"My father once told me," Lalbahadur observed, "that
there are only two kinds of men in the world. Normally,
I do not listen to such nonsense, since it is my thought
that the only two kinds of men in the world are those who
see only two kinds of men in the world and those who
do not." He stopped, slightly confused.

"Two kinds of men, your father said," Sten prompted.

"Yes. There are those who love to polish metal and
leather and there are those who would rather drink.
Captain, to which group do you belong?"

"Pass, Havildar," Sten said with regret. "I'm still on
duty."

Sten and the noncom saluted, then the small, stocky
man doubled off. Sten had a few minutes before guard
check, so he walked to the end of the tunnel to watch the
Praetorians parade.

They were very, very good, as befits any group of men
and women whose sole duties and training consisted in
total devotion to their leaders, an ability to stand motionless for hours on guard, and colorful ceremonious pirouet-
ting.

Sten was being unfair, but the few times he'd been told
off for parade duties, he'd found it a pain in the mouli-
nette. Parading soldiers may be interesting to some types,
but those people could never have spent the endless dull
hours of shining and rehearsal that a parade takes.

Although Sten had to admit that the Praetorians were
highly skilled. They paraded with archaic projectile weapons; the stubby, efficient willygun wasn't spectacular
enough for any manual of arms. And the willygun had no
provision for a bayonet. By the fortieth century, the ben-

efits of mounting a can opener on the end of a rifle were long gone, save for ceremonial purposes.

And so the Praetorians jerked to and fro in intricate array with near-four-foot-long rifles.

The soldiers initially had their weapons at the shoulder. On count, the weapons came down to waist-carry, the bayonets gleaming before them like so many spears.

Marching in extended order, on command, each rank would wheel and march back toward the next rank's lowered bayonets. Sten winced to think what would happen if a noncom missed a beat in the continual chant of commands.

The unit pivoted back on itself, then wheel-turned in ranks. By chant, they began a progressive manual of arms; as each line's boots would crash against the tarmac, that rank would move from carry arms to port arms to shoulder arms to reverse shoulder arms.

Simultaneously, squads broke apart and began doing by-the-count rifle tosses—continuing the progressive manual, but after the shoulder arms command each soldier would pitch his weapon straight up and backward, to be caught by the next person in ranks.

Sten, watching with give-me-strength cynicism, had never studied history enough to have met the old line: "It's pretty, but is it war?"

CHAPTER THREE

CERTAIN BEINGS EVERYONE loves on first sight: They seem to live on a slightly higher plane than all others. And yet those noble ones find an echo of themselves in all other living things. They see life as art, so therefore can be somewhat pretentious. Yet they also mock their own pretensions.

Marr and his lover, Senn, were two such beings, twittering superlatives over the Praetorian Guard.

"My, what lusty fellows," Marr said. "All those muscles and musk. Almost makes a creature want to be human."

"You wouldn't know what to do with even *one* of them if you were," Senn sniffed. "I should know. It certainly has been a long time since you tried your wicked way with me."

"I was merely admiring those wonderful young men. They please the eye. Nothing to do with sex. A subject you always seem to have on the cranium."

"Oh, gonads. Let's not fight, Marr, dear. It's a party. And you know how I *love* a party."

Senn softened. Perhaps he *was* behaving like an off-cycle human. He leaned closer to Marr and let their antennae twine. Parties always got to him, too.

In fact, there were very few beings in the Empire who knew more about parties than Senn and Marr. Celebrations of all kinds were their speciality—a little glitter, a little tack, interesting personalities tossed into a conversational salad. Their official function on Prime World was that of *the* Imperial Caterers. They were always deploring the fact that the Eternal Emperor's get-togethers put them in the red. They were, however, much too good businessbeings to deplore too loudly; the Emperor's "custom" was the reason their catering service was booked years in advance.

In an age not generally known for permanent bondings, the two Milchen stood out. They had been sexually paired for more than a century and were passionately determined that the relationship should go on for a century more. However, such stability was not unusual in their species; for the Milchen of Frederick Two, pairing was literally for life—when one member of a Milchen pair died, the other would always follow within a few days. Long-term pairings among the Milchen were always of the same sex. For want of a better description, call it male. The other gender—put the "female" label on it, it's easier—was called Ursoolas. Of all things in the many universes, the Ursoolas were among the most beautiful and delicate, beings of gossamer and many-changing perfumed colors. They lived only a few short months, and during that time it was all loving and sexual intensity. If a Milchen male pair was fortunate, it might enjoy two or three such relationships in its lifetime. Out of each bonding came a "male" pair and half-a-dozen dormant Ursoolas. The mother would whisper a few last loving words to her broadsac and then die, leaving the care of the young to the father pair.

For the Milchen, life was a never-ending breeding-cycle tragedy, that bred the kind of loneliness that can kill a loving race. And so they evolved the only system open to them—same-sex bonding. Like most of their people, Marr and Senn were passionately devoted to each other, and to all other things of beauty.

They were slender creatures, a meter or so high, and covered with a downy, golden fur. They had enormous liquid-black eyes that enjoyed twice the spectrum of a human's. Their heads were graced with sensitive smelling antennae that could also caress like a feather. Their small monkeylike hands contained the Empire's most sensitive tastebuds, and were largely the reason for Milchen's being among the Empire's greatest chefs. The Eternal Emperor himself grudgingly admitted they surpassed all other races in the preparation of fine meals. Except, of course, for chile.

The two Milchen cuddled closer and drank in the ultimate spectacle that was Empire Day. Busybodies that the Milchen were, the beings around them were at least as interesting to them as the Imperial display.

Marr's eyes swept the VIP boxes. "Everyone, but *everyone* is here."

"I noticed," Senn sniffed. "Including a few who ought not to be."

He pointed to a box across from them as an example— the box that held Kai Hakone and his party. "After the reviews of his last masque, I don't know how he can even hold up his pate in public."

Marr giggled. "I know. Isn't it delicious? And the silly fool is such a bore, he even agreed to be the guest of honor at our *party*."

Senn snuggled closer in delight. "I can hardly wait! The blood will flow, flow, flow."

Marr gave his pairmate a suspicious look. "What did you do, Senn? Or dare I ask?"

Senn laughed. "I also invited his critics."

"And?"

"They were delighted. They'll all be there."

The two chuckled over their evil little joke, and glanced at Hakone again, wondering if he suspected what was in store for him in few short days.

Marr and Senn would have been disappointed. Kai Hakone, a man some people called the greatest author of his day—and others the greatest hack—wasn't even thinking of the party.

Around him were a dozen or more fans, all very rich and very fawning. A constant stream of exotic dishes and drinks flowed in and out of the box. But it was hardly a party. Even before the celebration had begun, everyone had realized that Hakone was in "one of those moods." And so the conversation was subdued, and there were many nervous glances at the brooding master, an enormous man with unfashionably bulging muscles, a thick shock of unruly hair, heavy eyebrows, and deep-set eyes.

Hakone's gut was tightening, his every muscle was tense, and he was perspiring heavily. His mind and mood was ricocheting wildly. Everything is ready, he would think one minute, and his spirits would soar. But what if there's a mistake? Gloom would descend. What has been left undone? I should have done that myself. I shouldn't have let them do it. I should have done it.

And on and on, as he went over and over each detail of the plan. Thunder arose from the crowd as another spectacular event crashed to its conclusion; Kai Hakone barely heard it. He touched his hands together a few times, pretending to join in the applause. But his mind churned on with constantly changing images of death.

The last of the marching bands and dancers cleared the field, and the crowd slowly chattered its way into semisilence.

Two huge gravsleds whined through the end gates—gravsleds loaded with steel shrouding, lifting blocks, and ropes. They hummed slowly down the field, each only a meter from the ground, halting at frequent intervals. At each pause, sweating fatigue-clad soldiers jumped off the sleds and unloaded some of the shrouding or blocks. Ropes and cables were piled beside each assemblage. By the time the gravsled stopped next to the Imperial reviewing stand, the long field looked as if a child had scattered his building blocks across it. Or, as was the case, an obstacle course had been improvised.

As the sleds lifted up over the castle itself, two large targets—solid steel backing, plus three-meter-thick padding—were lowered from the castle walls to dangle 400 meters above the field. Then six bands marched in through gates and blasted into sound. Some military-trivia types knew the tune was the official Imperial Artillery marching song, but none of them knew the tune itself was an old, bawdy song sometimes titled "Cannoneers have Hairy Ears."

Two smaller gravsleds then entered the parade ground

through the gates. Each carried twenty beings and a cannon. The cannons weren't the gigantic combat masers or the small but highly lethal laserblasts the Imperial Artillery actually used. The wheeled cannons—mountain guns—were only slightly less ancient than the black-powder, muzzle-loading cannons staring down from the battlements.

After the forty men had unloaded the two mountain guns, they doubled into formation and froze. The leader of each group snapped to a salute and held it as a gunpowder weapon on the castle battlements boomed and a white cloud spread over the parade ground. Then the forty cannoneers began.

The event was variously called "artillery competition," "cannon carry," or "impressive silliness." The object of the competition between the two teams was fairly simple. Each team was to maneuver one mountain gun from where it sat, through the obstacles, to a site near the Imperial stand. There it was to be loaded, aimed at one of the targets, and fired. The first team to complete the exercise and strike the target won.

No antigrav devices were allowed, nor was it permitted to run around the obstacles. Instead, each gun had to be disassembled and then carried/hoisted/levered/thrown over the blocks. The competition required gymnastic skills. Since each team was moving somewhat over a thousand kilograms of metal, the chances of crushed body parts was very high. Nevertheless, qualification for the Cannon Carry Teams was intense among Imperial Artillerymen.

That year the competition was of particular interest; for the first time the finals were not between two of the Guards Divisions. Instead, one team of nonhumans, from the XVIII Planetary Landing Force, would challenge the top-ranked men and women of the Third Guards Division.

Another reason for spectator interest, of course, was that the cannon carry was one Empire Day event that could be bet on. Official odds were unusual: eight to five in favor of the Third Guards. However, actual betting ran somewhat differently. Prime World humans felt that the nonhumans, the N'Ranya, were underdogs, and preferred to invest their credits accordingly, non-humanoids felt somewhat differently; preferring to back the favorites.

Sometimes the gods back the sentimental. The N'Ranya were somewhat anthropoidal and weighed in at about 300 kilos apiece. Plus, their race, having developed as tree-dwelling carnivores on a jungle world, had an instinctual eye for geometry and trigonometry.

Working against the N'Ranya was a long tradition of How a Cannon Carry Should Work. The drill went as follows for the Guardsmen: The gun captain took the sight off, doubled to the first obstacle. Waiting for him there were two men who'd already secured the gun's aiming stakes. They literally pitched the gun captain and sight to the top of the wall. He helped his two men up, then went on toward the second obstacle.

By this time the gun had been disassembled into barrel/trail/carriage/recoil mechanism and was at the foot of that wall. Ropes were thrown to the first two men, and they became human pulleys and the guns went up the wall. Other men free-scaled that wall, grabbed the guns, and eased them down to the other side.

The N'Ranya, however, were more simple. They figured that two N'Ran could lug each component, and worked accordingly. Each part of the gun was bodily carried to the obstacle and "thrown" to two more N'Ran who waited at the top. Then it was dropped to two more on the far side.

And so it went, clever teamwork against brute force. The N'Ran moved ahead on the net lift, since the carrying N'Ran, without bothering to hand off their parts, simply swarmed up and over the net.

The Guards, on the other hand, went into the lead on the steel spider by uniquely levering the skeleton structure *up* and moving the cannon underneath it.

By the time the two teams staggered over the last obstacle and began putting the gun back together, the Guards team was clearly ahead by seconds.

The N'Ran barely had their cannon assembled when the Guards gun captain slammed the sight onto his gun and powder monkeys slotted the charge into the breech.

All that was needed for the Guards team to win was for the aiming stakes to be emplaced and the gun laid and then fired. Obviously this competition fired somewhat out of "real" sequence.

And then the N'Ran altered the rules. The gun captain ignored the sightstakes, etc., and bore-sighted the gun. He moved his head aside as the round was thrown home, then free-estimated elevation. The N'Ranya dove out of the way as their gun captain toggled off the round. It hit dead center in the target.

Protests were lodged, of course, but eventually the bookies grudgingly paid off on the N'Ranya champions.

At the same time, orders were circulated within the Guards Divisions that recruiters specializing in artillery would be advised to spend time on the N'Ranya worlds.

Tanz Sullamora wasn't happy with things, especially since his Patriotic Duty had just cost him a small bundle.

When he'd heard that for the first time ETs were to be permitted to compete in the cannon carry, he'd been appalled. He did not feel that it was good Imperial policy to allow nonhumanoids to be publicly humiliated on Empire Day.

His second shock was finding that Prime World betting was heavily on the N'Ranya. Patriotism required Sullamora to back the Guards team. It was not the loss of credits, Sullamora rationalized. It was that the contest had been unfair. The N'Ranya were jungle dwellers, predators just one step above cannibals. Of course they had an unfair advantage. Certainly they would be better at carrying heavy weights and so forth. The Emperor had better realize, Sullamora sulked, that while nonhumanoids were a necessary part of the Empire, they certainly should understand how far down the ladder of status they were.

Which inexorably brought to Sullamora's mind where he was sitting. After all he'd done for the Empire, from charitable contributions to funding patriotic art to assisting the Court itself, why had he not been invited to the Imperial box for Empire Day? Or even assigned a box that was close to the Imperial stand, instead of being far down the first circle, almost in the second-class area?

The Emperor, Sullamora thought, was beginning to change, and change in a manner that, the merchant thought righteously, was indicative of the growing corruption of the Empire itself.

Tanz Sullamora was certainly not enjoying Empire Day.

Of course, one major set piece was always planned for Empire Day. And, of course, each year it had to be bigger and better than the previous year's.

Fortunately the current celebration didn't have much to worry about. The previous year, the set piece had been assigned to the Eighth Guards Division, who planned to display the fighting prowess of the individual infantryman.

To that end, McLean units were taken off gravsleds, half powered, and lightened to the point that a unit could be hidden in one soldier's combat rucksack. The end result—a flying man; flying sans suit or lifebelt.

In rehearsal it looked quite impressive.

The plan was for the Eighth Guards to pull one massive Swoop, with each soldier functioning as a cross between a tiny tacship and a crunchie.

The Eighth Guards, however, forgot to check on the weather. Prime World was windy. And the normal twenty-gusting-to-thirty winds that blew across the parade field were magnified by the enormous ground's own weather effects. The end result was many, many grunts' being blown into the stands in disarray—not bad for them, since many made valuable instant friends—some bruised egos and bodies in the second area of seating, and an enormous gust of laughter from the Emperor.

That gust of laughter blew the Eighth Guards to the Draconian Sector, where they were spending morose tours keeping that group of dissident pioneer worlds in something approaching coherence.

This year, it was Twelfth Guards' turn in the barrel. And, after she spent considerable time in thought, the commanding General found a unique way to do a massive display. Laser blasts lanced into the arena and ricocheted from pre-positioned surfaces to bounce harmlessly into the atmosphere. Explosions roared and boomed. And then elements of the Twelfth Guards fought their way back into the arena.

The Emperor nodded approvingly; very seldom had he seen anybody schedule a fighting *retreat* for display.

Antennas went up, and signalmen began flashing. From over the horizon tacships snarled and realistically strafed the area just behind the parade ground.

Pickup ships snaked in as antiaircraft fire boomed around them (lighter-than-air balloons, painted non-reflective black and set with timed charges). The ships boiled in, grounded, and, in perfect dicipline, the troops loaded aboard. The pickup ships cleared, hovered, and suddenly the air just above the parade ground hummed and boomed and echoes slammed across the field. Screams rose from the stands, and the Emperor himself almost went flat—then reseated himself, while wishing he could figure out how anybody could fake a maser cannon.

Then the stars darkened and two Hero-class battle-wagons drifted overhead, their kilometer-long bulks blackening the sky. Lasers raved from the two battleships, and missiles flamed from the ships' ports. Eventually the "enemy ground fire" stopped, and the pickup ships arced up into the heavens and into the yawning bays of the battleships. Then the ships lifted vertically, Yukawa behind them, and suddenly vanished, sonic-booming up and out of Prime World's atmosphere.

The crowd went nuts.

The Eternal Emperor poured himself a drink and decided that the Twelfth Guards would not go to Draconia.

Godfrey Alain watched the battleships vanish over-head and shivered slightly. In his mind those same battleships were lifting away from the ruins of his own world. His private calculations showed that such an invasion was no more than a year away. Death in the name of peace, he thought.

Alain had faced Imperial Guardsmen before, both personally and strategically—he *knew* the might of the

Empire. But, somehow, seeing those battleships and the smooth efficient lift of an entire division of 12,000 struck more immediately home.

And I'm the only one who'll keep that invasion from happening. The Tahn will not do anything. My own people will just die. And my cause will be lost for generations to come.

Alain was not an egotist. All projections showed that he was the only one who could stop such an invasion.

Unfortunately, Godfrey Alain had less than twenty-four hours to live.

Everyone loves clowns and acrobats. Almost a thousand of them filled the parade ground. Doing clown numbers:

A new group of "drunk soldiers" deciding to salute the Emperor, not knowing how to do it, and building toward a fight that built toward a pyramid display, with the "drunkest" man atop the pyramid saluting perfectly and then doing a dead-man topple to spin through three tucks and land perfectly on the balls of his feet.

Men in barrels, rolling about and narrowly avoiding destruction; tumblers, spinning for hundreds of meters on their hands; gymnasts using each other, themselves, and sometimes, it seemed, thin air to soar ever upward in more and more spectacular patterns; boxers, who swung majestically, missed, and went into contortions of recovery to get back to the mock-fight; crisscross tumbling, with bodies narrowly missing other bodies as they cartwheeled over and over.

The crowd loved them.

The announcer's text said that the thousand clowns were part of the "Imperial Gymnastic Corps," but that corps never existed. Of those present, only the Emperor knew that the display of clowns was as close as his Mantis Section men—the superelite, superclassified commandos that did the Emperor's most private and dangerous skulking—could get to any kind of public display.

Besides, the children—which included the Emperor— loved that part of the evening.

* * *

In normal times, Dr. Har Stynburn would have attended Empire Day from a private booth. At the very least, it would have been in the second circle. More than likely he would have been a guest in the first area, a guest of one of the important people who were his patients.

But those were not normal times.

Stynburn sat far to the rear of the landing field in one of the uncushioned, unupholstered seats that were reserved for the Prime World residents themselves.

Residents. Peasants.

Stynburn was surely a racist. But the gods have a certain sardonic sense of humor. The entire row in front of him was filled with longshoremen: octopod longshoremen. Not only that, but drunk octopod longshoremen, who waved banners, unspeakable food, and even more unspeakable drink in Stynburn's face.

Still worse, the longshoremen expressed enthusiasm by opening their tertiary mouths, located atop their bodies, gulping in air, and then emitting it suddenly and explosively.

Stynburn had, he thought, expressed polite displeasure after one longshoreman had inadvertently shoved a snack that looked like a boiled hat into Stynburn's face. Instead of agreeing, the longshoreman had asked if Stynburn would like to be a part of Empire Day, and wound up two pitching tentacles to provide the means.

He ran fingers through his carefully coiffed gray hair— like his body, still young, still needing neither transplants nor injections.

Stynburn consciously forced his mind to another subject, and stared at the holographic screen across the way. The screen showed close shots of the clowns as they moved toward Stynburn's area, then a momentary shot of the Emperor himself, rocking with laughter in his booth, then other celebrities in their very private booths.

Stynburn was not feeling at his best. As he'd moved into the arena, carefully looking and thinking anonymous, he thought he'd caught a glimpse of the man he had hired.

He was wrong, but the moment had upset him. How

did he know that the man was in fact on his assigned post? Hiring professional criminals for a job was valid, he knew, but he also knew through experience that they were extremely unreliable.

Stynburn's train of depression was broken as a security guard came through the stands and told the longshoremen to pipe down or get thrown out. The guard continued up the steps, but paused to give Stynburn a sharp glance.

No, Stynburn's mind said. I know I do not belong here. It is possible that I do not look it.

But continue on, man. Do not stop, for your own life.

Stynburn was not exaggerating. Years before, other surgeons had implanted a tube of explosives where his appendix had been, and a detonator between his shoulder blades. All it took to set off his suicide capsule—and to destroy a twenty-meter-square area—was for Dr. Stynburn to force his shoulders back in a superexaggerated stretch.

But that would not be necessary; the guard continued up the steps and Stynburn forced his eyes back onto the arena, and his mouth to produce very hollow laughter at the antics of the clowns.

Icy fingers tailed up Marr's fragile spine, an instinct that had saved generations of Milchen from death in the long-ago days of Frederick Two. His heart fluttered, and he pulled slightly away from Senn.

"What's wrong, dear?"

"I don't know. Something is . . . I don't know."

Senn tried to pull him closer to comfort him. Marr shook his head and rose to his full slender height.

"Take me home, Senn," he said. "It doesn't feel like a party anymore."

CHAPTER FOUR

THE SNIFFER STIRRED as Sten approached the closet, micro-gears whirring and throbbing like a small rodent. The security bot hesitated a half second, filament whiskers quivering, and then scuttled inside, its little metal feet clicking on the floor of the closet.

Sten stepped back and examined the Emperor's wardrobe. It was crammed with hundreds of uniforms and ceremonial robes and suits, each item meant for a specific occasion, some as simple as a dazzling white togalike garment, others as complex as a form-fitting suit of many and changing colors.

A vid-book in Sten's room told the history of each piece of clothing. The toga, he remembered, had been for the Emperor's visit to the small system of Raza, where his official title was Chief Philosopher. And the suit of many colors, he was pretty sure, had something to do with something called Mardi Gras. Sten hadn't had time to memorize them all yet, since he'd only been on the job officially for a few months and his mind was still learning the hundreds of duties required of the captain of the Emperor's Own Bodyguard. So far, he had been concentrating on his primary function, which was to keep His Majesty safe from plotters, schemers, groupies, and other fanatics.

The Emperor's security was a many-layered force. First were the military and police forces on Prime World. Within the palace itself was an elaborate mechanical and electronic blanket. The Imperial Household had three Guards units. The most noticeable were the Praetorians. Not only

27

were they used as spit-and-polish, highly visible palace factotums, but they could double as riot police in the event of major disturbances, if there ever were any.

Second were the members of the Imperial Household itself, recruited to a man (or woman) from the ranks of Mantis Section, Mercury Corps, or the Guards.

Lastly were the Gurkha bodyguards, one company of 150 men from the Earth province of Nepal. Most came from the Thapa, Pun, Ala, and Rana clans, all char-jat aristocracy. They were technically mercenaries, as many of their people had been for more than two thousand years.

Small, stocky men, the Gurkhas combined cheerfulness, humor, devotion to duty, and near-unbelievable personal fortitude in one package. The Gurkha company was led by one Havildar–Major, Lalbahadur Thapa, who was overseen by Captain Sten, the official commander and liaison with the Emperor and the Imperial Household.

His new post was not like being in Mantis Section, the superthug unit that Sten had so far spent most of his military career assigned to. Instead of dressing casually or in civilian clothes, Sten wore the mottled-brown uniform of the Gurkhas. Sten was somewhat grateful that he was assigned a batman, Naik Agansing Rai, although he sometimes—particularly when hung over—felt that the man should be a little less willing to comment on the failings of superiors.

Sten would, in fact, through the rest of his military career, maintain two prideful contacts with the Gurkhas—his wearing of the crossed, black-anodized kukris emblem on his dress uniform and the kukri itself.

Now, waiting for the sniffer to finish, Sten was armed with a lethal kukri on one hip, and a small, Mantis-issue willypistol on the other.

The sniffer completed its tour of the closet and scuttled back out to Sten, squeaking its little "safe" tone. He palmed the off-plate, tucked the bot away, and stepped back. His Majesty's personal quarters were as safe as he could make them.

Sten began mentally triple-checking the security list

for the rest of the wing. Changing of the guard had already passed . . . He had trusted lieutenants posted at . . .

"Captain, I don't like to bother a man at his work, but—"

And Sten was whirling around for the voice just behind him, the fingers of his right hand instinctively making the claw that would trigger the knife muscles in his arm, and—

It was the Eternal Emperor, staring at him, a little bit amazed, and then relaxing into humor. Sten felt himself flush in embarrassment. He stiffened to attention, giving himself a mental kick in the behind. He was still a little too Mantis hair-trigger for palace duty.

The Emperor laughed. "Relax, Captain."

Sten slid into a perfectly formal "at ease."

The Emperor grinned, started to make a joke about Sten's way-too-military understanding of the word "relax," buried it to save Sten further embarrassment, and turned away. Instead, he plucked at the party clothing he was wearing and sniffed distastefully. "If it's okay with you, I'd like to change out of this. I smell like a sow in heat."

"Everything's fine, sir," he said. "Now, if I may be dismis—"

"You disappoint me, Captain." The Emperor's voice boomed back from the changing room. Sten flinched, running over his potential sins. What had he missed?

"You've been on the job now—how long is it?"

"Ninety-four cycles, sir."

"Yeah. Something like that. Anyway, ninety-odd days of snooping around my rooms, getting on my clotting nerves with all your security bother, and not once—not once have you offered to show me that famous knife of yours."

"Knife, sir?" Sten was honestly bewildered for a second. And then he remembered: the knife in his arm. "Oh, *that* knife."

The Emperor stepped into view. He was already wearing a gray, nondescript coverall. "Yeah. *That* knife."

"Well, it's in my Mantis profile, sir, and—and . . ."

"There are a *lot* of things in your Mantis file, Captain.

I reviewed it just the other day. Just double-checking to see if I wanted to keep you on in your present position."

He noted Sten's look of concern and took pity. "Besides the knife, I also noticed you drink."

Sten didn't know how to answer that, so he remained wisely silent.

"How well you drink, however, remains to be seen." The Eternal Emperor started for the other room. He stopped at the door.

"That's an invitation, Captain, not an order. Assuming you're off duty now." He disappeared through the door.

Sten had learned many things from Mantis Section. He knew how to kill—had killed—in many ways. He could overthrow governments, plot strategic attacks and retreats, or build a low-yield nuclear bomb. But one thing he had learned more than anything else: When the CO issues an invitation, it's an order. It just so happened that his current CO was the Big Boss Himself.

So he made an instant executive decision. He throat-miked some hurried orders to his second and rostered himself off duty. Then he braced himself and entered the Eternal Emperor's study.

The smoky liquid smoothed down Sten's throat and cuddled into his stomach. He lowered the shot glass and looked into the waiting eyes of the Emperor. "That's Scotch?"

The Emperor nodded and poured them both another drink.

"What do you think?"

"Nice," Sten said, consciously dropping the sir. He assumed that officer's mess rules applied even with the Eternal Emperor. "I can't figure why Colonel—I mean General—Mahoney always had a problem with it."

The Emperor raised an eyebrow. "Mahoney talked about my Scotch?"

"Oh, he liked it," Sten covered. "He just said it took getting used to."

He shot back another glass, tasting the smoothness.

Then he shook his head. "Doesn't take any getting used to at all."

It was a nice thing to say, at that point in the conversation. The Emperor had spent years trying to perfect that drink of his youth.

"We'll have another one of these," the Emperor said, pouring out two more shots, "and then I'll get out some heavy-duty spirits." He carefully picked up Sten's knife, which was lying between them, examined it one more time, and then handed it back. It was a slim, double-edged dagger with a needle tip and a skeleton grip. Hand-formed by Sten from an impossibly rare crystal, its blade was ony 2.5 mm thick, tapering to a less-than-hair-edge 15 molecules wide. Blade pressure alone would cause it to slice through a diamond. The Emperor watched closely as Sten curled his fingers and let the knife slip into his arm-muscle sheath.

"Clotting marvelous," the Emperor finally said. "Not exactly regulation, but then neither are you." He let his words sink in a little. "Mahoney promised me you wouldn't be."

Sten didn't know what to say to this, so he just sipped at his drink.

"Ex-street thug," the Emperor mused, "to Captain of the Imperial Guard. Not bad, young man. Not bad."

He shrugged back some Scotch. "What are your plans after this, Captain?" He quickly raised a hand before Sten blurted something stupid like "at your Majesty's pleasure," or whatever. "I mean, do you really like all this military strut and stuff business?"

Sten shrugged. "It's home," he said honestly.

The Emperor nodded thoughtfully.

"I used to think like that. About engineering, not the clotting military, for Godsakes. Don't like the military. Never have. Even if I am the commander in clotting chief of more soldiers than you could . . . you could . . ."

He left that dangling while he finished his drink.

"Anyway. Engineering it was. That was gonna be my whole life—my permanent home."

The Eternal Emperor shook his head in amazement at this thousand-year-old-plus memory.

"Things change, Captain," he finally said. "You can't believe how things change."

Sten tried a silent nod of understanding, hoping he was doing one of his better acting jobs. The Emperor caught this, and just laughed. He reached into the drawer of his antique desk, pulled out a bottle of absolutely colorless liquid, popped open the bottle and poured two glasses full to the brim.

"This is your final test, young Captain Sten," he said. "Your final, ninety-cycle-on-the-job test. Pass this one and I okay you for the Imperial health plan."

The Emperor slugged back the 180-proof alcohol and then slammed down the glass. He watched closely as Sten picked up the glass, sniffed it briefly, shrugged, and then poured white fire down his throat.

Sten set the glass down, then, with no expression on his face, slid the glass toward the bottle for some more. "Pretty good stuff. A little metallic..."

"That's from the radiator," the Emperor snapped. "I distill it in a car radiator. For the flavor."

"Oh," Sten said, still without expression. "Interesting ... You wouldn't mind if I tried some more..."

He poured two more equally full glasses. He gave a silent toast, and the Emperor watched in amazement as Sten drank it down like water.

"Come on," the Emperor said in exasperation. "That's the most powerful straight alcohol you've ever tasted in your life and you know it. Don't con me."

Sten shook his head in innocence. "It's pretty potent, all right," he said. "But—no offense—I have tried something stronger."

"Like what?" The Emperor fumed.

"Stregg," Sten said.

"What in clot is Stregg?"

"An ET drink," Sten answered. "People called the Bhor. Don't know if you remember them but—"

"Oh, yeah," the Emperor said. "Those Lupus Cluster

fellows. Didn't I turn a system over to them, or something like that?"

"Something like that."

"So what's this Stregg swill like? Can't be better than my pure dee moonshine—you got any?"

Sten nodded. "In my quarters. If you're interested, I'll send a runner."

"I'm interested."

The Emperor raised the glass to toast position.

"By my mother's," he said through furry tongue, "by my mother's... What was that Bhor toast again?"

"By my mother's beard," Sten said, equally furry-tongued.

"Right. By my mother's beard." He shot it back, gasped, and held on to the desk as his empire swung around him.

"Clot a bunch of moonshine," the Eternal Emperor said. "Stregg's the ticket. Now what was that other toash ... I mean toast. By my father's..."

"Frozen buttocks," Sten said.

"Beg your pardon. No need to get—oh, that's the toasshtt—I mean toast. By my father's frozen buttocks! Sffine stuff." He lifted his empty glass to drink. He stared at it owlishly when he realized it was empty, and then pulled himself up to his full Imperial Majesty. "I'm clotting fried."

"Yep," Sten said. "Stregg do that to you. I mean, does that you to—oh, clot. Time is it? I gotta go on duty."

"Not like that, you don't. Not in this Majesty's service. Can't stand drunks. Can't stand people can't hold their liquor. Don't trust them. Never have."

Sten peered at him through a Stregg haze. "Zzatt mean I'm fired?"

"No. No. Never fire a drunk. Have to fire me. Sober us up first. Then I fire you."

The Emperor rose to his feet. Wavered. And then firmed himself. "Angelo stew," he intoned. "Only thing save your career now."

"What the clot is Angelo stew?"

"You don't need to know. Wouldn't eat it if you did.

Cures cancer...oh, we cured that before, didn't we... Anyway...Angelo stew's the ticket. Only thing I know will unfreeze our buttocks."

He staggered off and Sten followed in a beautifully military, forty-five-degree march.

Sten's stomach rumbled hungrily as he smelled the smells from the Eternal Emperor's private kitchen. Drunk as he was, he watched in fascination as the equally drunk Emperor performed miracles both major and minor. The minor miracles were with strange spices and herbs; the major one was that the Emperor, smashed on Stregg, could work an antique French knife, slicing away like a machine, measure proportions, and...keep up a semilucid conversation.

Sten's job was to keep the Stregg glasses full.

"Have another drink. Not to worry. Angelo stew right up."

Sten took a tentative sip of Stregg and felt the cold heat-lightning down his gullet. This time, however, the impact was different. Just sitting in the Emperor's superprivate domain, added to the fact that it was indeed time to get his captain's act together, had the effect of clearing away the boozy haze.

The kitchen was four or five times larger than most on fortieth-century Prime World, where food was handled out of sight by computers and bots. It had *some* modern features—hidden cabinets and environmental food storage boxes operated by finger touch. It also was kept absolutely bacteria free and featured a state-of-the-art waste disposal system that the Emperor rarely used. Mostly he either swept what Sten would have considered waste into containers and returned them to storage, or dumped things into what Sten would later learn were simmering stockpots.

The most imposing feature of the room was a huge chopping block made of rare hardwood called oak. In the center of the block was an old stainless steel sink. Set a little bit lower than the chopping block, it was flushed by a constant spray of water, and as the Emperor chopped away, he swept everything that didn't make Angelo stew into the sink, where it instantly disappeared.

Directly behind the Emperor was an enormous black cast-iron and gleaming steel cooking range. It featured an oven whose walls were many centimeters thick, a single-cast grill, half-a-dozen professional-chef-size burners, and an open, wood-burning grill. From the slight smell it gave off, the stove obviously operated by some kind of natural gas.

Sten watched as the Emperor worked and kept up a running commentary at the same time. From what Sten could gather, the first act of what was to be Angelo stew consisted of thinly sliced chorizo—Mexican hard sausage, the Emperor explained. The sausage and a heaping handful of garlic were sautéed in Thai-pepper-marinated olive oil. Deliciously hot-spiced smells from the pan cut right through the Stregg fumes in Sten's nostrils. He took another sip from his drink and listened while the Emperor talked.

"Never used to think much about food," the Emperor said, "except as fuel. You know, the stomach complains, you fill it, and then go about your business."

"I understand what you mean," Sten said, remembering his days as a Mig worker.

"Figured you would. Anyway, I was a typical young deep-space engineer. Do my time on the company mission, and spend my Intercourse and Intoxication time with joygirls and booze. Food even seemed to get in the way of that."

Sten understood that as well. It was pretty much how he had spent his days as a rookie trooper.

"Then as I went up the company ladder, they sent me off on longer and longer jobs. Got clotting boring. Got so the only break you had was food. And that was all pap. So I started playing around. Remembering things my dad and grandma fixed. Trying to duplicate them."

He tapped his head. "Odd, how all the things you ever smelled or tasted are right up here. Then all you got to do is practice to get your tongue in gear. Like this Angelo stew here. Greatest hangover and drunk cure invented.

Some old Mex pirate taught me—clot, that's another story..."

He stopped his work and took a sip of Stregg. Smiled to himself, and tipped a small splash in with the chorizo. Then he went back to the task at hand, quartering four or five onions and seeding quarter slices of tomatoes.

"Jump to a lot of years later. Way after I discovered AM2 and started putting this whole clottin' Empire together..."

Sten's brain whirled for an instant. AM2. The beginning of the Empire. What this mid-thirties-looking man was talking about so lightly was what one read about in history vids. He had always thought they were more legend than fact. But here he was having a calm discussion with the man who supposedly started it all—hell, nearly twenty centuries in the past. The Emperor went on, as if he was talking about yesterday.

"There I was, resting on my laurels and getting bored out of my mind. A dozen or so star systems down and working smoothly. A few trillion-trillion megacredits in the bank. So? Whaddya do with that kind of money?"

He motioned to Sten to top up the Stregg glasses.

"Then I realized what I could do with it. I could cook anything I wanted. Except I don't like the modern stuff they've been doing the last six or seven hundred years. I like the old stuff. So I started experimenting. Copying dishes in my brain. Buying up old cookbooks and recreating things that sounded good."

The Emperor turned and pulled a half-kilo slab of bleeding red beef from a storage cooler and began chunking it up.

"What the hell. It's a way to kill time. Especially when you've got lots of it."

The Emperor shut off the flame under the sausage and garlic, started another pan going with more spiced oil, and tossed in a little sage, a little savory and thyme, and then palm-rolled some rosemary twigs and dropped those in on top. He stirred the mixture, considered for a moment, then heaped in the tomato quarters and glazed them. He shut off the fire and turned back to Sten. He gave the young captain a long, thoughtful look and then began talking again, rolling the small chunks of beef into flour first, and then into a bowl of hot-pepper seeds.

"I guess, from your perspective, Captain, that I'm babbling about things of little interest, that happened a long time ago. Old man talk. Nothing relevant for today."

Sten was about to protest honestly, but the Emperor held up an Imperial hand. He still had the floor. "I can assure you," he said quite soberly, "that my yesterdays seem as close to me as yours do to you. Now. For the crucial question of the evening."

He engulfed half a glass of Stregg by way of prepunctuation. "How the clot you doing, Cap'n Sten. And how the hell you like Court duty?..."

Sten did some fast thinking. Rule One in the unofficial Junior Officer's Survival Manual: When A Senior Officer Asks You What You Think, You Lie A Lot.

"I like it fine," Sten said.

"You're a clotting liar," the Eternal Emperor said.

Rule Two of said bar guide to drinking with superiors: When Caught In A Lie, Lie Again.

"No, really," Sten said. "This is probably one of the more interesting—"

"Rule Two doesn't work, Captain. Drop the con."

"It's a boring place filled with boring people and I never really gave a damn about politics anyway," Sten rushed out.

"Much better," the Emperor said. "Now let me give you a little career advice..."

He paused to turn the flame up under the sausage and garlic, then added the pepper-rolled beef as soon as the pan was hot enough.

"First off, at your age and current status, you are luckier than hell even to be here."

Sten started to agree, but the Emperor stopped him with a hard look. He stirred the beef around as he talked, waiting until it got a nice brown crust.

"First tip: Don't be here very long. If you are, you're wasting your time. Second thought: Your current assignment will be both a huge career booster and an inhibitor.

Looks great on the fiche—'Head of the Imperial Bodyguard at such and such an age.'

"But you're also gonna run into some superiors—much
older and very jealous superiors—who will swear that I
had a more than casual interest in you. Take that how
you want. They certainly shall."

The Emperor finished the beef. He pulled out a large
iron pan and dumped the whole mess into it. He also
added the panful of onions and tomatoes. Then he threw
in a palmful of superhot red peppers, a glug or three of
rough red wine, many glugs of beef stock, a big clump of
cilantro, clanked down the lid, and set the flame to high.
As soon as it all came to a boil, he would turn it down
to simmer for a while.

The Emperor sat down next to Sten and took a long
swallow of Stregg.

"I don't know if you realize it or not, but you have a
very heavy mentor in General Mahoney."

"Yeah. I know it," Sten said.

"Okay. You got him. You're impressing the clot out of
me right now. Not bad. Although I got to warn you, I am
notorious for going hot and cold on people. Don't stick
around me too long.

"When all is lost, I sometimes blame my screwups on
the nearest person to me. Hell, once in a while, I even
believe it myself."

"I've been there," Sten said.

"Yeah. Sure you have. Good experience for a young
officer. Drakh flows downhill. Good thing to learn. That
way you know what to do when you're on top."

The stew was done now. The Emperor rose and ladled
out two brimming bowlsful. Sten's mouth burst with saliva.
He could smell a whole forest of cilantro. His eyes watered
as the Emperor set the bowl in front of him. He waited
as the man cut two enormous slices of fresh-baked sour-
dough bread and plunked them down along with a tub of
newly churned white butter.

"So here's what you do. Pull this duty. Then get thee
out of intelligence or anything to do with cloak and dagger.

Nobody ever made big grade in intelligence. I got it set up that way. Don't trust them. Nobody should.

"Next, get thee to flight school. No. Shut up. I know that's naval. What I'm saying is, jump services. Get yourself in the navy. Learn piloting."

The Emperor slowly buttered his slice of bread and Sten followed suit, memorizing every word.

"You'll easily make lieutenant commander. Then up you go to commander, ship captain, and—with a little luck—flag captain. Form there on in, you're in spitting distance of admiral."

Sten took a long pull on his drink to cover his feelings. Admiral? Clot. Nobody but nobody makes admiral. The Emperor topped the glasses again.

"I *listen* to my admirals," the Emperor said. "Now do what I say. Then come back in fifty years or so and I may even listen to *you*."

The Emperor spooned up a large portion of stew.

"Eat up, son. This stuff is great brain food. First your ears go on fire, then the gray stuff. Last one done's a grand admiral."

Sten swallowed. The Angelo stew savored his tongue, and then gobbled down his throat to his stomach. A small nuclear flame bloomed, and his eyes teared and his nose wept and his ears turned bright red. The Stregg in his bloodstream fled before a horde of hot-pepper molecules.

"Whaddya think?" the Eternal Emperor said.

"What if you don't have cancer?" Sten gasped.

"Keep eating, boy. If you don't have it now, you will soon."

CHAPTER FIVE

THE EMPEROR HAD two problems with Prime World. The first was, Why Was His Capital Such A Mess? He had run an interstellar empire for a thousand years. Why should a dinky little planet-bound capital be such a problem?

The second was, What Went Wrong?

Prime World was a classic example of city planning gone bonkers. In the early days, shortly after the Eternal Emperor had taught people that he controlled the only fuel for interstellar engines—Anti-Matter Two—and that he was capable of keeping others from learning or stealing its secret, he'd figured out that headquartering an empire, especially a commercial one, on Earth was dumb.

He chose Prime World for several reasons: It was uninhabited; it was fairly close to an Earth-normal habitat; and it was ringed with satellites that would make ideal deep-space loading platforms. And so the Emperor bought Prime World, a planet that until then was nothing more than an index number on a star chart. Even though he controlled no more than 500 to 600 systems at the time, the Emperor knew that his empire would grow. And with growth would come administration, bureaucracy, court followers, and all the rest.

To control the potential sprawl, owning an entire world seemed a solution. So the finest planners went to work. Boulevards were to be very, very wide. The planet was to have abundant parks, both for beauty and to keep the planet from turning into a self-poisoning ghetto. Land was leased in parcels defined by century-long contracts. All buildings were to be approved by a council that included as many artists as civic planners.

Yet somewhat more than a thousand years after being set up, Prime World looked like a ghetto.

The answers were fairly simple: greed, stupidity, and graft—minor human characteristics that somehow the Eternal Emperor had ignored. Cynically, the Emperor realized he did not need the equivalent of the slave who supposedly lurked on Caesars during their triumphal processions to whisper "All this too is fleeting."

All he had to do was travel the 55-plus kilometers to Fowler, the city nearest to his palace grounds, and wander the streets. Fowler, and the other cities on Prime World, were high-rise/low-rise/open kaleidoscopes.

To illustrate: A building lot, listed in the Prime World plat book as NHEB0FA13FFC2, a half kilometer square, had originally been leased to the luxury-loving ruler of the Sandia system, who built a combination of palace and embassy. But when he was turned out of office by a more Spartan regime, Sandia sublet the ground to an intersteller trading conglomerate which tore down the palace and replaced it with a high-rise headquarters building. But Transcom picked the wrong areas and products, so the building was gradually sub sublet to such "small" enterprises as mere planetary governments or system-wide corporations. And as the leases were sublet to smaller entities, the rent went up. Annual rental on a moderate-size one-room office could take a province's entire annual product.

The Transcom building turned into an office slum until all the subleases were bought up by the Sultana of Hafiz, who, more than anything, wanted a palace she could use on her frequent and prolonged trips to Prime World. The high-rise was demolished and another palace built in its place.

All that in eighty-one years. Yet the Imperial records still registered the President of Sandia, who by then had spent forty-seven years forcibly ensconced in a monastery, as the lease-holder.

Given the subleasing system, even rent control did not work. "Single" apartments sometimes looked more like troopship barracks because of the number of people required to meet the monthly rent.

The Emperor had tried to help, since he was quite

damned aware that even in an age of computers and bots, a certain number of functionaries were needed. But even Imperial housing projects quickly changed hands and became examples of free enterprise gone berserk.

After nearly 800 years of fighting the sublet blight, in a final effort to control the pressure that drove such destructive practices, a limitation was placed on immigration to Prime World. Prospective emigrants were required to show proof of employment, proof that a new job had been created for them, or proof of vast wealth. The regulations were strictly enforced.

That made every Prime World resident rich. Not rich on Prime World, but potentially rich. Anyone, from an authorized diplomat to the lowest street vendor, could sell his residence permit for a world's ransom.

Prime Worlders being Prime Worlders, they did not. Most preferred to sit in their poverty (although poverty was relative, given guaranteed income, rations, recreation, and housing) than to migrate to be rich. Prime World was the Center, the Court of a Thousand Suns, and who would ever choose to move away from that if he, she, or it had any choice?

Sometimes the Emperor, when he was drunk, dejected, and angry, felt the answer was to nationalize all the buildings and draft everyone on the world. But he knew that his free-lance capitalists would figure a way around that one, too.

So it was easier to let things happen as they did, and live with minor annoyances such as population density or city maps that were outdated within thirty days of issue.

In addition to the cities and the parks, Prime World was full of estates. Most of the leased estates were situated as close to the Imperial ring as possible. The proximity of one's living grounds to the palace was another measure of social stature.

There was one final building located on the grounds of the Emperor's main palace. It was about ten kilometers away from Arundel, and housed the Imperial Parliament. It had been necessary to build some kind of court, after all. After the Eternal Emperor authorized its structure, he'd immediately had a kilometer-high landscaped mountain built between his castle and the parliament building. He may have had to deal with politicians, but he didn't have to look at them when he was on his own time...

Prime World was, therefore, a somewhat odd place. The best and the worst that could be said is that it worked—sort of.

The pneumosubways linked the cities, and gravsleds provided intrasystem shipping. Out-system cargoes arriving in Prime System were off-loaded to one of the planet's satellites or the artificial ports that Imperial expansion had made necessary. From there, they would either be transferred to an outbound freighter or, if intended for Prime World itself, lightered down to the planet's surface.

Five shipping ports sat on Prime World. And like all ports throughout history, they were grimy and violent.

The biggest port, Soward, was the closest to Fowler. One kilometer from Soward's main field was the Covenanter.

Like the rest of Prime World, Soward had troubles with expansion. But warehousing and shipping had to be located as close to ground level as possible.

Ancillary buildings, such as rec halls, offices, bars, and so forth, were built over the kilometer-square warehouses. Ramps—some powered, some not—swept up from the ground level to the spider-web steel frameworks that held the secondary buildings.

The Convenanter sat three levels above the ground. To reach the bar required traveling one cargo ramp, one escalator, and then climbing up oil-slick stairs. Despite that, the Convenanter was usually crowded.

But not in the night.

Not in the rain.

Godfrey Alain moved into the shadows at the top of the escalator and waited to see if he was being tailed.

Minutes passed, and he heard nothing but the waterfall sound of the rain rushing down the ramps to the ground far below. He pulled his raincloak tighter around him, still waiting.

Alain had left his hotel room in Fowler. Four other

rented "safe" rooms had given him momentary safety, a chance to see if he was followed, and a change of clothes. He appeared to be clean.

A more experienced operative might have suggested to Alain that he should have tried less expensive costuming; his final garb and his final position, a warehouse district, made him a potential target for muggers.

But Godfrey Alain was not a spy; the skills of espionage were secondary to him. To most of the Empire, he was a terrorist. To himself, his fellow revolutionaries, and the Tahn worlds, Alain was a freedom fighter.

What Alain was, oddly enough, was less a factor of politics than population movement. The Tahn worlds having originally been settled by low-tech refugees guaranteed that the Empire left them alone. The Tahn worlds being what they were—a multisystem sprawl of cluster worlds—guaranteed no Imperial interference. But the Tahn's lebensraum expansion also was a guarantee that sooner or later the Empire and the Tahn would intersect, as had happened some generations before when Tahn settlers moved from their own systems to frontier worlds already occupied by small numbers of Imperial pioneers.

The two very different cultures were soon in conflict, and both sides screamed for help. The Tahn homeworlds could not provide direct armed support, nor were they willing to risk a direct confrontation with the Empire.

The Empire, on the other hand, could afford no more than token garrison forces of second- and third-class units to "protect" the Imperial settlers from Tahn colonials.

The Caltor system Alain was born into was on one of those in conflict. Since the Tahn settlers ghettoed together socially and economically, they were guaranteed an advantage against the less united Imperial inhabitants. But the Imperial pioneers had Caltor's garrison troopies to fall back on and they felt that Imperial presence lent them some authority.

Such a situation breeds pogroms. And in one such pogrom Alain's parents were slaughtered.

The boy Alain saw the bodies of his parents, saw the local Imperial troops shrug off the "incident," and went to school. School was learning how to turn a gravsled into a kamikaze or a time bomb; how to convert a mining lighter into a transsystem spaceship; how to build a projectile weapon from pipes; and, most important, how to turn a mob into a tightly organized cellular resistance movement.

The resistance spread, from pioneer planet to pioneer planet, always disavowed by the distant Tahn worlds yet always backed with "clean" weaponry and moral support; always fought by the Imperial settlers and their resident "peace-keeping" troops; always growing.

Alain was a leader of the resistance—in the fifty years since he had seen his parents dead in the ruins of their house, he had become the chief of the Fringe Worlds' liberation movement.

And so he went by invitation to his home worlds as the representative of a huge, militant movement. Going home—to a political and ideological home he had never seen, the Tahn worlds, turned Alain into a lost man, because the Tahn system—those worlds the fringe worlds would unite with if his movement was successful—were not at all what he expected.

The government-encouraged population explosion was part of his disenchantment, as were the rigid social customs. But the biggest thing was the very stratification of the Tahn society. Coming from a pioneer world, Alain felt that any person should be able to rise to whatever level he was capable of. Intellectually he knew this was not part of Tahn culture, but what grew in his craw was the populace's acceptance of the stratification. As far as he could tell, the warrior had no intentions of becoming nobility, the peasant had no interest in the merchant class, and so forth.

It was the classic confrontation between a man from a culture which is still evolving and a society that has fixed on a very successful formula.

That was the first problem. The second, which he had been reminded of at gut level during the Empire Day celebration, was that, if the Eternal Emperor desired it, his revolutionary movement could be obliterated—along with the Tahn settlers Alain's freedom fighters moved and lived among.

Six months before, Alain had made very secretive overtures to an Imperial ambassador-without-portfolio. Initially, he had wanted to discuss a truce with the Empire, and with the fringe worlds that the Empire supported. And, over the months, the concept of truce had evolved.

Alain's final proposal, to be put before a direct representative this night, was broader. He wanted not just a cease-fire, but a slow legitimization of his people and his movement, recognizing the fringe worlds as an independent buffer zone between the Tahn worlds and the Empire itself.

Alain had only discussed the proposition among his oldest friends and most trusted advisors. It would be all too easy for Tahn intelligence to learn of the proposition, proclaim Alain a counterrevolutionary, and arrange for his death.

It would also be convenient for some of his long-term enemies on the Imperial side to have him killed. Alain was not afraid of dying—nearly fifty years as a guerrilla had blanked that part of his psyche out—but he was terrified of dying before his plan was in front of the Emperor.

The meeting had been most secretively arranged. Alain had been provided with false credentials, authorized "at the highest level," and arrived as just one more tourist to see the Empire Day display and sample the exotic life of the world that was home to the Court of a Thousand Suns.

Sometime during the Empire Day festivities, he was passed instructions on where the meeting was to occur, but the handoff was so subtle that even Alain was unsure how or when the time-burn message came into his pockets.

He felt relatively secure about the meeting, which had been set at a ship-port dive. It might prove fatal to Alain to have met with an Imperial representative in the long run, but it would certainly be damaging to the Emperor himself if anyone were to know his representative was meeting with a terrorist, especially a terrorist who had been the unsuccessful target of two Mantis Team assassination runs.

There were no followers.

Alain walked lightly up the stairs. His hand on the projectile pistol under the cloak, he checked behind him once again. Then he went down the ten-meter-wide catwalk of pierced steel plating. Alain could see the ground, long meters below. On either side of the catwalk hung the structural-steel plating which supported offices and small industrial shops. Gaps yawned between them.

The only overhead on the catwalk was also over the only lit building, a bright red bar faced with pseudo wood. Its holographic display morosely blinking T E COV ANTER.

He moved quite slowly down the catwalk, slipping from shadow to shadow. He saw no one and nothing outside the bar.

The man was diagonally across the catwalk from the Covenanter, on the open second floor of an unfinished warehouse. He stood well back from the window, just in case anyone was scanning the area with heat-sensitive glasses.

For two hours the bomber had been alternately sweeping the catwalk with light-enhancing binocs and swearing at the rain and his stupidity for taking the job—just as he had every night for three weeks from two hours after nightfall until the Convenanter closed.

This is a busto bum go, the bomber thought not for the first nor the five-hundredth time. Showed what happened when a man needed a job. The clots could sense it, and crawl out from the synth-work every time, somehow knowing when a real professional needed a few credits and didn't have much choice how he got them.

The bomber's name was Dynsman, and, contrary to his self-image, he was quite a ways from being a professional demolitionist. Dynsman was that rarity, a Prime World native. His family did not come from the wrong side of the tracks, because his older brothers would have torn those tracks up and sold them for black-market scrap.

Dynsman was small, light on his feet, and occasionally quick-minded.

All else being normal, Dynsman would have followed quite a predictable pattern, growing up in petty thievery, graduating to small-scale nonviolent organized crime until a judge tired of seeing his face every year or so and deported him to a prison planet.

But Dynsman got lucky. His chance at real fame came when he slid through a heavy traffic throng to the rear of a guarded gravsled. When the guards looked the other way, Dynsman grabbed and hauled tail.

The gravsled had been loaded with demolition kits intended for the Imperial Guards. The complete demo kit, which included fuses, timer, primary charges, and the all-important instructions, had zip value to Dynsman's fence. He had sadly found himself sitting atop a roof and staring into a box that he'd gone to Great Risk—at least by Dynsman's scale of danger values—to acquire. And it was worth nothing.

But Dynsman was a native Prime Worlder, one of a select group of people widely thought capable of selling after dinner flatulence as experimental music. By the time he'd removed three fingers, scared his hair straight, and been tossed out of home by his parents, Dynsman could pass—at a distance, after dark, in a fog—as an explosives expert.

Soon Dynsman was a practicing member of an old and valued profession—one of those noble souls who turned bad investments, buildings, spacecraft, slow inventory, whatever, into liquid assets—with more potential customers than he had time for. Unfortunately, the biggest of those turned out to be an undercover Imperial police officer.

And so it went—Dynsman was either in jail or in the business of high-speed disassembly.

He should have known, however, that something was wrong on *this* job. First, the man who had bought him was too sleek, too relaxed to be a crook. And he knew too much about Dynsman, including the fact that Dynsman was six cycles late on his gambling payment and that the gambler had wondered if Dynsman might look more stylish with an extra set of kneecaps.

Not that Dynsman could have turned down the stranger's assignment at the best of times; Dynsman was known as a man who could bust out of a dice game even if he was using his own tap dice.

According to the gray-haired man, the job was simple. Dynsman was to build a bomb into the Covenanter. Not just a *wham*-and-there-goes-everything bomb, but a very special bomb, placed in a very particular manner. Dynsman was then to wait in the uncompleted building until a certain man entered the building. He was then to wait a certain number of seconds and set the device off.

After that, Dynsman was to get the other half of his fee, plus false ID and a ticket off Prime World.

Dynsman mourned again—the fee offered was too high. Just as suspicious was the expensive equipment he was given—the night binocs, a designer sports timer, a parabolic mike with matching headphones, and the transceiver that would be used to trigger the bomb.

Dynsman was realizing he was a very small fish suddenly dumped into a pool of sharks when he spotted the man coming down the catwalk toward the Convenanter.

Dynsman scanned the approaching figure of Alain. Ah-hah. The first person to come near the bar in an hour. Expensively dressed. Holding the glasses in one hand, Dynsman slid the headphones into position and the microphone on.

Down on the catwalk Alain stopped outside the Covenanter's entrance. Another man stepped out of the blackness—Craigwel, the Emperor's personal diplomatic troubleshooter. He wore the flash coveralls of a spaceship engineer, and held both hands in front of him, clearly showing that he was unarmed.

"Engineer Raschid?" Alain said, following instructions.

"That is the name I am using."

Across the street, Dynsman almost danced in joy. This was it! This was finally it! He shut off the mike, dropped it, and scooped up the radio-detonator and the sports timer.

As the two men went into the Covenanter, Dynsman thumbed the timer's start button.

CHAPTER SIX

TEN SECONDS:

Janiz Kerleh was co-owner, cook, bartender, and main waiter at the Covenanter. The bar itself was her own personal masterpiece.

Janiz had no poor-farm-girl-led-into-trouble background, though she was from a farming planet. Fifteen years of watching her logger parents chew wood chips from dawn to dusk dedicated her to finding a way out. The way out proved to be a traveling salesman specializing in log-snaking elephants.

The elephant salesman took Janiz to the nearest city. Janiz took twenty minutes to find the center of action and ten more to line up her first client.

Being a joygirl wasn't exactly a thrill a minute—for one thing, she could never understand why so many people who wanted sex never bothered to use a mouthwash first—but it was a great deal better than staring at an elephant's anus for a lifetime. The joygirl became a madame successful enough to finance a move to Prime World.

To her total disappointment, Janiz found that what she had figured would be a gold mine was less than that. Not only were hookers falling out of Prime World's ears, but more than enough amateurs were willing to cooperate for something as absurd as being presented at Court.

Janiz Kerleh, then, was on hard times when she met

Chief Engineer Raschid. They'd bedded, found a certain similarity in humor, and started spending time in positions other than horizontal.

Pillow talk—and pillow talk for Janiz was the bar she'd always wanted to open. Twenty years' worth of dreaming, sketching, even putting little pasteboard models together when the vice squad pulled the occasional plug on her operation.

Paralyzed was probably the best way to describe her reaction when Raschid, a year or so after they'd known each other, and sex had become less of an overriding interest than just a friendly thing to do, handed her a bank draft and said, "You wanna open up your bar? Here. I'm part owner."

Raschid's only specification was that one booth—Booth C, he'd told her to name it—was to be designed somewhat differently than the others. It was to be absolutely clean. State-of-the-art debugging and alarm devices were delivered and installed by anonymous coveralled men. The booth itself was soundproofed so that any conversation could not be overheard a meter away from the table. A security service swept the booth once a week.

Raschid told Janiz that he wanted to use the booth for meetings. Nobody was permitted to sit there except him— or anyone who came in and used his name.

Janiz, who had a pretty good idea how much money a ship's engineer made, and knew it was nowhere near enough to front an ex-joygirl in her hobby, figured Raschid had other things going. The man was probably a smuggler. Or . . . or she really didn't care.

The Covenanter was quite successful, giving dockers and ship crewmen a quiet place to drink, a place where the riot squad never got called if evenings got interesting, and a place to meet colorful girls without colorful diseases. Raschid himself dropped by twice a Prime year or so, and then would vanish again. Janiz had tried to figure what ship he was on by following the outbound columns in the press, but she could never connect Raschid with any ship or even a shipping line. Nor could she figure who Raschid's "friends" were, since they ranged from well-dressed richies to obvious thugs.

So when the two men, Alain and Craigwel, asked for Booth C, in an otherwise totally deserted bar, she had no reaction other than to ask what they were drinking.

SEVENTY-TWO SECONDS:

When Dynsman had broken into the Covenanter to plant the bomb a week earlier, he had also paced out the detonation time. His man would enter the bar. Ten seconds. Look around. Fifteen seconds. Walk to the bar. 7.5 seconds. Order a drink. One minute. Pick up the drink and walk across the room to Booth C. The bomber made allowances for possible crowding—which the Covenanter certainly was not that night—then gave his time-sequence another two minutes just to be sure.

Alain eyed the vast array of liquors on display, then picked the safe bet. "Synthalk. With water. Tall and with ice, at your favor."

Craigwel, the professional diplomat, ordered the same. His next statement would kill both men. It was intended only to lubricate the discussion that was to follow. "Have you ever tried Metaxa?"

"No," Alain said.

"Good stuff on a night like this."

"Nonnarcotic?" Alain asked suspiciously.

"Alcohol only. It's also a good hullpaint remover."

Janiz poured the two shots, then busied herself making the synthalk drinks.

Alain lifted his shot glass. "To peace."

Craigwel nodded sincerely, and tossed his glass back.

Time ran out. On timer cue, Dynsman touched the radio det button.

The bomb exploded.

High-grade explosive, covered with ball bearings, crashed.

The three humans died very quickly but very messily. Dynsman had erred slightly in his calculations, since the bearings also slammed into the bar stock itself.

Across the street, Dynsman dumped his equipment into a case, ran to the rear of the building, dropped the thread ladder down two levels, and quickly descended. When he hit the second level, he touched the disconnect button, and the ladder dropped down into his hands. That ladder also went into the case, and Dynsman faded into the shadows, headed for his own personal hideaway, deep inside one of Prime World's nonhumanoid conclaves.

Ears still ringing from the explosion, he did not hear the clatter of boots on the catwalk above as they ran toward the shattered ruin that had been the Covenanter.

Moments before the explosion, Sergeant Armus had been trying to soothe the injured feelings of the other member of his tac squad. The sector was so quiet and the duty so boring that it felt like a punishment tour. They were an elite, after all, a special unit that was supposed to be thrown into high-crime-potential areas to put the lid back on, and then turn the area over to normal patrols.

Instead, they had been on nothing duty for nearly a month. Sergeant Armus listened to his corporal run over the complaints for the fiftieth time. Tac Chief Kreuger must really have it in for them. Nothing was going on in the sector that one lone Black Maria couldn't deal with. Armus didn't tell the man that he had been making the same complaint nightly! He had to admit there was a great deal of justification for his squad's complaints. Kreuger must be out of his clotting mind, assigning them to a dead sector, especially with the festival going on. Maybe the crime stat computer hiccupped. Maybe Krueger had a joygirl in the area who had complained about getting roughed up. Who could fathom what passed for the mind of a clotting captain?

In the interest of maintaining proper decorum, Armus kept all that to himself. Instead he ran the overtime bit past his squad members again—which was another thing that was odd. Because of the pressures of the festival, there were very few tac soldiers to spare, and the entire unit had been on overtime from almost the beginning. Now, how the clot was the chief going to explain that?

And then came the shock wave of the explosion. Almost before the sound stopped, the squad was thundering down the rampway and turning the corner—sprinting for the ruin that had been the Covenanter. Armus took one look at the shattered building and three thoughts flashed across his brain: fire, survivors, and ambulance. And, as he thought, he acted. Although no flames were visible in the ruins of the bar, he smashed an armored fist into an industrial extinguisher button and a ton or more of suds dumped into the building. He shouted orders to his men to grab any tool in sight, and thumbed his mike to call for an ambulance. Then he stopped as an ambulance lifted over the catwalk and hissed toward the bar. What was *that* doing here? He hadn't even called yet! But he had no time to waste; he unhooked his belt prybar and plunged into the ruins after his men.

BOOK TWO

LUNETTE

CHAPTER SEVEN

Dear Sten:

   Hi ya, mate. Guess you're surprised to hear from the likes
of me. Well, yours truly has finally landed some much-deserved
soft duty. This is duty, I might add, befitting a clansman of
such high rank. Sergeant Major Alex Kilgour! Hah, *Captain*!
Bet you never thought you'd live to see the day!

Sten pulled back to give the letter a disbelieving glance.
Kilgour! He didn't recognize him without the thick Scots
accent. But then, of course even Alex wouldn't write with
a burr. He laughed, and dove back into the letter.

   Of course, a sergeant major still can't drink at the fancy
officer clubs with an exalted captain, but an honest pint of
bitter is an honest pint of bitter, and it drinks much smoother
when it's never your shout. I've never seen such a brown-
nosing clan of lowly noncoms as I've got here. Although I do
not dissuade them of this practice. I'm sure that buying a pint
for the sergeant major is a ceremony of ancient and holy
tradition in these parts.
   To be honest with you, this tour is beginning to wear
thinner than a slice of haggis at a Campbell christening. The
powers that be have posted me as curator of the clotting
Mantis Museum. Now, as you well know, it requires a Q
clearance to even see the lobby of this godforsaken place, so
we don't get a lot of visitors. Just blooming security committee politicians getting their clotting expense tickets punched
on the way to some gambling hell. Although there was one
lass . . . Ah, never mind. A Kilgour doesn't kiss and tell, especially when the bonny one outranks him.
   Anyhow, here I am, performing the safest duty in my
wicked career as one of the Emperor's blackguards. I'm going

out of my clotting mind, I tell you. And the only thing that
keeps me sane is that you can't be doing much better in that
fancy-dan job of yours on Prime World. No, I'm afeared it
will never be the same since they broke up our team—Old
Mantis 13. They better well retire the number, I tell you, or
there'll be some explaining to do to a Kilgour.

Have you heard from the others? In case your news is
wearier than mine, I'll fill you in on what I know. Bet has
been promoted to lieutenant and is running her own team
now, although I'm not too sure what nasty business she's
about at the moment.

As for Doc, well, that little furry bundle of sharp edges
managed himself a sabbatical leave. Do you recall the Stralbo?
You know, The People Of The Lake? Those horrendous tall
blokes who supped on blood and milk? Sure, I thought you
would and wasn't Doc more than a giggle the way he got
blotto on all that blood? So, what Doc is doing is getting
drunk and staying that way all in the name of Mother Science.

The only one I haven't picked up any particulars on is
Ida. When her hitch was over, she refused to reup and did a
bloody Rom disappearing act. Although I imagine she must
have gnashed her teeth over all that filthy lucre they were
waving at her. One thing I have to say for her, though, she
did come through on my share of the loot she was investing
for us. It was a clotting big heap of money that took almost
all of one leave for me to go through. If you haven't got yours
yet, I suspicion that it's probably winging its way to you.
Truly, it's a nice bundle of credits. If by chance she's holding
out on you, howsomever, check the futures market columns.
Any big jump or dip in the exotics, and you'll find the plump
little beggar.

Well, I've about run out of time to get this into the next
post. Hope all is well with you, mate.

Yours, Aye.
Alex Kilgour

Sten chuckled to himself as he blanked out the letter.
Same old Alex, grousing when the tour is too hot, and
grousing when it's too soft. He did, however, have a point
about Prime World. It looked soft, and felt soft—danger-
ously so. Sten had pored over the records his predeces-
sors had left. For the last few centuries, they were almost
depressing in their lack of action. However, the few times

things did happen, he noticed, the situation tended to get very bloody and very political. After his years in Mantis Section, blood didn't bother Sten much. But politics— politics could make your skin crawl.

Forgetting how small his quarters were, Sten leaned back in his chair, bumping his head against a wall. He groaned as the thump reminded him of the royal hangover he was suffering from. The only effect the Angelo stew had was to mask the alcohol and allow him to stay up even later with the Emperor. Somehow, he had stumbled through his job the next day, leaving him no other cure the following night then to try to drink the residual pain and agony away. Sten had sworn to himself last night that today he would be pristine pure. Not a drop of the evil Stregg would wet his lips. That was the only way out of it. The trouble was, just then, it wasn't Stregg he wanted, but a nice cold beer.

He scraped the thought out of his mind, drank a saintly gulp of water, and looked around his room. The homely-looking woman on the wall stared back at him. Sten gave another mental groan and searched for another place to rest his grating eyes—only to find the same woman giving him the same stare. In fact, wherever he looked, there she was again, the skinny-faced homely woman with the loving eyes.

The walls of the room were covered with her portrait, a legacy, Sten had learned, from the man who had proceeded him. Naik Rai, Sten's batman, had assured him that the previous CO had been an excellent Captain of the Guard. Maybe so, but he sure was a lousy painter— almost as lousy as his taste in women. At least, that's what Sten had thought at first, when he had stared at the murals crowding his walls. After the first week living with the lady, he had ordered her image removed—blasted off, if necessary. But then she began to haunt him, and he had countermanded the order—he wasn't sure why. And then it came to him: The man must have *really* loved the woman, no matter how homely.

The records proved it: The captain had been every bit as hardworking, dedicated, and professional as any being before him. Although older than Sten, he had been assured of a long and promising career. Instead, he had pulled every string possible to win a lateral transfer into a dead-end job on some frontier post. And, just before he left, he had married the woman in the picture. The emperor had given the bride away. In his gut, Sten knew what had happened. In the few months he had been there, Sten had realized that his particular post was for a bachelor, or someone who cared very little about spouse and family. There just weren't enough hours in the day to do the job properly. And the good captain had realized that enough to throw it all away for the homely lady in the pictures.

Sten thought he had been a very wise man.

Once you got past the murals, the rest of Sten's room dissolved into a bachelor officer's dilemma: a jungle of items both personal and work-related. It wasn't that Sten didn't know where everything was; his was a carefully ordered mind that heaped things into their proper mounds. The trouble was, mounds kept sliding into one another, a bit like his current interests. His professional studies, for example, blended into a gnawing hunger for history— anyone's history, it didn't matter. And, along with that, the obvious technical tracts a fortieth-century military being might need, as well as Sten's Vulcan-born tech-related curiosity. Also, since leaving Vulcan, he had become an avid reader of almost everything in general.

Two particular things in the room illustrated the personal and professional crush: Filling up one corner was a many-layered map of the castle, the surrounding buildings, and the castle grounds. Each hinged section was at least two meters high, and showed a two-dimensional view of every alley and cranny and drawing room of the entire structure. Sten had traced the sectional map down in a dusty archive after his first month on the job, when he realized that the sheer size of the castle and its grounds made it impossible for him to ever see it all on foot. And without personal, detailed knowledge of every Imperial centimeter of the area, he would not be able to perform his primary function—which was to keep the Emperor safe.

Crammed a few meters away from the map was the other major feature in Sten's current life. Sitting on a fold-up field table was a very expensive miniholoprocessor. It was the biggest expense in Sten's life, not even counting the thousands of hours of time invested in the tiny box lying next to it.

The little box contained Sten's hobby—Model building: not ordinary glue-gun models set into paste-metal dioramas but complete, working and living holographic displays ranging from simple ancient engines to tiny factories manned by their workers. Each was contained on a tiny card, jammed with complex computer equations.

Sten was then building a replica of a logging mill. He had imprinted, byte by byte, everything that theoretically made the mill work, including the workers, their job functions, their tools, and the spare parts. Also programmed were other details, such as the wear-factor on a belt drive, the drunken behavior of the head mechanic, etc. When the card slid into the holoprocessor it projected a full-color holographic display of the mill at work. Occasionally, if Sten didn't have his *voilà* moves down, a worker would stumble, or a log would jam, and the whole edifice would tumble apart into a blaze of colored dots.

Sten glanced at the model box guiltily. He hadn't worked on it more than a few hours since he started the job. And, no, there wasn't time now—he had to get to work.

He palmed the video display and the news menu crawled across the screen. TERRORIST DIES IN SPACEPORT BAR EXPLOSION.

Sten thumbed up the story and quickly scanned the details of the Covenanter tragedy. There wasn't much to it at the moment, except for the fact that Godfrey Alain, a high-ranking Fringe World revolutionary, had died in an accident at some seedy bar near the spaceport. It was believed that a few others had also died, but their names had not yet been released. Mostly the article talked about what was *not* known—like what Alain was doing on Prime World, especially in a bar like the Covenanter.

Sten yawned at the story. He had little or no interest in the fate of terrorists. In fact, he had marked PAID to many terrorist careers in his time. Clot Godfrey Alain, as far as he was concerned. He noticed, however, that there were as yet no official statements on Alain's presence.

The only thing he was sure of was that the press had it wrong about the explosion being an "accident." Terrorists do not die accidentally. Sten idly wondered if someone in Mantis Section had sent Alain on to meet his revolutionary maker.

Sten yawned again and began to scroll on just as he got the call. The Eternal Emperor wanted him. Immediately, if not sooner.

CHAPTER EIGHT

THE ETERNAL EMPEROR was an entirely different person from the man Sten had drunk with. He looked many years older, the flesh on his face was sagging, and pouches had appeared beneath his eyes. His complexion was gray underneath the perfect tan. More importantly, the man Sten was observing was stern and grim, with hatred burning just beneath the surface. Sten stirred uneasily in his seat, goose-bumps on the back of his neck. Something was frightening there, and although Sten hadn't the faintest idea what was going on, he hoped to hell it didn't involve a transgression on his part. Sten would not have liked to be the being the Emperor was fixing his attention on at the moment.

"You've read this," the Emperor said coldly, sliding a printout across his desk.

Sten glanced at the fax. It was an update on the death of Godfrey Alain. Puzzled, Sten scanned it, noting that although there were a few more details, they involved mostly color, with few hard facts. "Yes, sir," he said after a moment.

"Are you familiar with this man's background?"

"Not really, sir. Just that he's a terrorist and that he's been a thorn in our side for some time."

The Emperor snorted. "You'll need to know a lot more than that. But no matter. I've given you clearance for his files. You can go over them after we've talked.

"I want the people responsible," the Emperor snapped. "And I want every single swinging Richard of them standing before me, not tomorrow or the next day, but yesterday. And I want them delivered in a nice neat package. And no loose ends. Do you understand me, Captain? No loose ends."

Sten started to nod automatically. Then he stopped himself—no, he didn't understand. And his survival instinct told him he'd better not pretend otherwise. "Excuse me, sir," he finally said, "but I do *not* understand. Perhaps I'm missing something, but what does Godfrey Alain have to do with the captain of your guard?"

The Emperor's face clotted with anger, and he started to rise to his feet. Then he stopped, took a deep breath, and sat down again, the anger barely under control. "You're right, Captain. I'm getting ahead of myself." He took another deep breath. "Fine, then. Let me explain.

"This . . . accident has put all of us in a world of hurt. And if you do believe that it was an accident, then tell me now, because I obviously have the wrong man for the job."

Sten shook his head. "No, sir. I don't think it was an accident."

"Good. Now let me fill you in on the background. And I'm sure I don't have to warn you that not one word I say is to be repeated.

"To begin with, Alain was here to see me."

Sten was surprised. The Eternal Emperor meeting with a terrorist? That was absolutely against Imperial policy. But then Sten remembered who *set* Imperial policy, and kept his mouth shut.

"He had a proposal—and I'm sure it was a serious

one, or I wouldn't have hung myself out like this—to defuse our problems with the Tahn System. Simply put, he wanted to set up a buffer zone, his Fringe Worlds—under my aegis—between the Tahn and the Empire."

"But wouldn't that make him a traitor to his own people?"

The Eternal Emperor gave Sten a grim smile. "One man's traitor is another man's patriot. The way I see it is that it finally got through the thick heads of Alain and his people that they are the ones doing all the bleeding.

"Every time the Tahn act and we retaliate, they're the ones who get it in the neck. And they are also the ones who take all the blame and get nothing in return."

"And so he set up a secret meeting with you?" Sten said, filling in the gaps. "The Tahn found out and short-stopped him."

"Not quite that simple. Yes, he was going to meet with me. Eventually. But first off, there was to be an initial meeting with one of my best diplomatic operatives. A man named Craigwel."

"One of the unidentified bodies in the bar?" Sten guessed.

"Exactly. And he's going to stay unidentified. Officially, that is."

"Any other victims in the bar I should know about?"

There was a long hesitation. And then the emperor shook his head, firmly, no.

"Just worry about Craigwel and Alain. Now, it was supposed to work like this. After exchanging the usual password, Alain and Craigwel were supposed to request Booth C. It had already been reserved for them and secured.

"Alain was then going to lay out his plan, and if he convinced Craigwel of his sincerity, we would have gone to the next step. A personal meeting with me."

"But then the Tahn stepped in," Sten said.

"Maybe. But don't be too sure of that. There are about five sides too many in this thing, each one of them with a reason to prevent any negotiations.

"Perhaps it was the Tahn. Perhaps it was someone from

our camp. And who knows—perhaps it was one of Alain's own people. Regardless. That's what I want you to find out."

"But why me, sir? it sounds like a job for a cop. And that I'm not. Clot, I wouldn't even know—"

"No, Captain. This is *not* a job for the police. It's much too delicate a situation. The police *are* investigating. And, officially, they will round up a few suspects and those people will be publicly punished."

He leaned closer to Sten to emphasize his next point. "And those people will be scapegoats. I don't even care how guilty they are. Just as long as we have somebody to feed the public lions. Because there is a good chance that what you find out will remain classified for the next hundred years."

He fixed Sten with a cold stare.

"Do I make myself absolutely clear, Captain?"

"Yes, sir." Sten came to his feet. "If that will be all, sir." He snapped a salute.

"Yes, Captain. That's all. For now."

Sten wheeled and was out the door.

CHAPTER NINE

"DRINK UP, CHEENAS," Dynsman shouted. "It's all on me today." He pounded on the table for the bartender's attention and made motions for six more brimming schooners of narcobeer with synthalk backs. His companions hissed their approval. Dynsman watched in fascination as Usige, his best pal in the group, grabbed a liter jug, unhinged his jaws, and poured down the whole thing without a gasp or even breathing hard. "That's it Usige, old buddy. Drink 'em down and make room for another."

Of course, downing a liter of narcobeer at a gulp was not a great accomplishment for Usige or the others. Their scaled abdomens could swell to almost any proportions, and the only visible signs of inebriation the Psaurus ever displayed was to turn a slightly darker shade of purple.

"I tell you, cheenas, today begins a whole new life for yours truly. I hit it lucky for a change. And I'm gonna keep hittin' that way. I can feel it in my bones."

Usige's grin framed serrated rows of needle-sharp teeth. "I don't want to pry, Dynsman dearest," he hissed, "but you've been flashing a wad of credits around that would even choke one of us." He waved at his yellow-eyed companions. "Your obvious good fortune delights us all. But..."

"You wanna know if I can put you in on it," Dynsman broke in.

"That would be lovely, old fellow. Business, as you no doubt know, has been a touch slow."

"Sorry, pal. This was a one-time number. The kind we all dream of. I pick up the rest of my pay in a couple of hours, and then it's party time for the rest of my life."

Usige tried to hide his disappointment, not an easy task; the skin of a Psaurus glows when the creature is disturbed. Dynsman noticed the change and leaned over to pat his friend's claw.

"Don't clottin' worry. Dynsman never forgets his cheenas. Fact, I might make a business of it, now that I'm comin' into all these credits.

"What the clot, you boys come up with somethin' tasty, need a little financing, you can always hit me up. Low interest rates, and maybe a small cut of the action if the deal's really sweet."

Usige's color returned to normal. There was an idea that appealed to him. Rates for the criminal element in Prime World tended to be not only enormous but also more than painful if payment was delayed.

"That is certainly worth considering, friend. We can discuss it later. Now, meanwhile..." Usige rose to his

full two-and-a-half-meter height and snaked out his foot-
long orange tongue as a signal to the others to follow.

"Unlike you, we still have to pay the rent."

"Anything nice?"

"Not really. Just a little warehouse B&E."

Dynsman sighed his understanding and watched his
friends slither out of the bar, their long tails scraping the
floor after them. He checked the time: still a little more
than two hours before his meeting. He had been hoping
that Usige would keep him company, because he hated
waiting alone. He was itching with impatience, and
although he didn't realize it yet, a tiny warning bell was
still tinkling at the back of his mind.

He ordered up another drink, dumped a credit coin in
the newsvid, and began scanning the sports menu. He
stifled a yawn as he picked through the sparse offerings.
Not much happening so soon after Empire Day—especially if you wanted to get a bet down. Bored, he flipped
over to the general news section. Dynsman had less than
no interest in anything involving the straight workings of
Prime World. But what the clot, maybe something juicy
was going on in his profession. He scanned the menu,
looking for anything involving crime.

He didn't have to scan far. The Covenanter bombing
headline jumped out at him like a holovid. Clot! Clot!
Clot! His target had been clotting political! Dynsman automatically gulped down his shot of synthalk and then almost
equally as automatically found himself gagging on his own
bile. He fought to keep it back.

Steady, man, steady. Gotta clotting think. Gotta clotting—And the first thing he realized was that he was as
good as a dead man. No credits would be waiting for him
when he met with his contact. Although the payment, he
was certain, would be quite final.

He ran over the possibilities. Obviously, he would have
to be satisfied with the roll in his pocket. Would it be
enough to pay for a hideout? How long would it take
before pursuers forgot about him? Dynsman groaned; he
knew the answer. It had been set up just as skillfully as
Godfrey Alain. There would be no forgetting.

There was only one solution, and the thought frightened him almost as much as the cold-faced man he knew would soon be tracking him. Dynsman had to get off Prime World.

CHAPTER TEN

LIEUTENANT LISA HAINES, Homicide Division, wanted to kill someone. At that particular moment, she wasn't particular who it would be, but she wanted the method to be interesting, preferably one that involved parboiling.

And *evisceration*, she added, as the combat car with the Imperial color-slash on it grounded on the crosswalk.

The man who climbed out wasn't the pompous beribboned bureaucrat she'd expected when her superiors advised that an Imperial liaison officer would be assigned to the case. The man who came toward her was young and slender, and wore only the plain brown livery of the Imperial Household. He appeared to be unarmed.

Sten, on the other hand, was nursing his own attitude. He barely noticed that the woman was about his own age and under different circumstances could have been described as attractive. Sten was flat irked. He still had no idea why the Emperor had picked him for the assignment, since he knew less than nothing about police procedures and murder investigations. He'd spent more of his career on the other side.

From his earliest days Sten had hated cops—the sociopatrolmen on his home world of Vulcan through the various types he'd encountered in Mantis to the military policemen who attempted to keep control on the Intoxication and Intercourse worlds.

"Captain, uh, Sten?"

Two could do that. "Uh, Lieutenant . . . what was your last name again?"

"Haines."

"Haines."

"I assume you'd like to see the report," Lisa said, and, without waiting for an answer, shoved the plate-projector at him.

Sten tried to pretend that he knew what the various forms and scrawled entries meant, then gave up. "I'd appreciate a briefing."

"No doubt."

2043 Tacunit 7-Y reported an explosion, arrived at scene at 2047, Tacunit commander reported ratcheta-ratcheta, response ratcheta ratcheta, ambulance, no suspects, description, blur.

Sten looked at where the Convenanter had been. The entire baseplate the bar had stood on was enclosed in what appeared to be an enormous airbag. On one side, next to the catwalk, was an airlock.

"Step one," Haines explained, "in any homicide is to seal the scene. We put that bubble around the area, pump all oxygen out, and replace the atmosphere with a neutral gas, if you're interested in details."

"I am interested in details, Lieutenant." Sten began once more with the report. On second reading, it was no more (or less) confusing than any military afteraction report. Sten reread it a third time.

"Would you like a guided tour, Captain? It's messy, by the way."

"If I start to get sick, I'll let you know."

The bubble suits looked a little like close-fitting shallow-water diving dress, except that the lower chest area had a large, external evidence bag and the upper chest area bulged, making the wearer look somewhat like a pouter pigeon. Inside the bulge was a small alloy table where an investigator could put notes, records, etcetera. The suit also had a backpack with air supply and battery plate.

Sten thumbed his suit closed and followed Haines

through the airlock into the ruins of the Covenanter. Of course it wasn't the first time Sten had examined a bomb site, but it was the first time he wasn't busy running away from it or expecting another one momentarily. He'd learned, years ago, not to consider that gray, pink, or yellow dangling ropes, snaillike particles, and bas-relief facial bones had once been human. Sten oriented himself. There . . . there was the door. That low parapet would have been the bar. Along . . . there . . . would have been the booths.

Two other cops were inside the bubble, laboriously scraping fire-foam from the floor and walls.

"You're right," Sten said conciliatorily. "A mess."

"Two of them," Haines said bitterly.

"Ah?"

"Captain, I'll—" Haines caught herself, shut off her radio, clicked Sten's off, and touched faceplates. "This is for your information only. This crime scene is so mucked up that we'll be very lucky if we ever get anything on the case."

"You know, Lieutenant," Sten said thoughtfully, "if you'd said that with an open mike I'd have figured you were setting up an alibi. So GA. I'm not sure I track you."

Haines thought that maybe the liaison type wouldn't be quite the pain in the sitter she'd expected. "SOP, Captain, is very explicit. Whatever officer comes on a homicide scene, he is to first take appropriate action—looking for the killer, requesting med, whatever.

"Second, is to notify homicide. At that point, we take charge.

"But that isn't what happened." She waved her arm helplessly.

"That tac unit responded just before 2100 last night. Homicide was not notified for ten hours!"

"Why not?"

"Hell if I know," Lisa said. "But I could guess."

"GA."

"Our tactical squads think they're the best. The Imperial Guards. I guess, since they were first on the scene they wanted it to be their case."

Sten thought back through the report. "Is tac presence normal in this area?"

"Not especially. Not unless there's some kind of disorder, or maybe for security on some classified shipment. Or if the area's high-crime."

"And?"

"The tac sergeant said his squad had been pounding these catwalks for three weeks, and nothing had happened."

Odd. Sten wondered: Since the last two weeks had been the pandemonium before Empire Day, it *did* seem as if the tac unit was misassigned. However, in Sten's experience cops had always found a way to stay away from where they could get hurt. But the tac squad's assignment could be something to ask about.

"Look at this," Haines continued. "No fire, but the tac sergeant opened up the extinguishers. He and his people went in. Three bodies. Dead dead. And so he and his people spend the next ten hours galumphing around trying to play detective. For instance..."

Lisa pointed down at the flooring. "That size-fourteen hoof is not a clue—it's some tac corporal's brogan right in the middle of that bloodstain."

Sten decided that he still didn't like cops that much and cut her off. "Okay, Lieutenant. We've all got problems. What do you have so far?"

Haines started a court singsong: "We have evidence of a bomb, prior planted. No clue as to detonation method, or explosive. The bomb specialists have not arrived as yet."

"You can hold on them," Sten said dryly. "Maybe I know a little about that."

He'd already spotted the blast striations on what remained of the ceiling. Sten lifted an alloy ladder over to the center of the striations. Sten may have been ignorant of police SOP, but he knew a great deal about things that went *boom*.

"Lieutenant," Sten said, turning his radio back on, "you want to put a recorder on?"

Haines shrugged—now the Imperial hand-sitter was

going to play expert, so let him make an ass of himself. She followed orders.

"The bomb was mounted in the ceiling light fixture. We've got . . . looks like some bits of circuitry here . . . the explosive was high-grade, and shaped. The blast went out to the sides, very little damage done to the overhead.

"Your bomb people should be able to figure out whether the bomb was set off on a timer or command-det. But I'd guess it was set off by command."

"We have a team checking the area."

Sten got down off the ladder and reexamined the striations. They occupied almost a full 360 degrees. But not quite. Sten hummed to himself and ran an eyeball azimuth from that area toward the wall.

"Thank you, Lieutenant." Sten went toward the airlock and exited. Outside, he stripped off his suit and walked well away from the bustling techs around the bubble.

Haines removed her suit and joined him. "Are you through playing detective, Captain?"

"I'll explain, Lieutenant Haines. I got stuck with this drakh job and I don't know what the hell I'm doing. That sends me into orbit, Lieutenant. Now what lit your stupid fuse?"

Haines glowered at him. "Item: I'm in the same mess you're in. I'm a cop. A very good cop. So I come down here and see what I've got to work with.

"And *then* I get some—some—"

"Clot?" Sten offered, half smiling. He was starting to like the woman.

"Thank you. Clot, who comes down here, says one thing, and then is going to go back to the palace and get his medal. Let me tell you, Captain, I do not need any of this!"

"You through?"

"For the moment."

"Fine. Let's get some lunch, then, and I'll bring you up to speed."

The restaurant sat very close to Landing Area 17AFO. Except for clear blast shields between the field and the patio area, it was open-air. The place was about half-full of longshoremen, docking clerks, and ship crew. The combination of one man in Imperial livery and one woman who was obviously the heat guaranteed Sten and Haines privacy.

Dining was cafeteria-style. The two took plates of food, paid, and went to the far edge of the dining area. Both of them saw the other reflexively checking for parabolic mike locations, and, for the first time, smiled.

"Before you get started, Captain," Haines said through a mouthful of kimchi and pork, "do you want to talk about that booth?"

Sten chewed, nodded, and pretended innocence.

"Thank you. I'd already spotted that the bomb was directional. Actually, semidirectional. It was intended to garbage the whole joint—except for one booth."

"Good call, Lieutenant."

"First question—the one booth that wasn't destroyed was rigged with every antibugging device I've ever heard of. Is there any explanation, from let us say 'top-level' sources? What was a security setup like that doing in a sleazo bar?"

Sten told her, omitting only Craigwel's identity and position as the Emperor's personal troubleshooter. He also didn't feel that the lieutenant needed to know that Alain was planning a meeting with the Emperor himself. Any meeting with any Imperial official was enough for her to work on, he felt. Sten finished, and changed the subject, eyeing a forkful of kimchi cautiously. "By the way—what is this, anyway?"

"Very dead Earth cabbage, garlic, and herbs. It helps if you don't smell it before you eat it."

"Since you know about bombs," Sten asked, "did you figure out why no shrapnel?"

Haines puzzled.

Sten dug into his pocket and set a somewhat flattened ball bearing on the table. "The bomb's explosive was semidirectional. To make sure the bomb took care of anyone in the bar, the bomber also taped these on top of the explosive. Except the area facing that booth.

"Prog, Lieutenant?"

Haines knew enough military slang to understand the question. She pushed her plate aside, put her fingers together, and began theorizing.

"The bomber wanted everybody in that bar dead—except whoever was in that booth."

"If Alain and your man *had* been in that booth when the bomb went off, they would have been . . . concussed, possibly, or suffering blast breakage at the worst, right, Captain?"

"Correct."

"The bomber knew about that booth . . . and had to have known Alain would be in that booth on that particular night."

Haines whistled tunelessly and drained her beer. "So for sure we have a political murder, don't we, Captain? Clot!"

Sten nodded glumly, went to the counter, and brought back two more beers.

"Not just a political murder, but one done by someone who knew exactly what Alain's movements were supposed to be, correct?"

"You're right—but you aren't exactly making my day."

"Drakh!" Lisa swore. "Clottin' stinkin' politics! Why couldn't I get stuck with a nice series of mass sex murders."

Sten wasn't listening. He'd just taken the reasoning one step further. Impolitely, he grabbed the plate-projector from under Haines' arm and began flipping through it.

"Assassination," Lisa continued, getting more depressed by the minute. "That'll mean a pro killer, and whoever hired it done will be untouchable. And I'll be running a precinct at one of the poles."

"Maybe not," Sten said. "Look. Remember the bomb? It was just supposed to knock Alain cross-eyed, yes? Then what was supposed to happen?"

"Who can tell? It never did."

"Question, Lieutenant. Why did an ambulance *not* called by this tac sergeant show up within minutes of the blast? Don't you think that maybe—"

Haines had already completed the thought. Beer unfinished, she was heading for Sten's combat car.

CHAPTER ELEVEN

PORT SOWARD HOSPITAL bore a strange resemblance to its oddly shaped cnidarian receiving clerk. It just grew from an emergency hospital intended to handle incoming ship disasters, industrial accidents, and whatever other catastrophe would come up within a ten-kilometer circle around Soward itself. But disasters and accidents have a way of growing wildly, so Soward Hospital sprawled a lot, adding ship-capable landing platforms here, radiation wards there, and nonhuman sections in still a third place.

All of that made Admissions even more a nightmare than in most hospitals. In spite of high-speed computers, personal ID cards, and other improvements, the hospital's central area went far toward defining chaos.

Sten and Haines waited beside a large central "desk," the outer ring of which was for files and such. The second ring contained a computer whose memory circuits rivaled an Imperial military computer. In the center swam the clerk(s), a colony of intelligent polyps—cnidarians, beings which began life as individuals and then, for protection, grew together—literally, like coral. But most cnidarians did not get along. The one in front of Sten—he mentally labeled it A—burbled in fury, snatched a moisture-resistant file from Polyp B, tossed it across the ring to Polyp R, Sten estimated, brushed Polyp C's tentacles off A's own terminal, and finally turned to the two people waiting. Its "voice" was just shrill enough to add to the surrounding madness as white-clad hospital types steered lift gurneys past, patients leaned, lay, or stood against the walls, and relatives wailed or wept.

"You see what it's like? You see?" The polyp's feeder tentacles were bicycling wildly against the bottom of the tank.

"Police," Lisa said dryly, holding out a card with one hand. She touched the card with an index finger, and the "badge" glowed briefly.

"Another cop. This has been one of those days. Some wiper comes in, bleeding like—like a stuck human. Drunk, of course. He doesn't tell me that he's union, and so I send him to the Tombs. How was I know to he was union? Job-related and all that, and now I've got all this data. He'll probably die before I get the paperwork through. Now what do *you* want?"

"Last night, around 2100 hours, an ambulance responded to a call."

"We have thousands of ambulances. For what?"

"An explosion."

"There are many kinds of explosions. Ship, atomsuit, housing, radiation. I *can't* help you if you don't help me!"

Haines gave the polyp the file. The being submerged briefly, only the plate-projector, held in one tentacle, above the surface. Then another tentacle wove behind the being to a terminal and began tapping keys.

"Yes. Ambulance GE145 it was. No input on who summoned it. You see what my trouble is? No one seems to *care* about proper files."

Sten broke in. "Where would this ambulance have been routed to."

"Thank you, man. At least someone knows the proper question. Since it was sent to a . . . drinking establishment . . . unless other data was input, it would have gone to the Tombs."

"The Tombs?"

"Human emergency treatment, nonindustrial." The polyp pulled a square of plas from the counter and touched the edges of it. An outline of the sprawling hospital sprang into life on it. Further tentacling and a single red line wound its way through the corridors.

"You are...here. You want to go *there*. They'll be able to help you. Maybe."

Sten had one final question. "Why is it called the Tombs?"

"Because this is where our—I believe the phrase is down and under—go. And if they weren't before, they are when they get to the Tombs."

"GE145. Weird." The desk intern was puzzled. "No entry on who dispatched it—came from out-hospital. Three DOA's. They're...um, being held for autopsy results, Lieutenant."

"Question, Doctor. Assuming this ambulance had arrived with live victims, what would have happened then?"

"Depends on the injury."

"Blast. Shock. Possible fractures," Sten said.

"Um...that would have gone to—let me check last night's roster...Dr. Knox would have treated them."

"Where is he?"

"Let me see...not on shift today. Pity."

"Would he be in the hospital?"

"No, not at all. Dr. Knox was hardly one of us. He was a volunteer."

"Do you have a contact number on him?" Lisa asked.

"It should be right—no. No, we don't have anything on his sheet. That's unusual."

"Two unusuals, Doctor. I'd like to see your files on this Knox."

"I'm sorry, Lieutenant. But without a proper court order, not even the police—"

Sten's own card was out. "On Imperial Service, Doctor."

The intern's eyes widened. "Certainly...perhaps, back in my office. We'll use the terminal there. Genevieve? Would you take the floor for me?"

Ten minutes later Sten knew they had something.

Or rather, by having nothing, they had something.

KNOX, DR. JOHN, began the hospital's scanty info card. No such doctor was licensed on Prime World, as Sten quickly learned. Yet somehow a "Dr. Knox" had convinced someone at Soward Hospital—either a person or a computer—that he was legitimate. His listed home address was a recently demolished apartment building. His supposed private clinic was a restaurant, one which had been in existence at that address for almost ten years.

"So this Knox," Sten mused, still staring at the fiche, "shows up from nowhere as a volunteer two weeks ago."

"He was an excellent emergency surgeon, the intern said. "I prepped some patients for him."

"What did he look like?"

"Tall," the intern said hesitantly. "One eighty-five, one ninety centimeters. Slender build, almost endomorphic. Seventy kilograms estimated weight. Eyes...I don't remember. He was very proud of his hair. Gray it was. Natural, he swore. Wore it mane-style."

"Not bad," Haines said. "You ever think of being a cop?"

"In this job I sometimes think I am one."

"You said he was 'hardly one of you.' Did you mean just because he was a volunteer?" Sten asked.

"No. Uh—you see, we don't exactly get Imperial-class medicos here. The pay. The conditions. The patients. So when we get a volunteer as good as Dr. Knox, well..." And the intern interrupted himself: "His room!"

"Knox had a room?"

"Of course. All of us do—our shifts are two-day marathons."

"Where would it be?"

"I'll get a floor chart."

"Very private sort, this Knox," Lisa said. "His room card specifies no mechanical or personal cleaning wanted. Maybe *we'll* get something."

Sten suspected they would get nothing, and if they got as thorough a nothing as he feared...

"Four thirteen."

Lisa took the passcard from the back of the room file.

"Hang on. And stay back from the door."

Millimeter by millimeter, Sten checked the jamb around the slide-door's edges. He found it just above the floor—a barely visible gray hair stretched across the doorjamb.

"We need an evidence team," Sten said. "Your best. But there won't be a bomb inside. I want this room sealed until the evidence team goes through it."

Lisa started to get angry, then snapped a salute.

"Yes, sir. Captain, sir. Anything else?"

"Aw drakh," Sten swore. "Sorry. Didn't mean to sound like, like—"

"A cop?"

"A cop." Sten grinned.

The room was ballooned, then gently opened. Finally, the tech team went in.

The three spindars—one adult and two adolescents—were not what Sten had thought expert forensic specialists would look like. As soon as the room was unsealed and the adult lumbered into the bedroom, the two adolescents rolled out of its pouch and began scurrying about with doll-size instruments and meters taken from the pack strapped to the adult's pouch.

The adult spindar was about two meters in any direction and scaled like a pangolin. It surveyed the scuttlings of its two offspring with what might have been mild approval, rebuttoned the instrument pack with a prehensile subarm, scratched its belly thoughtfully, and sat down on its rear legs in the center of the room. The being chuffed three times experimentally, then introduced itself as Technician Bernard Spilsbury. Spindars having names unpronounceable to any being without both primary and secondary voice boxes, they found human names a useful conceit—names selected from within whatever field the spindar worked in.

"Highly unusual," it chuffed. "Very highly unusual. Recollect only one case like that. My esteemed colleague Halperin handled that one. Most interesting. Would you be interested in hearing about it while my young protegés continue?"

Sten looked at Haines. She shrugged, and Sten got the

idea that once a spindar started, nothing short of high explosives could shut him up.

"Out on one of the pioneer worlds it was. Disremember at the moment which one. Pair of miners it was. Got into some unseemly squabble about claims or stakegrubs or whatever miners bicker about.

"First miner waited until his mate got into a suit, then shot him in the face. Stuffed the corpus into the drive, suit and all."

One young spindar held up a minidisplay to his parent. Columns of figures, unintelligible to Sten, reeled past.

The young one chittered, and the older one rumbled.

"Even more so," the spindar said. "If you'll excuse me?" His forearm dug larger instruments from the pack, then he waddled to the bed, half stood, and began running a pickup across it. "Curiouser and curiouser."

"Speaking of curious," Haines said quietly to Sten. "You wondered about that tac squad? I think I'll check on just *why* they were assigned to that area.

"I owe you a beer, Captain."

They smiled at each other.

Before Sten could say anything, the spindar was back beside him. "That took care of one sort of evidence, of course."

"You found something?"

"No, no. I meant the miner. To continue, he then dumped the ship's atmosphere and disposed of all of his mate's belongings and went peaceably on his way.

"Questioned some months later, said miner maintained that he had shipped solo. Contrary to the ship's lading, no one had been with him. Claimed the other party had never showed at lift-off, and he himself had been too lazy to change the manifest. There was, indeed, no sign that anyone had ever been on the ship besides this individual.

"But Halperin produced evidence that it was physically impossible for one human to have consumed the amount of rations missing from the ship. The miner contradicted him. Swore that he was a hearty eater. Pity."

Evidently that was the end of the spindar's story. By then, Sten knew better, but asked what happened anyway.

"The planetary patrols in the frontier worlds are somewhat pragmatic. Not to say ruthless. They purchased an equivalent amount of rations and sat the suspect down in front of them. Gave him thirty days to prove his innocence. Trial by glut, I suppose you would refer to it. A definite pity."

Again the spindar dug out instruments and, attaching extensions to them, swept the ceiling area. "The man died of overeating on the third day. Odd system of justice you humans have.

"This case," the spindar continued, reseating himself, "is even stranger. You do, just as you warned me, Lieutenant, appear to have a great quantity of nothing."

For Sten, that was the first positive lead toward finding the disappeared Dr. Knox.

CHAPTER TWELVE

"AND WHAT, CAPTAIN, does nothing give you?" the Eternal Emperor asked.

The Emperor might appear less angry, but Sten was determined to keep the briefing as short as possible. As long as he stuck to business, he probably couldn't get in much trouble.

"This Knox did not want the room cleaned. My theory is that he was afraid some personal evidence might still be in the room's automatic cleaning filters.

"We found no fingerprints. No traces of dead skin, no urine traces in the bed, no sweat or oil stains in the pillow. Also, there was no IR residue in the bed coverings."

"Thank you, Captain. I will now assume you and the

techs produced every sort of zero-trace science can look for. Explain."

Sten did. Knox not only cleaned the room minutely, but also used sophisticated electronics to remove *all* traces of his occupancy.

"So. Your, uh, Knox character's more than just a professional doctor."

"That's the assumption," Sten said carefully. "Haines—she's the police OIC on the case—is tracing doctors who might have learned another set of skills."

"If your Knox is as good as you say, Captain, I'd assume he was an offworlder."

"Haines is checking all Prime World arrivals within the last E-year, sir."

"Good luck. Prediction, Captain: You're going to draw a big fat blank."

"Probably. Which is why we're working angle B—the bomber."

The Emperor shrugged. "If you've got one pro, why couldn't the bomber be just as faceless?"

"Because the bomber—" Sten caught himself before he could say "blew it."—"made a mistake."

The Emperor considered. "All right. Work that angle. Is there anything else?"

Sten shook his head—there was no point in mentioning the tacsquad's mysterious presence until Haines had more information.

"One more thing, Captain. For your information only. The Tahn Embassy's Principal Secretary has requested an interview with me. I think we may both assume what it will be regarding.

"And I really would like to be able to tell him more than 'I got plenty of nothing.'

"That's all, Captain. You may go."

CHAPTER THIRTEEN

STEN FINGERED THE pore-pattern key on his mailbox and absentmindedly fished out its contents. It was the usual junk—*The Imperial Guard Times*, *Forces Journal*, the palace's daily house organ, the latest promotion list, an ad from a military jeweler—all of which went into the disposal. Sten tucked one fiche—reminder of his somewhat past-due bill from a uniform tailor—into his belt pouch and started to close the little door. Then he saw something else and fished it out curiously.

It was a real paper envelope, addressed by hand to "Captain Sten, Imperial Household." Sten fumbled the envelope open. Three other pieces of paper dropped into his hand. The first was a blank envelope. The second was a thick engraved paper card:

MARR & SENN
Request the Honor of
Your Attendance
At a Dinner Reception
for
KAI HAKONE

RSVP   Guest

Perplexed, Sten stared at the invitation. Of course he knew Marr and Senn as the Imperial caterers and unofficial social arbiters at Court. The brief meetings he'd had with them had been purely official, even though he was personally intrigued by their bitchy humor and warmth. He wondered why they'd invite a lowly captain, regardless of position, to what must be a Major Social Event.

The third piece of paper, also hand-written, explained it. The card said simply, "It's time for old friends to meet again," and was signed Sofia.

Umm. Sten knew that the woman he'd had a brief but very passionate affair with during a previous assignment was on Prime World—he'd been responsible for getting Sofia off Nebta before the shooting started—but had semideliberately not looked her up, having no idea any longer what he felt toward her.

Sten decided he needed some advice. In the Imperial Household, unofficial advice for officers was the province of the Grand Chamberlain. His offices were only a few hundred meters from the Emperor's own business suite.

The Grand Chamberlain, Fleet Admiral Mik Ledoh (Ret.), looked like everyone's favorite grandsire. Sten, however, had looked up the admiral's record as part of his routine security check while settling into the job.

A hundred years before, Ledoh had been a fireball. Literally. During the Palafox rising, his tacship flight was ordered to provide cover for a small plantery landing. Unfortunately, intelligence had erred, and the planet was strongly defended by hardened orbital satellites.

Ledoh had supervised the conversion of the tacships into pilot-aimed nuclear missiles, and then led the strike himself. He and three other pilots managed to jettison their capsules successfully.

Then, over the next decades, he'd become the Imperial fleet's prime specialist in planetary assaults. Promotion came rapidly for a man who, basically, specialized in logistics. By the time of the Mueller Wars, Ledoh was a fleet admiral.

The Mueller Wars were one of the more confusing conflicts of the Empire, since the battles were fought near-simultaneously on dozens of different worlds. During the wars, Ledoh commanded the landings in the Crais System, and in a war noted for its bloodiness and ineptness, took the system with minimal losses—minimal, at least, compared to the fifty to seventy percent casualties the war's other battles produced.

After peace was signed, Ledoh retired for some years,

then emigrated to Prime World. When the previous Grand Chamberlain died in office following an unfortunate surfeit of smoked eels, Ledoh, with his combat record and, more important, logistical ability, was a natural for the job.

Sten could never figure out how Ledoh managed to juggle the various official and unofficial requirements of a household the size of a medium city and still maintain benevolence. Sten was very grateful that he had nothing more to worry about than keeping the Emperor alive, and the welfare of 150 Gurkhas.

Sten stepped inside Ledoh's office and paused.

Ledoh, Colonel Fohlee, CO of the Praetorians, and Arbogast, the Imperial Household's paymaster, were staring at a wallscreen readout.

"Colonel," Arbogast said, "I am not attempting to involve myself in militaria. All I am doing is trying to clear this inquiry from Himself regarding the, and I quote, inordinately high desertion rate in your unit."

"What does the Emperor expect to happen when you dump a lot of young soldiers into the middle of Prime? Any virgin can be seduced."

"Another area which isn't my expertise," Arbogast said. He and Fohlee quite clearly hated each other. Ledoh attempted mediation.

"There were four desertions this month alone, Colonel. Perhaps you should examine the selection method for your Praetorians."

Fohlee turned on Ledoh. "Does not compute, Admiral. Candidates for the Praetorians are personally vetted by myself or my adjutant."

Arbogast came in before Ledoh could respond. "No one is trying to assign blame, Colonel. But your records indicate that almost forty men from your unit have disappeared in the last E-year alone. And none of these deserters has turned himself in or been arrested. The Emperor feels that something is wrong."

"I'm aware of that," Fohlee said. "My staff is devoting full attention to the problem."

"Perhaps," Ledoh said, "we're putting too much demand on the young soldiers."

"Perhaps," Fohlee said reluctantly. "I'll look into it myself."

"Thank you, Colonel. I'll report to the emperor that you have taken over full personal responsibility." Arbogast gathered his file, nodded to Ledoh and Sten, and disappeared back toward the rabbit-warren filing system.

"Clotting clerks," Fohlee snarled, then turned and saw Sten. "Captain."

"Colonel Fohlee."

"I've been trying to contact you for most of today."

"Sorry, Colonel," Sten said. "I was under special orders."

Fohlee snorted. "No doubt. I've been observing your troops, Captain. And, while I never believe in telling another commander his business, it appears to me that some of your soldiers are less than adequately concerned about their appearance."

"Gurkhas are pretty lousy at spit and polish," Sten agreed.

"It's been my experience, having commanded soldiers from every race, that none of them cannot be taught proper military appearance."

Even though Fohlee was nowhere near Sten's chain of command, there was little benefit in getting into a slanging match with a superior officer.

"Thank you for bringing the matter to my attention," Sten said formally. "I'll check into it."

Fohlee nodded a very military nod. Once up, once down. He collected his file, came to attention, saluted Ledoh, and brushed past Sten.

Ledoh waited until the colonel's metal-tapped boot-heels resounded down the corridor, then smiled. "Offload, young Sten. What's the prog?"

Sten was still staring out the door.

"Don't fret the colonel, boy. He's just grinding his molars."

"I see. But what the hell do I have to do with why his toy soldiers are disappearing?"

"Jealousy."

"Huh?"

"Colonel Fohlee is deeply disturbed that—by Fohlee's thinking at least—the Eternal Emperor puts so little faith in his Praetorians, and chooses the Gurkhas for immediate security."

Sten blinked. "That—no offense, sir—is damned silly."

"The smallness of the military mind in peacetime, young Sten, should never be overrated. At any rate. Your problem, now."

"It's, well, unofficial. And personal."

"Oh-hoh." Ledoh touched a key on his desk and the door behind Sten slid shut and the CONFERENCE light on the exterior went on. "Timecheck?"

Sten looked at his watch finger. "Seventeen forty-five."

Ledoh sighed contentedly and fished a flask out of his desk. Two pewter cups went beside it, and Ledoh gestured with the bottle. "Join me in a libation of this substance our Eternal Distiller refers to as Scotch."

"Uh, I'm not sure if I'm off duty."

"As my prerogative as Household Chamberlain, you are officially off duty."

Sten grinned as Ledoh filled the cups.

"I have no idea," Ledoh said plaintively, "why His Highness insists on gifting me with this vile swill."

The two men drank.

"GA, young man."

Sten passed Ledoh the invitation.

Ledoh's eyebrows slithered slightly in amazement. "Great Empire, but you rate, young man. *I* wasn't invited to this bash."

Sten handed the personal note across.

"Ah. Now I see. Who is this Sofia?"

"A, uh, young woman I am—was—friendly with."

"Suddenly it all becomes very clear. Pour yourself another, son."

Sten followed orders.

"Firstly, this event is, as the vid-chatter says, the primo social event of the season."

Sten didn't want to seem ignorant, but—"Who is this Hakone?"

"Tsk. Young officers should read more. He is an author. Very controversial and all that. Writes about, generally, the military, from, shall we say, a somewhat unique point of view.

"Were the Eternal Emperor not who he is, in fact, Hakone's writing might be termed borderline treason."

"That settles that, then."

"Negative, young man. The Emperor encourages dissent—short of anyone's actually putting it into practice. And as you may have discovered after Empire Day, he likes his officers to think freely."

"So I should go?"

"You should go. Excellent visibility for career and all that. However, there remains one problem. This young lady . . . Sofia."

"Yeah," Sten agreed.

"Without prying, young Sten, what are your current feelings toward the lady?"

"I'm not sure."

"Then there *is* a problem—besides the fact that both our glasses are empty. Thank you.

"Marr and Senn believe in keeping, shall we say, a lively household. By this I mean that they have in residence some of the most marriageable beings in the Empire."

"Oops," Sten said, almost spilling his Scotch.

"Exactly. If this Sofia is able to invite you to the fete, she must be one of Marr and Senn's Eligibles."

Sten couldn't believe it. "Me?"

"Of course, Captain. You could be considered very desirable. I assume this Sofia comes from some off-planet nobility or other, and probably has wealth. For her, marrying someone who has the appropriate hero awards, someone who is part of the Imperial Household, and, most important, someone who has been selected at a very young age for a fairly important command, might, shall we say, signify?"

"I'm not going!"

"Do not be so absolutist, Sten. Consider the invitation. It says 'Guest,' does it not? The answer to your problem is simple. Contact an incredibly lovely young lady of your acquaintance and take her. That should defuse the Sofia situation handily."

Sten poured his drink down and shook his head sadly.

"Admiral, all I've done since I've been on Prime is my job. I don't know any young ladies—let alone any incredibly lovely ones."

"Ah well. Perhaps the Emperor will be willing to give the bride away, then."

Sten blanched.

CHAPTER FOURTEEN

THE TOWER WAS a shudder of light at the end of a long, narrow valley. A gravcar flared over the mountains, spearing the valley with its landing lights—hesitating as the autopilot oriented itself, and then *whoosh*ed toward the tower along the broad avenue that was the valley. Moments later, other gravcars followed its route, hovering momentarily then bursting for the tower in a rush.

Marr and Senn had invested half their credits and most of their ultraartistic souls in the tower. It needled up from a broad base to a slender penthouse perch. The tower was constructed of every imaginable mineral, metal, or crystal that responded pleasingly to light. For *their* living quarters, Senn and Marr had had no interest in conventional building materials. Nor were the materials uniform in shape or size—a vaguely oval lump might be placed next to a perfect square. Light in all its forms was all that counted. Red light fired by emotional changes; blue from the musk of wild valley animals; and all the other primary colors from the constantly changing humidity and temperature of the valley itself. Some lights flickered from hue to hue in constantly shifting moods; others stayed one color for hours on end—the bass notes in the color orchestra.

Marr and Senn thought of the tower as a simple place, a place they called home. And that night it glowed more frantically than most others as the guests arrived. Because that night they were having a special party.

Sten's throat was suddenly filled with abrasive phlegm. Cough as he would, he couldn't clear it, it just seemed to clog his throat more. What's more, his ears burned and his toes and fingers felt frostbitten and his tongue plascoated. He was trying to figure out what to do with the gorgeous woman pressed up against him. His arms waggled on either side of her body, trying to make up their minds whether to paddle in or paddle out. It didn't help that the woman's musk was designed—well designed—to incite lust in any male dead less than ninety-six hours. Finally, he put his hands on the woman's slender hips, hugged them slightly for politeness' sake, and then pushed her away. "Uh . . . nice to see you, too, Sofia."

Sofia stepped back and took him in with melting eyes. She was looking at him with, well, approval, Sten thought, wishing a guy could wear something resembling underwear beneath the skin-tight formal uniform of a Gurkha officer.

She crammed herself against him again in another full-body melt and whispered in his ear. "It's been so long, Sten, love . . . I could . . . I could—You know . . ."

Yeah, Sten *did* know. He could remember quite well, thank you, and all of his memories were pleasant. The trouble was, he almost hadn't recognized Sofia when she appeared before him. Not that she was unpleasant to look at; far from it. But he had fixed in his mind a portrait of the straightforward woman of nineteen or twenty, with a dark short-cropped halo of hair and eyes that questioned and judged things as they were. Instead, he was staring at a surgically perfect curve of a woman, with a glittering tumble of hair that reached just below her buttocks. It was also her only covering. Sofia was fashionably naked, her skin pricked here and there with highlights of color. Still, it was Sofia, after a fashion, a Sofia with hungry, knowing eyes.

Sten was sorrier than hell that he had ever had her introduced at Court. "You . . . look great, Sofia," he said, trying again to edge her gently away. It wasn't that he didn't like having a naked woman in his arms, he just liked it better without everyone watching him.

"We have so much to catch up on," Sofia draped an arm in his. "Let's go someplace private and talk."

Sten felt himself being led away like an obedient little dog.

"Here's our drinks, Sten," came the welcome voice from behind him. "You can't believe the cute little robo-server they . . . oh . . . uh . . . Sten?"

And Sten turned with great relief. Police Lieutenant Lisa Haines was standing with two drinks in her hands and a puzzled-going-to-hurt look on her face.

With the numb but still nimble fingers of a born survivor, Sten jumped for the rope she was dangling out. "Lisa," he said, his voice a little high, "you're just in time to meet an old friend of mine, Sofia Parral."

Sofia stared coldly at the woman. "Oh," she said, her voice steel-edged.

"Sofia, I'd like you to meet Lieutenant Haines. She's uh . . . I mean, we're . . . uh . . ."

Lisa extended a hand to Sofia. "I'm his guest—a *new* friend of Sten's," Lisa purred. "So nice to meet an old one. Knowing the captain, I'm sure we have a great deal in common."

Sofia coldly took her hand and shook it. "Yes," she said. "I'm sure we do."

She turned her attention back to Sten. Frost coated her eyes. "Forgive me, Sten, but I simply must not ignore the other guests. Perhaps we can talk later." She turned a smooth, lovely back to him and ankled away. Sten was not quite sure what he had escaped, but clotting glad he had. He absently reached for one of the drinks Lisa was holding and was brought up short by the smile on her face.

"I didn't realize you knew anyone here, Sten."

He swallowed his drink and then found the other one being thrust into is hand.

"Oh, maybe one or two." Then he laughed, suddenly at ease. "Put it at one. Just one. And thanks a hell of a lot."

He looked Lisa over approvingly. Her body was curved richly and deep, and displayed in a very uncoplike white gown that hugged and hollowed in all the proper places. She took the glasses from him.

"Now, let's go find a refill," she said. "And enjoy the party. Assuming there are no more surprises. Mmmm?"

"No. No more surprises. I hope."

Sten couldn't have been more wrong. In seconds he had a refill, Lisa was close against him, an orchestra was playing, and there was just enough room on the dance floor. Sten figured he could fake it, especially since the orchestra was playing what even Sten could recognize as a three-quarter-time slow dance.

He bowed to Lisa and led her onto the polished metal floor. That, he realized later, should have been the key.

But there he was, settling gently into Lisa's arms, moving his feet along the floor, and then he started to understand why Marr and Senn's events were superparties.

When the band began the song's reprise, someone turned the generators on and surprised dancers found themselves floating straight up, then drifting sideways into counteractive generators.

The ballroom instantly became less a dance floor than a flurry of slow-motion acrobatics.

Sten blessed his null-grav training when Lisa, looking bewildered as her gown billowed around her waist, floated past him. He tucked and swam toward her, grabbing an ankle first, then working his way up until he had her by both hands.

Lisa recovered, smiled, and resorted to the traditional "'nother fine fix."

Sten had no idea what she was talking about, but decided to seize the instant.

Weightless kisses taste about the same, even if there does seem to be a sudden excess of saliva.

Seizing the instant also meant that Sten, watching out of the corner of his eye, dolphin-bent his legs, waiting. Until a flustered matron floated nearby.

Sten used his feet as a kickoff point, and the drive sent Lisa and him spinning down toward the floor. They bounced near the edge of the field, close enugh for Sten to pirouette Haines sideways onto a normal-grav floor. She in turn dragged him out of the McLean field.

"Nice party," Sten managed.

"Mmm," Lisa said. "So zero-gee winds you up, Captain?"

"Isn't heterosexual love odd in its incarnations?" Marr whispered after closely watching Lisa and Sten's slow orbit.

"Perambulations is the word you're looking for," Senn corrected. "Shall we arrange those for later?"

"Regardless. We should take them under wing, and—Sr. Hakone! You honor us!"

Hakone had approached them unnoticed. He sipped from his half-empty glass of quill.

"As the guest of honor, may I comment on the evening thus far?"

Senn opened his liquid-black eyes in mock astonishment. "Is anything wrong?"

"For a party that purported to be in my honor," Hakone said, "I find too many people here who would like to use my bones for toothpicks."

"We made our invitations before your masque was previewed, Sr. Hakone," Marr said. "We had no knowledge—"

"Of course you hadn't," Hakone said dryly. "You two aren't the sort who believe a party is best gauged by the number of duels it creates."

"You offend!" Senn hissed.

"Perhaps." Hakone was indifferent. He drained his glass and fielded another from a passing tray. "My idea of a gathering, after all, is a group of comrades, with something in common to share. Evidently we differ in that regard."

"If we had known," Marr pacified, "that you wished a group of fellow ex-soldiers to sit around and become comatose while sharing lies of your long-gone youth, we would have done so."

Hakone allowed a smile to crawl across his face. The writer was dressed entirely in black, close-fitting trousers and a flowing tunic. "As I said before, we differ. By the way—one man I would like to meet."

"There is someone we didn't introduce to you? Our failing."

"Him."

Hakone waved a hand toward Sten, who was recovering his sense of gravity with a full glass.

Marr flicked a glance at Senn. Puzzlement. Then took Hakone by the hand and led him over to Sten.

"Captain Sten?"

Sten, who was about to kiss Lisa again, turned, recognized his hosts and, thanks to his cram course in the palace files, the guest of honor.

"Sr. Hakone."

"This is a young man," Marr said, "who we believe will progress greatly. Captain Sten. And?"

"Lisa Haines." Like most good cops, Lisa didn't believe in unnecessarily letting anyone know what she was.

Hakone smiled at her, then effectively shut Lisa, Marr, and Senn out of the conversation. "You command the Emperor's bodyguard, isn't that correct?"

Sten nodded.

"It must be interesting work."

"It's . . . different," Sten said neutrally.

"Different? What were you doing previously?"

Sten's background, as a member of the Emperor's Mantis Section, was of course never to be admitted. For that period his record showed service on some far worlds, enough to justify a double row of medal ribbons that had been won for far stealthier and dirtier deeds.

"Guards. Mostly out in the pioneer sectors."

"Unusual," Hakone said, "for someone—and I mean no offense—as young as yourself to be picked for your current post."

"I guess they needed somebody who could climb up and down all those stairs in the palace without having heart failure."

"You have a mentor," Hakone pursued.

"I beg your pardon?"

"Never mind. Captain, may I ask you something frankly?"

"Yes, sir."

"I note from your ribbons that you've seen combat. And now you're here. At the heart of the Empire. Do you like what you see?"

"I don't understand."

"You joined the service, I assume, like all of us. Expecting something. Expecting that you were serving a cause."

"I guess so." Sten knew damned well why he'd joined— to get the hell off the factory world known as Vulcan and to save his own life.

"When you look around"—and Hakone's expansive hand took in the bejeweled Court denizens that had flocked to the party—"does this match what you expected?"

Sten kept his face blank.

"Don't you find this all a little, perhaps decadent?"

Not a chance, Sten's answer should have been. Not when you come from a world where boys and girls go into slavery at three or four. But that wasn't the right thing to say. "Sorry to be so thick, Sr. Hakone," Sten said, "but on the world I come from, *animals* are normal sex partners."

Hakone's face flashed disgust, then he realized. "You joke, Captain."

"Not very well."

"Do you read?"

"When I have the leisure."

"Perhaps at another time we can discuss this further. In the meantime, I would like to send you some of my works. Will you receive them at the palace?"

Sten nodded. Hakone bowed formally and turned away. Sten looked after him. Question: Why would the guest of honor decide to look him up? And then stand there and play games? The evening was increasingly surprising.

The party was ending on a muted note. It had gone from a mass of egos forced together to a swirl of excuses for other appointments. Sten and Lisa, not being very experienced in Prime World high society, were among the last to add themselves to the swarm of beings making polite exit.

Marr grabbed them just before they hit the pneumotube to their sled. "Too soon, my loves," he cried. "Much too soon."

And he latched on to their hands and began pulling them back through the crowd. Sten tensed—soldiers, like cats, don't look back. He felt equal tension through Lisa's fingers. Somehow that made him feel more at ease and very close to her. It was a sharing of distrust. "Really, Marr," Sten said. "We gotta go. We both have duty tomorrow, and there really isn't time for—"

Marr broke in with a sniff. "As you might say, clot duty. And as for time—that's just something the science types use to keep everything from happening at once."

He pulled them forward, out of the crowd and into a long, pulsing yellow hallway. Sten hesitated once again, and then felt Lisa's fingers tense before tugging him on. They turned a corner and were instantly confronted with a tricolored split, tunnels leading in different directions. Marr urged them toward left—blue—and Sten realized from the tension in his calves that they were moving upward.

"Senn and I have had our eye on you," Marr said. "Through the whole party. Both of you are a bit out of place, aren't you?"

"I'm sorry," Sten apologized. "I'm not very used to—"

Marr waved him down. "Don't be foolish. Our gatherings are not about social niceties. In fact, people's general appreciation is that we provide just the opposite."

"Oh, my god," Lisa said. "I knew I'd foul this up." She glanced down and checked the gossamer that was her dress. "You can see through it, right? I knew I should have—"

Sten pulled her close to him, shutting her off.

"I think he's trying to tell us something else," he said.

Marr pulled them onward, seemingly ignoring their hesitations. They rushed past rooms gleaming in haunting colors or dimmed to impossible shades of blackness. They were near the top level—the gallery section—and although the two guests didn't realize it, each room represented a fortune in art works. Scents and sounds slipped out, taunting, urging, but Marr pressed on, babbling all the time.

"This is special," Sten realized Marr was saying, "Something only the two of you would understand. You'll see—see for yourselves—why Senn and I built our home here."

The hallway suddenly blossomed into the open and Sten felt a soft, perfumed breeze.

"See," Marr said. "See." He waved a small, furry arm around, taking in . . . everything.

They were standing on what could most easily be described as a roof-top garden. Strange and exotic plants shadowed in close to them, nestling their bodies, caressing . . . what? Lisa, a bit fearfully, tucked in closer to Sten.

"Through here," Marr said.

And they followed him along a winding, darkened path. It was like walking through a series of bubbles. Scent and perfumed light tugging . . . tugging . . . and then bursting through into another pleasure. Sound, perhaps, or a combination of sound and light and tingling feeling. Sten felt Lisa's body loosen in his arms.

Then the violin curve tensed and stopped. For a moment all Sten could feel and know was the swell of her hip. Marr was talking again, and as he talked, Sten found himself looking upward.

"It only happens three times a year," Marr was saying.

"A work of art that can only be seen, not purchased." He pointed to the shimmer of glaze that separated the roof garden from the real world.

Sten saw the huddle of mountains, picked out by moonlight, that pressed in toward the dome sky. He shifted his weight and felt his leg brush a flower. There was a slight hiss of perfume, and he felt Lisa's body ignite his skin everyplace it touched.

"Watch," Marr said.

And Sten and Lisa watched. The crag of cliffside just beneath the moon suddenly darkened. It became a deeper and deeper blackness until it formed into a knotted, pulsing ball.

"Wait," Marr droned. "Wait . . . wait."

And then the black ball exploded. A soundless fury of storm clouds formed themselves into crayon swirls of black against the Prime World moon. Then they began to twist into a funnel shape that powered across the valley, hurling itself against the mountains on the other side of the valley.

This, Sten and Lisa didn't see. Because all they could observe was the broad, open end of the funnel, sweeping across the lights of the night sky.

It was over very quietly and softly. Somehow, Sten found himself holding Lisa in his arms. Above them, the dome was dark. Beneath them, the garden was shadow soft. Sten looked at Lisa, a dim halo of light, just below his height. "I . . ."

Lisa held a finger to her lips. "Shhh," she whispered.

He pulled her closer, and he felt the garden around him hush and soften even more . . .

Marr and Senn watched the two lovers embracing under the dome. They cuddled closer in bed when they heard Lisa's soft "shhh."

Senn turned to Marr and pulled him nearer. "There's only one thing nicer than a new love," he said.

Marr palmed the switch and the vidscreen went respectfully blank. He leaned over Senn. "An old love," he finished. "A very old love."

As Sten tightened his embrace, he could almost feel Lisa blush a very unlieutenantlike blush. A hand on his chest gentled him away a step. And Sten watched as the white gown shimmered off. Then there was only Lisa.

CHAPTER FIFTEEN

"YOU CLOTTIN' INCOMPETENT," Lisa hissed at the corpse. Sten had an idea that if he and the spindar techs weren't present she might have kicked it a couple of times.

Former Tac Chief Kreuger grinned up at them, blackened scavenger-gnawed flesh drawn back from his teeth. One arm had been torn off and, half-eaten, was lying almost five meters from the body, near the edge of the cliff.

"You humans have the most unusual idea of sport," Spilsbury rumbled, his subarms tapping busily on a small computer keyboard. "What pleasure can conceivably be derived from the stalking and slaughter of fellow beings? Beyond me. Quite beyond me."

"Sometimes they taste pretty good," Sten offered.

"Cause of death?" Haines asked. She was not in the mood for philosophical discussion. The phone call had, fortunately, come not quite at the crucial moment, but rather early the next morning, just as Sten and Lisa were awake enough to be getting reinterested in each other again.

"Hunting accident. We have an entry wound characteristic of that from a projectile weapon.

"Plus—and this will please you, Lieutenant—there

are no signs of an exit wound. I would assume the projectile remains in the body.

"Shortly one of my offspring should have it retrieved for you. Cause of death, therefore, I would theorize as emanating from a hunting accident."

"Very clottin' convenient," Haines said. Spilsbury's computer rattled, and the spindar handed the readout to the policewoman.

"Time of death . . . time of death. Here." Haines mentally ran time back. "One cycle prior to the bombing."

"Plus or minus three hours," Spilsbury said. "The precise time will be available momentarily."

Haines started to say something else, and Sten nodded her away from the tech. They walked to the cliff edge.

"Like you said, Lieutenant. Real convenient."

Since it was the first time it had happened, Haines had been wondering just what one called a person you worked with who you'd just made love to. She decided Sten's reversion to formality was probably the most sensible. "Cops don't believe in coincidence," she said.

"I don't either." Sten was trying to keep his theorizing under control. Coincidence *did* exist—every now and then.

Spilsbury waddled up behind them, holding a visenvelope out. "This is the projectile."

Sten took the envelope. The projectile—a bullet—was evidently made of some fairly soft metal; its tip had mushroomed until the bullet was fully twice as wide at its tip as at its base.

"I cannot identify the exact caliber," Spilsbury went on, "but it is indeed a hunting-type bullet.

"From the entry wound it appears that the corpse turned to face down the mountain just before the bullet struck him.

"It is a pity you humans were constructed with such soft epidermi, unlike more cleverly designed beings."

"Yeah. Helluva pity," Sten said. "Lieutenant, do you have any idea what kind of critters they hunt on this preserve?"

"Dangerous game."

"Like what, exactly?"

"I'll call the preserve center." She busied herself with a belt talker.

Sten chewed on his lower lip. Haines, the talker to her ear, turned and began reciting the list of target game the preserve featured. Two or three times Sten had to ask particulars about an animal. Lisa finished the list and waited. Sten nodded at her, and she broke com.

"Dangerous game," he said. "All designed to be real efficient."

Lisa looked puzzled.

"Efficient like the tech just said. Hairy, scaled, armored, or whatever. The kind of critter that'd take some serious killing."

Haines still didn't get it.

"When you are trying to stop something big and nasty, especially something that's got skin armor, you use a big bullet," Sten explained. In his Mantis career, there had been times he'd encountered said big and nasties in the performance of his duties and had to drop them. "A big bullet," Sten went on, "made out of some heavy dense alloy. You don't want the bullet to mushroom when it hits skin armor."

Lisa took the envelope from Sten. "So you wouldn't want a nice soft slug like this one. Not unless you were hunting a nice, soft-skinned animal."

"Like a man," Sten finished.

"I don't like this, Captain. Not worth a drakh."

Sten had to agree.

"You know what my bosses are going to say," Haines continued, "when I report that Tactical Chief Kreuger was involved in this conspiracy? That he put a tac squad in position knowing what was going to happen—and then got his chest blown in as a payoff?"

Sten looked at her, and knew that wasn't what the homicide detective was worried about. If one high-level police officer was involved, was he the only one?

"Something tells me there's going to be more than one boss with his tail out of joint," Sten said.

"Drakh, drakh, drakh, Captain. Come on, let's get back and see what else can ruin our day."

CHAPTER SIXTEEN

"DYNSMAN IS OUR mad bomber," Lisa said glumly.

Sten wondered why no joy, but that was less important than making sure the police identification was correct. He knew it would be far better to give the Emperor a "no report" than a wrong one. "Are we operating on a most-likely suspect or do we have the clot nailed?"

"Nobody's ever nailed until they confess. But I don't see anybody else but Dynsman being the nominated party. Item: He's the only professional Prime World bomber who's unaccounted for."

"How do you account for mad bombers?" Sten asked curiously.

"People who blow things up for a living tend to get watched pretty closely by us," Haines said. "And since they tend to be self-eliminating, there aren't that many of them."

"We're assuming that the bomber was a Prime World native?"

"We've got to start somewhere—plus no outworlder who pays the rent that way has come to Prime World within the past year."

"GA."

"This Dynsman specializes in insurance jobs. Using military explosives."

"Whoever blew the Covenanter used military demo."

"Second, this clown's never been offworld in his life. A few cycles before Alain got hamburgered," Haines went on, "Dynsman was in hock to his eyebrows to every loan shark around.

"Then he paid his debts and was flush. He hung out with the Psauri—don't bother asking: They're small-time lizards and even smaller-time crooks.

"Suddenly he was picking up the tab and promising even bigger parties to come.

"All at once he hit up every ten-percenter in Soward. Since he'd paid them off, his credit was good.

"Then he disappeared."

Sten ran through what Lisa'd given him. Contemplating, he walked to the railing of her "houseboat" and stared down at the forest below.

Since housing on Prime World was at a shortage, and strictly controlled, some fairly creative homes had been developed. Lisa lived in one such. Her landlord had leased a forest that was legally unsettleable. No one, however, said anything about overhead. So large McLean-powered houseboats were available, moored above the forest. They were built in varying styles, and rented for a premium. The occupants had supreme privacy and, except in a high wind, luxury.

The interior of Haines' houseboat was a large, single room, with the kitchen and 'fresher located toward the stern in separate compartments. Lisa divided the room with movable screens, giving her the option of redesigning the chamber with minimum work any time she had a spare afternoon.

Furnishings consisted of static wall hangings of the single-stroke color school, plus low tables and pillows that served as chairs, couches, and beds.

Sten, on the whole, wouldn't have minded living there without changing a thing. He went back to business. "You've got more."

"Uh-huh. This Dynsman went to the port and ironed a securicop who was guarding some richie's yacht. Exit yacht, two minutes later."

"Where'd Dynsman learn how to run a spaceship?"

"You've been in the military too long, Captain. Yachts are built for people with more money than brains. All you have to do is shove a course card in the computer; the boat does everything else. So the boat did everything else, and Dynsman was offworld."

"Clottin' wonderful."

"Yeah. Well, I got more. Including where Dynsman went."

"So why the glum?" Sten asked.

"The glum is for the real bad news. Background, Sten. When I made Homicide, I figured out that sometime I'd want to file something that nobody could access. So I set up a code in my computer. And just to be sneaky, in case somebody broke the code, I set up a trap. If somebody got into my files, at least I'd know it had happened."

"Drakh," Sten swore, seeing what came next. He stalked across the room."

"Pour me one, too. Right. Somebody got inside my computer. Somebody knows everything I've got."

Haines shot her drink back.

"Still worse, babe. I ran a trail on the intrusion: Captain, whoever broke my file's inside the Imperial palace!"

CHAPTER SEVENTEEN

"I DO NOT think I needed this," the Eternal Emperor said, quite calmly.

"Nossir," Sten agreed.

"Congratulations, Captain. You're doing an excellent job. I'm sorry as all hell I gave you the assignment."

"Yessir."

"Go ahead," the Emperor continued. "From the gleam, I know you've got something worse than just having a spy here in the palace."

"Yessir. This Dynsman took the yacht as far as the fuel would go, then abandoned the ship."

"Do you have a track?"

"Lieutenant Haines's report said that Dynsman signed on a tramp freighter in that port—Hollister, it was—and transshipped."

"How in the blazes could he get a berth? You didn't say this jerk has any deep-space experience."

"He doesn't. But the tramp, according to Lloyds, shouldn't be too particular. It carries high-yield fuels."

"Mmm. Continue."

"Uh . . . the tramp's single-load destination was Heath, sir."

"You are truly a bundle of joy, Captain Sten."

Heath was the capital of the Tahn worlds.

"Captain, have you been drinking?"

"Nossir. Not yet."

"We'd better start." The Emperor poured shots from the 180-pure flask and drained his.

"Captain, I will now let you in, on an example of Eternal-Emperor-type reasoning. Either (A) the Tahn *were* responsible for greasing Alain"—the Emperor's tone changed—"plus some . . . others, and are running this whole operation, or (B) this whole thing is turning into the most cluster-clotted nightmare going."

"Yessir. I dunno, sir."

"Lot of help you are. Fine, Captain, very fine. Pour another one, don't come to attention, and stand by for orders.

"I'll start with the assumption that I can trust you. You're too damned young, junior, and fresh on the job to be involved with whatever's going on.

"I trust the Gurkhas. By the way, how good a man is your subudar-major? Limbu, isn't it?"

"None better, sir."

"I want you to turn the guard over to him. You're detached. I will be quite specific since I remember from your Mantis days that you sometimes . . . freely interpret orders. You are to go find this Dynsman; you are to bring him back unharmed; he is to be capable of answering any and every question that I can come up with.

"I do not want revenge, I want goddamned answers, Captain. Is that clear?"

"Yessir." Sten touched the glass to his lips. "I'll need support, Your Highness."

"Captain Sten, you figure out your ops order. You can have any clottin' thing you want, up to and including a Guards Division if you think it'll help.

"I want that Dynsman!"

CHAPTER EIGHTEEN

THE PORTAL SLID shut behind Tarpy's back. Reflexively, he moved to put a wall at his back while his eyes adjusted to the semiblackness. His pupils dilated, and now he could see overhead the spots of light that were stars and space-ships.

The scene in the hemispherical chamber shifted, and it was daylight, as one sun swam into closeup, and the Imperial landing force hung "below" it, above the slightly larger dot that was the planet.

Across this moved the black strut-beam that supported the chamber's control chair, and Tarpy could make out the figure of Hakone outlined in the seat.

Again the scene shifted, and now the battleships and assault transports floated above the planet's surface, which swept to either side of the chamber. Tacships flared out and down, and remote satellites engaged them.

Five battleships split from the main force, their Yukawa-drives pushing them up toward the planet's pole, as the transports drifted down toward the landing.

Tarpy ran battles through his head, then snickered as he got it. Of course. Saragossa.

He could never understand why soldiers couldn't let go of the past. To him, the battles he'd fought in were meaningless. All they gave him was promotion, perhaps a medal, and that never-to-be-admitted satisfaction of close-range killing.

Saragossa. As far as Tarpy was concerned, the battle was not only long-lost but one that never could have been won. Hakone's laboring for some kind of culprit had never signified. But he caught himself. Not to reason why as long as somebody's paying the bills. He dug out a tabac and, making no move to shield the flame, set fire to its tip.

Hakone caught the reflection from a dial in front of him and spun the booth on its arm. "Is that you?"

Tarpy did not bother answering. He couldn't be bothered with nonsense—none of Hakone's servants had entry permit to the battle chamber. Therefore, whoever was inside would be whoever was expected.

The long beam swung down, out of the chamber and level with the chamber's lobby. Hakone climbed out, walked to Tarpy, and brought his hand through a 360-degree loop. The "battle" above died as the lights came up in the chamber. "The Emperor has saved us all some research," Hakone said. "We now have a line on this bomber our associate used."

He took a handful of fiches from his coverall's breast pocket and passed them to Tarpy. "The man fled into the Tahn worlds," Hakone said.

Tarpy half smiled. "It should be hard for him to go to ground there."

"You have whatever resources you need. If you wish, take a few of our Praetorian deserters with you for backup."

"Will it matter how I do it?"

"Not at all. He's a small-time criminal, adrift in a very violent society. No one will inquire."

Tarpy palmed the exit switch, and the chamber's portal swung open.

"By the way—the Emperor also has a man in pursuit."

"Do I worry?"

"No. He's inconsequential—some captain named Sten. I met him. Quite sloppy for an Imperial soldier."

"But if he gets close?"

Hakone shrugged. "The issue at stake is a great deal larger than the life of one Imperial grunt, Tarpy."

Tarpy stepped through the portal, palmed it shut, and was gone.

BOOK THREE

MOUTON

CHAPTER NINETEEN

SERGEANT MAJOR ALEX Kilgour, detached Mantis Section Headquarters, parent unit First Imperial Guards Division, glowered down at his tasteful purple and green loose tunic and pantaloons and then across the cobbled street at the schoolyard. In the yard, a uniformed and elderly Tahn officer was drilling eight-year-olds in some sort of arms drill. When y' gie th' bairns pikes before th' war starts, Alex thought sourly, p'raps y' should be thinkit ae nae fighting.

The march-and-countermarch he was watching, however, was very low on Kilgour's pissoff list. There were many, many others. Waiting for Sten, he ran through them.

There was nothing wrong with being detached for special duty. In the back of Alex's mind, he had been considering a certain sense of morality. He'd spent enough years in Mantis to realize that sooner or later the ticking clock would stop. Just lately Alex had been hearing his personal clock slowing.

But that, he protested to himself furiously, was nae the prime reason. Ah join't th' Guard ae ah soldier, he went on. An' somehow now Ah'm on some strange world, dressed ae a panderer. One of these aeons, Alex promised himself, prob'ly on my retirement, Ah'll gie th' Emperor what Ah serve the full story. The poor wee lad cannae know.

The strange world was Heath, capital of the Tahn worlds. Alex and Sten had gone in covertly. Kilgour, however, quibbled at their cover—Sten had figured that high-credit pimps would never be questioned as to their real motives.

Whatever Alex had been expecting, in a long career that specialized in inserting him in the middle of bizarre cultures, Heath proved a great deal more.

The Tahn culture consisted of rigid, stratified sub-cultures. At the top were the warlords, landed hereditary politico/commanders. Under them fell the lieutenants, the tactical leaders and warriors. Then the merchant class, and, finally, the peasants. The peasants did all the drakh work, from spear-carrying in the growing Tahn military to agriculture to menial jobs.

That, Alex thought to himself furiously, dinna makit me fash. But th' stinkit peasants no seem to *mind* bein' serfs. A thousand years earlier, Alex Kilgour would prob-ably have made a very acceptable revolutionary.

An' not only that, he went on, th' food's nae whae a civilized body should eat. Ocean weed, food frae' bottom-scuttlin' beasties, drakh-planted carbos dinna make a diet frae a human, he thought, and burped.

Alex, not being the sort who could keep himself at the bottom of a brooding barrel for long, was consoling him-self with the thought that at least the Tahn beer and alk were strong and readily available, when Sten slouched up beside him.

"Y'r mither dresses you funny," he said. Sten's garb was even more extreme—which in Heath's underworld culture meant even less noticeable—than Alex's. His knee-length smock was striped in orange and black, and the leotards under them were solid black. It was, Sten had been assured, the height of fashion among those who sharked through the sexworld of prostitution.

Sten merely grunted at Alex's sally. He, too, stared at the schoolyard. The Tahn warrior had discovered an error in some child's performance and was systematically shaming him in front of his fellow. Sten motioned his head, and the two men moved away, headed toward the red-light district they were quartered in.

"Hae'y found our mad bomber?" Kilgour asked.

"Yeah."

"Ah, Sten. P'raps y' dinna be telling me. It's aye worse'n Ah thought."

"Even worse," Sten began angrily. "The clottin' idiot went and did it again."

Lee Dynsman was an idiot. After he'd jumped ship on Heath, found a hidey-hole, a drink, a woman, and a meal, which consumed what was left of his credits, he'd put the word out in the underculture bars that he was an expert bomber and Very Available. A small gang with large ambitions had quickly recruited him to blow the vault on a Tahn credit repository. For once in Dynsman's career, the job had gone flawlessly, dropping the thick cement/steel back wall into rubble. The gang scooped up the loot, took Dynsman to their hangout, and drank him into celebratory oblivion. No dummies, they realized that since the Tahn "police" (actually paramilitary, seconded for special duties from the army) needed a culprit, they narked Dynsman.

"So our wee lad's in the clank," Alex said.

"Still worse."

"Ah, lad, lad. Dinna be makit aye worse. Y'know, Sten, when Ah was runnin' th' museum, Ah was considerin' m'leave. M'mum's castle's in Ross Galen Province, aye the loveliest part ah th' planet a' Edinburgh. An the castle sits on a wee loch, Loch Owen. Ah could'a gone there instead't bein' here wi' these barbarians."

"Shut the hell up." Sten was in no mood for Alex's meanderings. "Dynsman isn't in jail," he went on. "The clot's been transported."

"Oool." Alex understood.

"I thought you would, you refugee from a clan of criminals. Transported. To a clottin' prison planet."

"Ah need a drink."

"Many, many drinks," Sten agreed. "While we figure out how the hell we tell the Emperor there is no way in the world to lift Dynsman off the Tahn worlds' worst penitentiary."

Alex then saved the day by spotting a bar that was just opening. The two men pivoted and swerved inside.

CHAPTER TWENTY

TARPY, TOO, HAD tracked down Dynsman. His cover for travel to Heath hadn't been nearly as clever as Sten's. He and the five Praetorian deserters with him masqueraded as a touring public fight team. Arriving unannounced, they had very few bookings, which left the assassin and his men more than enough time to look for the disappeared bomber.

Tarpy twirled the cup of tea in his hands and wished for something stronger in celebration. But he had rules—absolute rules that had kept him alive for nearly seventy-five years, rules that were never broken. Among the strongest was no mind alterants on the job.

He shot the tea back and motioned for his legman, a former corporal, Milr, to continue.

Milr did, and the warm glow that spread inside Tarpy came from more than the tea.

Very seldom had he taken a job that did not require violence, toil, and blood. But the current one showed every sign of being simple, painless, and well-paid.

Tarpy scanned the fiche on the prison planet. Prehominid. All prisoners sentenced for life. Average prisoner life expectancy—five years, local. Number of escapes—zero.

Unlike most people who kill for a living, Tarpy believed an old adage—Kill Without Joy. He had taken the adage one step further—don't kill if there's no need.

Dynsman's chances of returning to the Imperial worlds were near zero. All these people, Tarpy thought. Running around scheming after something, and none of them realize that the gods always take care of those who play with fire.

Tarpy stood, pulled the fiche from its reader, and crossed to the hotel-room sink. He rinsed out his cup, opened a cupboard, and took out a bottle of pure quill. He poured a cup for himself, then, as an afterthought, a glassful for Milr. Milr swilled the alk, without bothering to wonder about the unannounced suspension of The Rule.

He drained his glass. "Reassemble the team, Corporal. We'll transship back to Prime World on the next available."

Dynsman was no longer a factor, nor was that Imperial officer. Tarpy next considered exactly how much of the commission he would have to pay the ex-Praetorians to keep them from feeling cheated.

CHAPTER TWENTY-ONE

A WRY JOKE on Heath was that the huge river running through the middle of the capital city was the only river that had ever caught on fire.

It burned for days, seriously scorching the surrounding waterfront. But even after the fire on the polluted channel had died, the Tahn lords had done nothing to clean it up, in spite of their loud and frequent avowals of love for simplicity and nature. After all, the warlords had immaculate gardens to wander through and in which to compose the Tahn's superstylized poetry. The peasants could—sometimes did—eat drakh.

On the other hand, since all waterfronts throughout history have been the same, perhaps the fire could have been considered instant urban renewal. Not that it took long for the same abattoirs to spring back to life.

The Khag was a prime example. Its popularity was twofold: Not only was it close to both the onworld water shipping and the spaceport, but at the port anything or anyone illicit was available.

The two men at the bar fit right in—except for their soiled gray uniforms and pants bloused in knee-high swamp boots. They were armed, but so was almost everyone else in the Khag. Their weapons—stunguns, truncheons, fighting knives, and gas sprays—were hung on leatherette Sam Browne belts. Their voices were as raw as they were loud and semidrunk. One of them—Keet—owled at the ticket packet on the bar in front of them.

"Last day, partner. Last day."

His cohort Ohlsn nodded. "You know, I have been figuring our problem, Mr. Keet."

"We sure have a lot of them."

"Not really," Ohlsn continued. He was in that stage of drunkenness where brilliant ideas occur, still sober enough so that some of them make some degree of sense. "The problem with us is we're betwixt and between."

"I don't track."

"Keep drinking. You will. We sit out there for three planet-years at a stretch, and what do we want more'n anything?"

"To get our butts back to homeworld."

"Shows why we aren't warrior-class. 'Cause that's dumb."

"You've been sluicing too heavy."

"Not a chance. Look at it. Out there, we got power, right? How many times you taped somebody 'cause you didn't like his looks? How many times you had some konfekta show up at your quarters wanting anything but to go out there with Genpop?"

"That's part of the job, Ohlsn."

"Sure it is. So look at the two of us. We're peasant-class, right? But when we're walkin' our post, for three years we do better 'n any warrior or warlord I know."

"This is a new assignment. Maybe it's gonna be a drakhheap."

"Come on, man. Think about it. The job's the same as we been doin' for years—how in hell could the two of us do any better?"

Keet considered. Part of his consideration was emptying the liter-size carafe of quill in front of them into their glasses.

That was what Sten and Alex had been waiting for. They were at a small table, about three meters behind the two men. Sten waved, and the previously overtipped waitress was beside them.

"Those two," Sten said. "Buy them another round." He slipped her more than enough credits, then looked at Kilgour.

"Och aye," Alex agreed to the unspoken question. "Those are our boys."

By that time, another carafe had been set in front of Keet and Ohlsn, and they'd quizzed the barmaid on who was buying. Keet turned and puzzled at them. Sten hoisted his own mug and smiled. Keet and Ohlsn exchanged glances, considered their diminished drinking fund, and came to the table. They both were highly unimpressed with Sten and Alex, who were glowing gently in their pimpsuits.

"Don't like to drink alk from somebody I don't know," Keet growled.

"We're the Campbell brothers," Alex smoothed.

"Yuh. And I know what you are."

"In our trade, it pays to advertise," Sten said. "You don't get the girls if you don't look like you can afford them."

"Got no use for pimps," Ohlsn said. "You ought to see what happens to 'em out there."

"An experience I plan to avoid," Sten said, refilling their mugs.

"Knock off the drakh," Keet said. "You know what we are. You ain't buying us 'cause you like our looks."

"Nope," Sten agreed. "We've got a problem."

"Bet you have."

"We thought maybe to take care of it before it happens."

"Lemme guess," Keet said. "One of your whores got staked, right? And she's headed out."

"This man's a mind reader," Sten mock-marveled to Alex.

"You know the rules, chien. Once they're gone, they don't come back. Unless they're stiff. So don't bother trying to buy us so that you can rescue your hole. Don't happen. Never has happened."

"We're no stupid," Alex said.

"So why the free?"

"Our friend, see," Sten began haltingly. "She's cuter'n leggings on a k'larf. But she ain't too swift. She went and got hooked up with somebody up there." Sten jerked his thumb upward, in the Heath-universal sign for any class above your own or the people you were dealing with.

"His third wife didn't like it. My friend ended up being took as a receiver."

"Hard hash," Keet said.

"She was a real moneymaker," Sten sighed. "And so I'd like to see she gets taken care of. She's the delicate type."

Keet and Ohlsn eyed each other.

"What are you looking for?"

"Somebody to take care of her. Don't want to see her end up on the wrong side."

"You want one of us to tuck her under a wing?"

"You have it."

"Don't make sense. Why do you care? She ain't never coming back."

"It's an investment. See, Din's got sisters growing up. And they're even cuter'n she is. So if I protect the family..."

Ohlsn grunted happily. From his point of view, he was in the bargaining chair.

"Fine, chien. We take care of her. But what's in it for us? Now? Here?"

Alex lifted a roll of Tahn credits from his pocket.

"Drakh," Keet said. "Should'a hit us at the beginning

of the leave. That won't do us any good for the next three plan-years out there, now will it?"

"Drop an offer."

Keet lifted the ticket packet. "This says we ship eight hours from now. Means if you're trying to buy us, you got to come up with something we can do 'tween now and then. And something that won't mess us. Which means don't even bother offerin' something in your own... organization?"

"Man drinks quill, he starts thinking about other things," Ohlsn steered them.

Sten widened his eyes. "Sorry, men. I guess I'm a bit slow. That's clottin' easy."

"Bro," Kilgour added. "We could set 'em um wi' any piece a' fluff. But these gens sound like they're willin' to treat us on the square. What about Din's sisters?"

Keet licked his lips. "You've already got them?"

"Clot yes," Sten said. "Folks don't care. They breed 'em like k'larf. Wait till they hit ten, then sell 'em. We've had two for about a month. Breakin' 'em in right."

"Then there's the deal," Keet said. "Plus you provide the rations and the drink—and make sure we hit the transport on time."

The four beamed at each other, and Sten signaled for another pitcher to seal the arrangement.

Outside, the salt air hit and instantly sobered Sten. He'd had just enough drink to seriously consider telling the two men in gray what was going to happen to them, and why. Instead, he fell back from Keet one half a pace and dropped his hand. His curled fingers freed the muscle holding the knife securely in his arm, and the blade dropped free into his hand. He gave the nod to Alex.

Alex spun and swung, knotted three-gee muscles driving his fist straight into Ohlsn's rib cage. Ribs splintered, and the punch-shock impacted the man's heart.

Ohlsn was dead, blood gouting from his mouth, before he could even realize.

Keet's death was somewhat neater, but no less sudden,

as Sten's knife slid into the base of the man's skull, severing the spinal cord.

Old Mantis reflexes took over. They caught the corpses as they toppled and eased them to the boardwalk.

The bodies were quickly stripped of weapons, uniforms, and ID packets. From a nearby piling, Alex grabbed weighted bodybags they'd stashed earlier; and they struggled the corpses into them.

Minutes after they'd died, the two bodies splashed into the harbor to sink tracelessly and dissolve quickly. Ten hours, and nothing but a revolting slush would remain for forensics specialists.

Alex bundled the uniforms together and tucked them under one arm. "Of a' the sins Ah hae on m'conscience," Alex mused. "Ah never consider't pollutin' th' ocean'd be one a them."

"Alex, help," Sten said plaintively.

"A min, lad. A min. Ah'm lockit up noo." Alex was indeed quite busy in the tiny slum flat they'd rented. Kilgour was feeding the ID cards, personal photos, and such from Keet and Ohlsn into one of the few Mantis tools they'd brought with them. The machine was copying the ID cards and personal data from the two originals then altering them so that Sten and Alex's pictures and physical characteristics were implanted on the documents.

"Sergeant Major Kilgour, I still outrank you, damn it!"

The final photo clicked out a shot of Keet arm in arm with some female-by-courtesy who must have been the love of his life. The new photo, however, showed Sten as the erring lover. Kilgour beamed and fingered a button. The machine began hissing—in less than a half a minute the original documents in the machine, and the guts of the machine itself, would be a nonanalyzable chunk of plas. He turned to see what Sten's problem was.

"I am not," he said firmly, "a clottin' seamstress. I am a captain in the Imperial Guard. I do not know how to sew. I do not know how to alter uniforms to fit, even with sewing glue and this clottin' knife. All I know how to do is glue my fingers together."

Kilgour *tsk*ed, poured himself a now off-duty drink, and sadly surveyed Sten.

"How in hell did y'manage to glue *both* hands together? M'mum w'd nae have trouble wi' a simple task like that."

Before Sten could find a way to hit him, Alex solved the problem by dumping his mug of alk over Sten's hands, dissolving the sewing glue, which Sten had rather ineptly been using to retailor Keet and Ohlsn's uniforms. The mug was swiftly refilled and handed to Sten, who knocked it back in one shot.

"Ah," Alex pointed out wisely after Sten had finished choaking and wiping the tears from his eyes. "Y've provit th' adage."

Sten just stared lethally at his partner.

"Ah y'sew, tha's how y'weep."

Kilgour, Sten decided, was definitely rising above his station.

CHAPTER TWENTY-TWO

HIS MUSCLES COMPLAINING as he automatically tensed his legs against the greasy tug of the water, Dynsman waded out through the receding tide. He was still way too new at the game yet, and hadn't learned to let the steady pull of the sea help him walk. It was the same at Conch time, when the day was officially ended by the shoreline horn. Then it was a matter of walking with the incoming tide and trying to keep one's balance. Dynsman still fought it. And the penalty was sleepless nights of agony as his legs knotted and cramped.

Adding to his problems was the knife-sharp sea bottom, littered with gnarled rocks and razor-edge mollsk shells. He had only thin plas boots to protect his feet.

"Clot!" A misstep, and a tiny slice of flesh was nipped off by a shell. He stopped, dragging himself back against the tide. His heart pounded wildly for an instant as he looked about him. He could almost feel the blood oozing from the tiny abrasion. Dynsman thought about all the things that sniffed for blood in the mollsk bed and shuddered.

He fought back the panic and tried to regain his bearings. On each side of him, forty other prisoners of Dru eased out through the surf like slow-beating wings. They moved cautiously through the water, watching for the telltale bubbles of frightened mollsks.

Dynsman had never worked so hard or been so frightened in his life. He would much rather disarm a sloppy bomb then pursue the wily mollsk. Dynsman really wasn't good with his hands even when working on the delicate mechanisms that make things go bang; his seven remaining fingers were mostly numb, blunt objects. He had lived at his trade as long as he had by being canny and what-the-hell-let's-go-for-it lucky.

"Dynsman!" came the bellow from the shoreline. "Get your ass behind it or I'll put my boot in."

The bellow hit him like an electric shock, and Dynsman stumbled clumsily forward, his mollsk-plunger held somewhat at the ready.

Like most tasks on Dru, what Dynsman was about involved a product that was exceedingly exotic, expensive, and lethal. The tender mollsk was prized in many systems for its incredible taste and mythological aphrodisiac qualities. It was a mutant Old Earth bivalve creature, containing on average a kilo of delectable flesh, guarded by a razor-sharp shell about a half meter in diameter.

It had been bred to its present delicious state over many centuries. The problem being, for the hunter, that the same genes that made it so large and tasty went along with a highly efficient system of mobility. The creature lived in the mud and preferred chill; krill-swarming seas.

When it fed, it opened its huge top shell like a fan, guiding the microorganisms into its stomach-filter system. The mollsk could not see or feel, but judged the environment for mating or danger by a highly evolved system of smell. Which, in addition to convenience, is why mollsk hunters worked as the tide rushed out. In theory, the smells of the decaying shore life would mask the odor of an approaching mollsk hunter. But only until the last moment, when the hunter was a meter or so away. Then the mollsk would smell the hunter, take fright, and burrow deeper into the mud, leaving a trail of roiling bubbles. That's when the hunter captured it. Or if you were Dynsman, tried for it.

Like the other hunters, Dynsman was provided with a mollsk-plunger. It consisted of two handles, a little more than a meter and a half long, that connected to a pair of very sharp shovel jaws that were spring-loaded and sieved. The plunger was held at the ready as the intrepid hunter waded out through the surf watching very carefully for the bubbles that marked panicked mollsks. Aiming at the point where the bubbles just disappeared, and making allowances for light refraction, the tool was plunged into the mud at just the right moment, triggering the spring. Then the mollsk-plunger was hauled to the surface spewing mud and water, and the creature was popped into the bubble raft towed behind the hunter.

Dynsman was about as bad at the job as anyone could be. He could never time the bubbles correctly, and, about every other shift, he dumped his raft over as he was wading to shore. That meant he lived on very, very short rations because on Dru, a prisoner's food intake and the availability of luxuries depended upon performance. After only a month on Dru, Dynsman's ribs stood out from his hollow stomach at about a thirty-degree angle. To add injury to starvation, every time he fouled up, Chetwynd, the behemoth who was the boss villain, put his wrist to the nape of Dynsman's neck and made him do what Chetwynd called "the chicken."

Dynsman moved slowly forward again, his feet feeling for the uncluttered spaces along the bottom. A streak of bubbles suddenly shot for the surface and Dynsman almost panicked. Blindly, he slammed the mollsk-plunger downward and triggered the release. A myriad of bubbles exploded upward and then Dynsman was laughing almost hysterically as he tugged up on the plunger, a large mollsk snared in its jaws. He pressed the release lever and hurled the creature into the raft. There, he thought to himself. You're finally getting it. With a great deal more confidence, he strode forward. But then the old doubts and fears came crowding back. All the stories he had listened to in the village about the things that wait for a guy and are most likely to attack during rookie false confidence.

Dynsman had yet to witness one of the attacks, but he had seen the bodies dragged up on shore by Chetwynd and his cronies. There were many, many beings to fear in those waters, it was said, but two creatures in particular were the source of constant conversation and mid-sleep perspiration. The second most deadly being that *also* preyed on the mollsk was the morae. It was shaped a bit like a serpent and powered its three-meter length through the seas by constantly moving ribs—the tail streaming out behind for a rudder, or more awfully, as a brace in attacking.

The morae had an enormous head with jaws that could unhinge, allowing it to rip into morsels much larger than the circumference of its tubular body. And, like most animals of the deep, its flesh was very dense, giving its enormous strength, even for its size. Eyewitness accounts had one morae going for a leg dangling out of a boat and dragging leg, boat, and all under water. Fortunately, Dynsman reassured himself, the morae rarely fed during an outgoing tide. It was during the return home, with the seas pounding back at the shore, that the hunters worried.

Most dreaded of all, however, was the gurion. This was a *thing* that was always hungry and hunted at all times. Dynsman noticed that he was about waist-deep, a depth most favored by the gurion when it was on the stalk. He had never seen a gurion, and sure as hell wanted to keep it that way. Apparently they looked a bit like an Earth starfish but enormously larger—perhaps two meters across. On their many legs they could rise up out of the water over a three-meter tide. A gurion could run through the water as fast as a human being could on land. It was impossible to escape them. They were an almost obscene white, covered with a thick bumpy skin. The huge sucking discs on their legs could rip a mollsk apart then evert its stomach, which was lined with rows of needle-teeth, over its prey, grasp the soft flesh, and pull it back into its body, ripping and digesting the living organism at the same time.

Dynsman never wanted to meet a living gurion.

All in all, after being condemned to Dru, Dynsman wasn't sure if he wouldn't have been better off facing Prime World justice. He felt that he had always been an unappreciated man, but on Dru his talents were going completely without use. He thought of himself as the kind of a fellow who could get along in any society. He had not a prejudice in him. He just wanted to be allowed to do what he did best—blow things up—and then enjoy the companionship of his fellow professionals in a bar after the bloody task was done.

Chetwynd had changed all that. Dynsman did not blame the Tahn system for his present state. He had made a misstep and then been caught. Dynsman blamed it on evil companions. What happened later was only to be expected.

Chetwynd was only one of many prisoner bosses who ruled the isolated villages sprinkled across Dru. The Tahn, fascists that they were, created the prison colony of Dru for only one purpose: to imprison criminals, both political and societal. Rob a bank or hoist a picket sign, it was all the same to the Tahn. But, fascists or not, they were also eminently practical. If they had to have a prison world, it should pay for itself. Better yet, it should make a profit.

In Dynsman's area, the Tahn had seeded a vast mollsk bed. Twenty grams of mollsk flesh went for a small fortune in Tahn high society. Deeper inland, musk-bearing plants rolled like tumbleweeds across an enormous desert landscape. Since they also sprayed a highly caustic acid all about them when they were halted, it cost many prisoner lives to harvest them. And across the face of Dru, ranches, farms, and mines produced items worth a warlord's dowry at the cost of many "worthless" lives.

Dynsman had figured out the system even before he was transported to Chetwynd's village, and was determined to keep himself alive. With Chetwynd, it was a plan that almost could have worked.

Chetwynd had been a labor organizer on the docks at the Tahn's main spaceport. In his somewhat colorful past there had been more than a modicum of murder and robbery and mayhem. But when he led his fellow workers out on strike over some now obscure benefit-parity issue involving in-flight feelies for deep-space workers, it was just the final straw for the Tahn. He was put in manacles and told there were many many *many* mollsks in his future.

By the time Dynsman came on the scene, the enormous being that was Chetwynd had staked out the village for himself. He dressed in the best of clothes, confiscated all the luxuries for himself and his cronies, and had gathered a little harem of prisoner lovelies. The ladies were there, it would be noted, more for his charm and prowess than his relative riches as boss thug.

Dynsman himself had fallen under the giant's spell when he was dumped from the flitter and assigned to Chetwynd's work party. The big man had already pored over a stolen copy of his rap sheet. "Bomber, huh?" he had mused. "You gotta be the clot I was always lookin' for back on Heath."

Chetwynd had immediately put Dynsman to work building bombs. The materials were far from right, but Dynsman did his damnedest to produce, bragging all the while about the sophisticated things he could do if given the right tools and materials.

He never asked Chetwynd what the bombs were for because the obvious targets—the guards—would bring thousandfold retaliations if any of them were even scratched. Eventually Dynsman managed to produce a double-throw-down explosive device, triggered by the narcobeer breath that always seemed to exude from Dru guards. The test was unfortunate. The problem was,

Dynsman had made a minor error involving the pheromone trigger, and when Chetwynd threw a party for the first blast, the musk favored by Chetwynd's latest passion set the bomb off well before schedule.

Dynsman expected to be killed on the spot. Instead, Chetwynd merely smashed him about for a while and then, after a long conference with his bullyboys, assigned him to the main mollsk work party. As he waded through the surf, waiting for the first *crunch* of the morae, or the gurion, Dynsman had mixed feelings about his reprieve.

There was a shout from his left. Dynsman whirled to see that entire side of the work force flailing at the water, desperately struggling to reach shore. Another shout rose to his right, and Dysnman knew that somehow it was too late. The others were already heading back, and he had been daydreaming about his problems, ignoring everything about him.

He tried to get his feet to move, but instead stared in awful fascination at the black shapes that were whipping through the sea toward them. Morae! By clotting hell, morae! Somehow he turned and started plunging his knees up and down, but made almost no headway against the outgoing tide. His heart was hammering, his muscles straining, and still it wasn't enough; he could almost feel the gaping jaws moving in on his legs. The legs felt so thin and brittle. Then he was on the shore, and people were pulling him onto the beach and he was gasping and laughing and messing himself in fear. They dumped him and ran back. Dynsman heard a scream and rolled over to look.

Chetwynd was standing in the surf, his huge body braced against some terrible pulling weight as he tugged at one of the mollsk hunters. Chetwynd had the man beneath both arms, and the hunter's body was wracked back and forth in fast, terribly agonizing motions. The man screamed and screamed and screamed. But Chetwynd kept his hold. He kept pulling, and finally whatever had the man let go. Chetwynd staggered back with him and collapsed on the sand to a ragged cheer from the others. Dynsman himself almost yelled out in relief until he saw the thing that was in Chetwynd's arms. The morae had won. Nothing existed below the waist. The worker grinned at Chetwynd, and then his eyes rolled up in his head and blood burst out of his mouth.

Dynsman turned aside to vomit.

CHAPTER TWENTY-THREE

"ONE TO YOU, Mr. Ohlsn!"

"Acknowledged, Mr. Keet!"

Prodded by Sten's club, the prisoner double-timed from the white line chalked on the ground across the compound toward Alex. Kilgour saluted, in the flat-hand outstretched salute of the Tahn, then motioned the prisoner out the gate, onto the world of Dru itself. He slammed and triple-print-locked the gate, then doubled, knees high, toward his partner. Again they exchanged salutes, then started toward their quarters.

"Ah ha' been a lot of things f'r the Emperor, young Sten," Kilgour said heavily, "but y've forced me into roles Ah dinna ken a' all. I wasna bad bein't a cashiered soldier when we were dealin't wi' those mad Taliemaners. But this time y'hae me ae first a pimp, an' noo a screw."

"M'mum w'd nae likit you."

Kilgour had been sniveling since the two had boarded the guard transport for Dru. Their identities hadn't even been questioned. Evidently even the security-conscious Tahn could not figure why anyone, for any reason, would want to go to the prison world of Dru.

Not that a guard's life was without its comforts. A good percentage of Dru's luxury goods were filtered into the guards' compound. And of course there were human amenities, since any prisoner condemned to Dru quickly learned that his or her life expectancy would be significantly enlarged by volunteering to share a guard's bed.

Sten and Alex had evaded the situation by claiming that on leave they'd both bedded the same woman, and been given the same social disease, which was slowly responding to treatment.

Ohlsn had been right—for the peasant-class men and women the Tahn routinely recruited as prison guards, life was very sweet indeed.

"Young Sten," Alex whispered, just outside the security door to the guards' barracks, "are you *sure* that all we hae t'do is lift this mad bomber? Wha' would happen if we set a wee bomb ae our own in the center ae this compound before we hauled?"

"Good idea, Sergeant Major. No."

Kilgour sighed and they entered their quarters.

Alex waited until the machine finished cycling, lifted the plas door, and took the two mugs of narcobeer to the table he and Sten were sitting at.

All of the recreation rooms in the barracks were the same—overly plush chambers that attempted to copy what the vids showed of warlord quarters. With additions. Like the narcobeer machines. Alex winced, and sipped. Coming from a free world and the Imperial military, he'd never experienced the dubious joys of narcobeer. Sten had slugged down more than his share on the factory world of Vulcan.

"Nae only d' these Tahn no eat right," Alex grumbled, "but th' dinna ken beer."

"That's not quite beer."

"Aye. A camel pisseth better ale than th' Tahn make."

"It's fermented grain of one sort or another. Plus about five percent opiate."

Alex chugged the mouthful he'd been swilling straight back into his glass. "Y'r jokin't."

Sten shook his head and drank. It tasted even worse than he remembered.

"Wha's the effect?"

"You get glogged, of course. Plus there's a slight physical addiction. Takes . . . oh, may be a cycle or two of the cold sweats to shake."

"Bleedin' great. First Ah'm a pimp, then Ah'm a screw, an' noo Ah'm becom'it a clottin' addict. The Emp'll ne'er know wha' troubles Ah seen."

Sten noticed, however, that the information didn't keep Alex from finishing his glass. Further complaints were broken by loud, raucous cheers from the other guards as they welcomed two others into the rec room—guards Sten and Alex hadn't seen during their three weeks on Dru.

"The Furlough twins!"

"How'd the luck of the draw play?"

The slightly older and beefier of the two women motioned for silence. Eventually, the other guards shut up.

"Y'wan a report? Awright. The late prisoner, our lamented whatever his clottin' name was—or was it her? —successfully passed to his reward and was recycled."

"Clot the villain. Who cares?"

"Me'n Kay found a new way to spend time back on Heath."

Great interest was obvious among the other guards.

"You people been using the body detail to hit the resorts. Lemme tell you, there's somethin' better. With the fleet bein' built up, there's a whole bunch of recruits.

"Young they are. Stuck on post. Me an' Kay figured that they got credits, and nobody to spend 'em on."

"Tell you, they spent 'em on us, since we used our guaranteed right an' spent time on base, in the R&R center."

"Good times," someone snickered.

"Tell you," the woman went on. "Back there, it's better. They sack with you 'cause they want to, not 'cause there's pressure. Tell you women a little secret," she leered. "It's a lot . . . stronger that way. Plus *they* pick up the tab."

A watch sergeant stood and ceremoniously waved his mug at them. "We're glad to see you people back. Sounds like your stories are gonna be great. But the next time the lottery rolls around, if you guys take it again, some-body's gonna get dead. This is the third time in two years you two went back to Heath."

Sten and Alex were looking at each other. There wasn't any need to discuss matters. They tabbed new narcobeers from the machine and joined the fray.

The problem they'd never solved was, once they found Dynsman, how to get him—and themselves—offworld. Being experienced covert operators, they'd always assumed there was a way. But in three weeks they had not yet been able to find one. Dru was ringed by manned and unmanned guard ships. The only way on or off was in prisoner transshipments or on robot freighters lifting out the luxury exports. The prisoner ships were manned by heavy guard contingents, and not even Sten and Alex felt competent enough to take over a ship guarded by a hundred people. The export ships were uniformly refrig-erated and nitrogen-atmosphered. This "lottery" sounded interesting.

It was. The Tahn were very proud of Dru. Not only was the prison planet operating in the black, but the pris-oners themselves were used, even beyond their death.

Under stress, the human animal's pituitary gland pro-duces a painkilling drug. The greater the stress, the greater the production. Since most prisoners who died on Dru died under extreme stress, their bodies were filled with the drug. The problem was acquiring the body, and freez-ing it before corruption set in. Prisoners died on Dru very frequently—but all too many of them died under condi-tions that made body recycling impossible. That was one reason why any of the prisoners sent to Isolation never reemerged, except in bodybags.

A "good" body, Sten and Alex found out, went off-world, to Heath. The cycling was not done on Dru, for two reasons: the difficulty of getting skilled techs to accept assignment to an armpit like Dru, and the fact that the pituitary gland extract was, like all painkillers, a joyful opiate. Whichever one of the Tahn warlords came up with the idea of using prisoners for opiates, he or she was bright enough not to want an already troubled world like Dru to have access to a supernarcotic. When enough prisoners had died and been frozen and bagged in time, the bodies were escorted offworld by two guards. That was the only way off Dru other than the normal Recreation leave following the three-year tour of duty. And the escorts were chosen by lottery.

By the end of the evening Sten and Alex were eyeball-crossing on narcobeer. But they had their way out. For Dynsman and themselves.

CHAPTER TWENTY-FOUR

STEP ONE WAS Alex's story. "Ah," he mock-yawned. "Nae a month on Dru, an a'ready Ah heard y'r best stories."

"You got a better one, Ohlsn," a guard jeered. The tubby Scotsman had already established himself as a character and a favorite among the guards. Especially since he was more than willing to buy his round and another.

"Since Ah'm buyin't, shouldna ye be shuttin' y'r mouth?"

Silence fell.

"Ah'm tellin't a story aboot Old Earth. Before e'en the Emperor. Back when we Scots ran free an' bare-leggit on a wee green island.

"But e'en then, afore the Emperor, there was an Empire. Romans, they were call't. An because they were sore afrait a' the wee Scots, they built this braw great wall across the island. Wi' us on one side, an' them on the other.

"Hadrian's Wall, it was namit.

"But e'en then, bus'ness was bus'ness. So a' course, tha' were gates in th' wall, for folks to go backit an' forth.

"A' course there were guard on th' gate.

"On th' evenin' in question, there wa' two guards on th' wall, Marcus and Flavius . . ."

Step Two was Sten.

The first thing they needed was to find Dynsman. The third thing Sten and Alex needed was a way to mickey the lottery.

Either task depended on having a terminal and accessing Dru's central computer.

Guards were not encouraged to have personal terminals, and the terminals that existed were carefully controlled and voice-sealed to the appropriate authorities.

However, Sten had discovered that the game machines in the recreation room were very sophisticated. If a guard won on them, he could be paid immediately in narcobeers (delivery through the slot) or by credits added to his or her banked salary. Losses, of course, meant immediate deductions. Sten had grinned in glee—the machines were exactly like those he'd grown up with on Vulcan—and exactly like those the Mantis team had boogered in their destruction of that factory world.

So while Alex was occupying the guards, Sten seemed to be pinballing his heart out on one of the machines. Actually he was taking over the machine and using its lines to access the central computer itself. His tools were a microbluebox that they'd smuggled onto Dru in the guise of a music machine, a secondary high-power source that also had been smuggled, and Sten's occasional bashing left foot against the game machine itself.

Sten reacted as the game screen flashed; he tapped keys and cut himself out of the circuit. Antiaccess device, but toad simple. He considered for a minute, then tried an alternate code. Another step forward.

". . . Now here's Marcus, who's been on this wee isle for years an' years. But puir Flavius, he's only been there for a month or so. An' the puir lad's scarit solid. He dinna like th' food, he dinna like th' weather, an' most a' all, he's messin' his tunic aboot th' Scots.

"'Dinna Fash,' Marcus tells him. 'Aboot nine a' th'

evenin't, y'll be hearin't a braw whoopin't an' hollerin't an' carryin't on.

"'Tha'll just be the Scots comin't oot a' th' grogshops. But y'll noo have to worry.'

"But Flavius is worrin't..."

Sten was also worrying. He looked around—every eye in the rec room seemed intent on Alex's story. Sten slithered a microdrill from his pocket and touched it to the rear of the game machine. The drill whined in. Sten plugged the connection on the drill handle into an outlet on the microbluebox and keyed the ANALYSIS button. The bluebox hummed concernedly.

"... So noo it's nigh nine, and sure enow, there's whoopin't an hollerin't an' carryin't on. And aye, doon the street toward our wee Romans comit this braw great cluster a' Scots. An' they're hairy an' dirty an' wearin't bearskins and carryin't great axes a' claymores.

"And Flavius knows he's gone to die, here on this barren isle light-years from his own't beautiful Rome. So he's shakin't an' shiverin't.

"But Marcus, he's got this braw smile on his face a' this horrible horde comit staggerin't up.

"'Evenin', he says.

"'Clottin' Romans,' comit th' growl, an' somebody unlimbers a sword.

"'You're lookin't good a' this night,' Marcus goes on.

"'Clottin' Romans' is th' solo thing he gets back, an' th' Scots are e'en closer, an' Flavius can smell their stinki't breath, an' he's a dead mon.

"'Nice night tonight,' Marcus keeps goin't.

"'Clottin' Romans,' comes again.

"Flavius hae his wee eyes shut, not wantin' t' see the blade tha' rips his guts out an' all. But nae happen't. All th' braw hairy killer monskers pass through the gate.

"An Flavius is still alive.

"He relaxes then. Takit twa deep breaths, grins a' Marcus, an' says, 'Y're right. Tha Scots na be so bad.'

"'Aye, lad. You're learnin,' Marcus comes back. 'But in another hour, when their *men* get done drinkin't, p'raps there'll be a wee spot a' trouble.'"

As usual when Alex finished one of his stories, there was uncomprehending silence. Broken by two things:

The game machine flashed the correct code. Sten now was inside the main computer; and:

His microdrill had evidently gone too far, since the PAYOFF sign started flashing, and narcobeers began dropping down the slot. As Sten quickly palmed the bluebox and microdrill, the guards whirled at the *whirclunkthud* of beermugs dropping into the serving pickup. A throng gathered instantly around the machine.

"Clottin' luck," one guard said. "I've been ringing this game for a year, and the most I got was two beers. Look at that." The PAYOFF sign read 387 narcobeers.

"And what the hell am I gonna do with all that," Sten wondered.

"Mr. Keet," one guard said, "you been takin' dumb lessons? We're gonna drink 'em, that's what we're gonna do."

Sten and Alex exchanged glances, then braced themselves for what would prove a very, very long evening...

CHAPTER TWENTY-FIVE

THE BIG MAN lolled on the beach, lazily watching the mollsk hunters plod across the bed. He was surrounded by half-a-dozen lovelies who were sunning themselves, but keeping one eye out in case Chetwynd should want something. Chetwynd barely stirred when he heard the flitter dust up behind him. And he pretended not to notice the whine of the engines cutting off, then bootheels grounding through the sand.

"Chetwynd?"

"Yar."

"Get up when I talk to you!"

Chetwynd slowly turned his huge head, then pretended surprise when he saw the two guards. Just as slowly, he creaked to his feet and struck a mock pose of respect.

"Sorry, mister—I didn't know..." He let his voice trail off in pretended nervousness. "We wasn't expecting a visit."

"Yeah, well too bleeding bad. Hate to inconvenience an important villain like you." Sten measured the bulk that was Chetwynd with his mind. Only the insolence in his eyes gave Chetwynd away. Everything else was as humble and respectful as any guard could wish from a villain of Dru. A very dangerous man, Sten thought.

"We're lookin' for a villain," Sten snapped.

"Came to the right place, mister," Chetwynd drawled.

Sten ignored the subtle rudeness. "Name's Dynsman."

"Dynsman...Dynsman..." Chetwynd puzzled, then he let his eyes brighten. "Yar. He's still alive. We got a Dynsman."

"Where?"

Chetwynd pointed, and Sten turned to see their target at the shoreline cleaning out a flat-bottomed skiff.

"Useless bugger, if you don't mind me saying so, mister. Can't do a clotting day's decent work. I'd put him washin' pots if I didn't figure he'd poison us all with his carelessness."

Sten and Alex ignored Chetwynd and began stalking across the beach, their bootheels grating heavily.

Dynsman barely had a chance to see them coming. Just as he raised his head, Alex grabbed him by the base of the neck and lifted him off the ground.

"Villain Dynsman?"

"Yeeeesss, mister."

"Wanna talk wi' y', lad."

Alex tossed the little man into the boat, gave Sten a glance, caught the nod, and climbed in after him. He picked up the oars as Sten tossed off the tie, and clambered in after him. Alex began rowing out into the sea.

"Honest, mister," Dynsman wailed. "I didn't do

nothin'..." Then in a flash of inspiration, he pointed an accusing finger at the receding mountain that was Chetwynd. "He *made* me build that bomb!"

"Is that right?" Sten said. "You're a bomb builder, are you?"

Dynsman was in instant terror. Maybe they didn't know...oh, clot, what was he into?

"Tell us aboot it, lad," Alex soothed.

"Well, see, he asked me...and...and I said I had some experience at explosives...and..."

"Shaddup," Sten hissed. "We don't give a clot about Chetwynd."

Dynsman just stared at Sten as it occurred to him that something terrible was about to happen.

"Tell us about the Covenanter," Sten snapped.

"Oh, my god," Dynsman breathed.

Alex gave him a cuff. "Ah canna abide blasphemy."

"Forget it," Sten said. "Let's just kill him now. Get it over with."

Sten curled his fingers and let the slim needle that was his knife spring into his palm. Dynsman saw it and began to sweat in real horror. "I didn't know it was political. I never do political work. Ask anybody. Ask 'em, and they'll tell you. I'm just a...just a..." He looked Sten full in the face, then burst into tears. "I don't do political," he sobbed.

Sten felt like a bugsnipe.

"For clot's sake's, Alex! We got the right guy. Do him, would you?"

Alex nodded and reached into the pocket of his uniform.

Dynsman screamed, coming halfway to his feet. It was the most chilling sound Sten had ever heard—despite enormous experience in listening to soon-to-be dead men scream. Then he realized that Dynsman wasn't screaming because of them.

Sten turned his head.

A *thing* was running toward the skiff through the water at about fifteen knots, closing so quickly on its spindly legs that it almost appeared to be walking on the surface of the water.

Dynsman screamed again. "It's a gurion!"

Alex desperately tried to spin the clumsy skiff around, but it had no centerboard and just spun freely on its axis. Sten grabbed for a punting pole, and just as the creature rose to its full height, vomiting out the awful stomach-mouth with its bleeding veins, he heard the sound of rushing water behind him.

Whatever *that* was, he had to leave it for Alex, and he rammed the pole straight into the gurion's maw. The tip of the pole splintered and gave as it speared past the scores of rows of teeth into soft flesh. The gurion howled but continued its rush forward, lifting the skiff upward and slamming it over.

Alex had even less time than Sten to react. A second after Dynsman's scream, he saw another gurion charging his side. He flailed out at it with an oar, and then felt a huge wave pressing under him, the sky rushing down at him, and then he was gobbling water. A thick arm clasped his body and squeezed hard as a tentacle tore at his uniform. He tried to get his feet under him—the water wasn't very deep at this point—and desperately fought for a grip on the animal.

Sten was afraid he was being dragged toward the gurion's maw, and he lashed out at the thing in front of him with his knife and slit straight across the delicate membranes of the gurion's stomach. Suddenly he was hurled away. He twisted his body in midair, and then was plunging into the water. He landed with a jolt and found himself standing thigh-deep in water. A geyser of blood was fountaining from the first gurion. Sten immediately put the creature out of his mind and whirled in the water, looking for Alex.

The heavyworlder's lungs were bursting, but he had managed to get a hand on a frontal ray, and another on a ridge graining upward from the gurion's back. Other rays were closing around him, suckers grasping his thick body. Under the water, Alex saw the blood-red maw, centimeters from his face. He strained mightily, a huge bubble of what little remained of the air in his lungs bursting out. Slowly, very slowly, he began forcing the ray toward the gurion's own stomach-mouth. Reflexively, the needle teeth began swarming as they sensed flesh approaching. Finally, with a last mighty shove, the tip of the ray entered the maw.

A high whine almost pierced Sten's eardrums. Then the gurion that had Alex rose to its full height out of the water, and Alex kicked off from the creature's body. The gurion had one of its own rays crammed into its mouth and was gobbling it down, shrieking in pain as its own digestive juices and teeth ripped into its own flesh. The animal was devouring itself; and its weird physiology— especially the peristaltic motion of its rows of inward-pointing teeth—would not let it stop.

Sten felt something thump at his side, and he grabbed into the water for Dynsman. The man was struggling hysterically; Sten felt for his carotid, pinched, and after a few moments Dynsman went limp. Sten began hauling the man to shore.

"There's more!" Alex shouted.

About a quarter of a klick away, three more shapes had risen out of the water and were charging toward them. Alex was at his side now, and the two of them grabbed Dynsman by the collar and began wading for their lives.

On the shore, Chetwynd and the others had been watching the battle with great interest. Chetwynd saw the two Dru guards rescue the little creep they called Dynsman. He glanced lazily over at one of the skiffs. If he gave the word, he and his cronies could rescue the three.

From many meters away, Sten could read Chetwynd's mind: the other skiffs, just lying there, plenty of hunters, and many makeshift weapons to boot. Even before it happened, Sten knew what Chetwynd was about to do.

The laugh came from his toes and burst up along his tremendous bulk. Chetwynd had never seen anything so funny. He collapsed to the ground, howling with mirth. Around him, the other prisoners caught the humor of the whole thing. If they didn't help, the guards would die.

And there was no way Chetwynd and his mates could be blamed. The entire shore rippled with laughter.

Sten and Alex dug in for one last effort as the water prowed behind them and a gurion closed in. With a final yank, they dragged out of the last few meters of muck and collapsed on the beach.

Sten lay there for a very long time. He could hear the laughter all around him. He waited there, gathering his breath, his eyes closed. Finally there was silence. He turned over on his back and looked upward. Chetwynd was grinning down at him.

"Anything I can do to help, mister," Chetwynd said.

Sten stared up into the mocking eyes. He felt the thin haft of his knife in his hand, and thought about how it would feel to...

"What the clot!" Sten gasped.

And the feeling was gone, and Sten found himself convulsed with laughter. All one had to do was to look at events from Chetwynd's point of view.

The aircar slid across the barren landscape, Alex at the controls. Dynsman was stuffed safely between them and a course was set for headquarters. There was a groan, and Alex glanced down at the stirring Dynsman. "A hard lad to kill," he commented.

"Yeah, well I guess we can settle that. Gimme."

He motioned to Alex, and Kilgour fished through a pocket and came up with a tiny hypo. He handed it to Sten, who began peeling up Dynsman's sleeve. The little bomber opened his eyes, spotted Sten, and tried to struggle up. Sten pushed him down with a hard hand and pressed the hypo to his flesh.

"Sweet dreams, you little clot," he said, and plunged it in.

CHAPTER TWENTY-SIX

STEN THOUGHT IT was too easy. The max-variation chip in Dru's central computer that determined the draw of the escort lottery turned out to be near–Stone Age, its random-variable generator only controlled by a pickup that measured the magnetic flux from Dru's sun and the other two worlds in the system.

His fellow guards didn't.

"Clottin' hell. I said this man was lucky," a guard marveled. "Not two months on-post, and you get the bag detail."

"Ah, tha's m'partner Mr. Keet," Alex covered.

"He cannae play cards worth a whistle, an' his choice on the racin' beasties is horrific.

"But gie the wee lad a pure-chance game, an' he always walks."

Their shift sergeant was more then irked.

"Mr. Keet. Mr. Ohlsn. I find it upsetting that you two new assignees to Dru are this lucky."

"Yessir," Sten said. He and Alex, in formal grays, were locked at attention.

"Consider this, gentlemen. While you're escorting this prisoner's body back to Heath, I plan on a full investigation."

"Investigation? A' wha?" Alex said.

"Of . . . we'll just call it luck. But I expect, when you two return here, there shall be great surprises."

"Aye, Sergeant," Alex put in fervently. "When next y' see us, surprises will be all around."

141

Before Alex could continue, Sten side-kicked him into silence, saluted, and the two about-faced and exited.

The robot ship, just out-atmosphere, automatically shut off the Yukawa drive and kicked in the AM2 drive for the stars.

Alex and Sten had already broken the lock to the control chamber and were standing over the pilot.

"Th' Tahn dinna be a' bright a' they think," Alex said. "This autopilot's a' easy to reprogram a' bacon through a goose." And Alex busied himself at the tapeplotter, changing the ship's course. "Dinna y' want to be unfreezin't wee Dynsman?"

"Why bother," Sten said. "A dead villain's not a worry."

"Aye. Time enow to lazarus the lad when we rendezvous."

Rendezvous was with a superspeed Imperial destroyer lurking just outside the Tahn sector, with instructions to monitor a given wave frequency for pickup. Once Alex and Sten were picked up, the robot ship would be returned to its old course for Heath. But a spacejunk fragment lay in its future. The robot ship would never arrive at its destination.

"W' hae our mad bomber, w' hae our health, wha' more could a man want?"

"A good healthy drink," Sten offered, and headed for the guards' living section to see if anybody had been humane enough to pack a liter or so of alk.

CHAPTER TWENTY-SEVEN

THE BLUE PANEL on Ledoh's desk began blinking. Ledoh quickly shut down the inconsequential conversation he'd been having with the Imperial Commissariat, hit the buttons that locked the entrance to his office, and set off the CONFERENCE lights. He crossed to the doorway into the Imperial chambers and tapped with a fingertip, then entered.

The Emperor had his chair swung around and was staring out at the parade grounds as Ledoh entered. Two full flasks sat on the Emperor's desk, one of what the Emperor called Scotch, the other—Ledoh shuddered when he recognized it—pure medical alk.

Without turning, the Emperor growled, "You feel like a drink, Admiral?"

"Uh . . . not particularly."

"Neither do I. What's the worst thing that's happened to you this shift?"

Ledoh sifted through unpleasantries. "The Tahn Embassy's Principal Secretary expressed dissatisfaction with the meetings."

"He thinks *he's* dissatisfied!"

"To continue, sir. His dissatisfaction has been communicated, through the usual channels, to the Tahn lords. I, uh, have here their response."

"Go ahead. Ruin my day."

"The communiqué is on my desk, if you'd like the exact wording," Ledoh said. "No? Roughly, in view of the situation on the Fringe Worlds, the Tahn lords would like to meet with you."

143

"Is that all?"

"Not quite. Because of the death of Alain, they are reluctant to meet here on Prime. They request a meeting on neutral ground in deep space, further conditions, to include the proper security by both sides, to be negotiated. Said meeting to occur within one Prime year."

"Clot, clot, clot. They are shoving it in my face."

"Yessir."

"What about the riots on the Fringe Worlds?"

"Four capitals overrun. No word from provincial capitals. Guard support units are moving into position. Casualties? We have an estimate of somewhere approaching twelve thousand. On both sides."

"You know," the Emperor said evenly, "at one time I figured that any problem I faced could be met with sweet reason, the Guards, or enough alk to blind me out. Turns out I was wrong, Admiral. This appears to be one of those situations. I'll summarize. See if you agree: Fact A: The Tahn worlds are using the death of Alain to pressure me. They want the Empire to back out of the Fringe Worlds. Correct?"

"Very possibly," Ledoh said.

"I pull out—and that'll leave those settlers who moved in dumb, fat, and happy on the assumption that the Empire will protect them forever and ever amen swinging in the wind. Im-clottin'-possible, even if I could convince those yokels to uproot and haul.

"Fact B: Alain's dissidents, who never got the word that unification with the Tahn worlds would probably mean their instant demise or at least the destruction of everything they're fighting for, are equally beyond reason. Check me, Admiral."

"You are making no mistakes that I can see."

"So the only solution that I've got is to figure out who murdered Godfrey Alain—and it *better* be nobody Imperial—and then go off and meet with these Tahn. On their turf. And eat a measure of drakh. Is that the only way out?"

"No comment, sir."

"You are a lot of clottin' help. Mahoney would have

had an idea." The Emperor glared at Admiral Ledoh, and then his expression softened. "Sorry. That was a cheap shot.

"What I'm thinking is that, way back when I was a ship engineer, I had another solution to things."

"I'm very interested in hearing it."

"That was to drink all the alk in sight and then punch up everyone involved."

"Very humorous," Ledoh said.

"You are a clottin' heap of help," the Emperor snarled as he got up and headed for the door into his private chambers.

Ledoh, before he left, carefully replaced both flasks in their cabinet.

CHAPTER TWENTY-EIGHT

THE GURION RUSHED straight for him, its blood-red stomach brushing across his face, leaving a trail of digestive saliva that burned through the first layer of skin. Dynsman screamed in horror and hurled himself backward. From the corner of his eye he saw the Dru guard plunge a pole into the creature's maw, and then the boat flipped over against the combined weight of the gurion and Dynsman's panicked attempt to escape.

He clawed his way to the bottom. He was in total hysteria, breath bursting out of his lungs, yet too frightened to surface. Blindly, he grabbed hold of a razor-sharp outcrop and felt the edges bite deeply into his hands. Despite the pain, he held on as long as he could. He could feel the awful roil of the water and taste the rusty sweetness of blood. Something hard touched him and Dynsman screamed again, losing the little hold he had over his sanity. Water rushed into his lungs and he battled his way to the surface. A huge *whoosh* of air knifed in, and Dynsman saw the guardsman closing on him, gore dripping from a slim flash of silver in his hand. Dynsman struck out at the man in a panic. In slow motion the knife hand reached toward him. Dynsman was helpless, and watched in awful fascination as the knife slid into a mouth beneath the arm, and then the hand shadowed past his head. There was a sudden heavy pressure between his shoulder blades and neck, and Dynsman felt himself . . . dying . . . dying . . . dying . . .

His body flopped against its restraints on the table. A huge flipper appeared and just barely touched the slide-pot, and soothing sedative trickled into his veins. Dynsman's body went very still again.

Rykor's face was a portrait of odobenus-contemplation. She woofed at her dripping whiskers and then daintily brushed them aside with a front flip. Rykor sighed and leaned back into her gravchair. The bot mechanism shrilled in complaint as it tried to adjust itself to her enormous bulk.

"It's difficult, young Sten," she said. "The man keeps replaying the same memory patterns."

Rykor was one of the Empire's chief psychologists, specializing in the Imperial military. Her subspecialty, never publicly mentioned, was screening people for the Guard's Mercury Corps—intelligence—and for the secret Mantis teams. She also handled the occasional special project, such as Dynsman's in-progress brainscan. But Dynsman's brain was locked in trauma and insisted on rerunning the moments of his near-death.

Sten glanced at the helpless bomber, almost obscene in his nakedness, dripping with a myriad of probes and intersyn connects. He had seen Dynsman relive the moments a dozen times, and so far nothing went past the gurion attack. Even the moment when he came awake on the flit was a ghostly instant that flashed back again and again to the terrible moment of the gurion.

Sten rose and walked to Rykor's side. She reached out

an affectionate flipper and gently caressed him. "You were always one of my . . . special people," she said softly.

Sten ran his hand across the bulk that was her shoulder.

Rykor brought her mind back from the Dynsman place. "Do you still have the knife in your arm?" she asked suddenly.

Sten just grinned and kept patting, bringing her down from the link.

Rykor hoisted herself up suddenly, the gravchair groaning. "We must go deeper. Smash past the trauma block."

"It's important," Sten said. "Others have died."

Rykor nodded and eased back into a full rest. She concentrated fully on the brainscan and gave the slidepot a heavy tap. Dynsman moaned.

Above him, the screen came to life again. First it was in black and white, and then a swirl of color bars. The bars fuzzed together and formed a picture. Softness at first, and then the gurion threatened for an instant, and then gradually collapsed against a persistent crease of yellow. Stan watched as Dynsman relived his life, in full color.

The tall slender man with the thick shock of gray hair leaned a narcobeer across the table. Dynsman's screen hand reached in and pulled it forward.

"Next shout's on me," Dynsman's voice echoed.

The man smiled into the screen at "Dynsman," and from the monitor's empathy-banks Sten could tell that it was a smile Dynsman didn't quite trust. In fact, he was more than a little frightened.

". . . If you don't mind, Dr. Knox," Dynsman continued, his voice trembling a little.

The gurion extended a long ray toward Dynsman, and he shrieked as he felt the cold band whip around his neck—

"Stop!" A shout from Sten.

Rykor took one look at the frozen horror on the screen and leaned her flipper onto the slidepot. Dynsman's body relaxed on the table. Rykor waited for Sten's instructions.

"Knox," Sten said. "Enhance."

The mind-vid screen blanked then blurred as it reversed itself to Knox. It held there as Sten studied the figure. "That's our boy," he said. "Fits the hospital description. Now, what else can we find out about him? Smell? Any special scent he uses."

Rykor keyed in the sniffers. "Nothing at all," she said. "Quite out of the ordinary for a man who obviously cares so much about his appearance." She ran her cursor up to his carefully coiffed hair for an example.

"As a matter of fact," she said, after studying her monitors, "there is nothing about this man at all—except for his visual appearance—that should attract any being... smell, no register... voice, firm, but no register... aura press, no register..."

She turned her head lazily toward Sten. "Nothing marks this human at all. Highly suspicious. Body motion empathy... verbal... forget it. It's all zed, zed, zed."

Sten studied the frozen picture that was Dr. Knox. At the moment, Knox was the complete cutout man. No one, except a superpro, is completely two-dimensional. Then Sten noticed something: a dull of yellow on Knox's left hand.

"Enhance, left hand," he told Rykor.

The hand filled the brainscan screen. The dull yellow was a ring, with a very clear emblem stamped on its flat surface. Sten peered at it, knowing what it was, but not quite believing it. The stamped emblem was a foot, elongated with its emphasis on the heel. And on the heel...

"Magnify," Sten said.

Blossoming from the heel were two wings.

Sten groaned and relaxed back into his chair. Matters had gotten even worse than he had expected.

Even Rykor was a bit overcome. She sneezed loudly. "Mercury Corps," she said, puffing through wet whiskers.

"Yeah," Sten said. "And I hope to god he's just a renegade."

The gurion's ray encircled Dynsman's neck... nestling, and then with a sudden burst, pulling him close. Dynsman felt his lungs collapse and saw the last precious

stream of air explode outward. And then a knife hand—
Sten's?—swept into view...and...

"The rest of the way!" Sten ordered.

Rykor's flipper paused at the slidepot. She glanced
over at Dynsman's flopping body, where he was reliving
the horror again and again. Her empathy glands were
weeping at the edges of her eyes.

"I don't know if I can," she said.

"Do it!" Sten said.

And Rykor startled, sliding the pot full on. The brainscan flurried far ahead...

The holograph to one side of the screen that was Dynsman's brain was the body of a curling worm. On its main
body, winking colors of blue and red and yellow, mapped
the parts that Sten and Rykor had already explored. The
gurion marked the only red. The blue points were connected by thin capillary pink. Those blue spots already
touched were blinking at them.

"Where?" Sten urged. "Where?"

Rykor studied the holograph. An infinite number of
blue spots to go...empathy...empathy...

"There," she breathed. And Rykor wept as she zeroed
in.

The image of the bar that was the Covenanter filled
the screen. The laser brights of the sign were swallowed
by the fog that drifted in from the nearby spaceport. Dynsman didn't know the scientific reason for it, but at night,
many kilometers surrounding the main port were surrounded by fog. And, this was a special night. He was
waiting for...

"This is a busto bum go," Dynsman's thoughts whispered across the screen to Sten and Rykor.

Dynsman was as unsure of himself as he had ever been.
A huge picture of one hand suddenly filled the screen.
Two missing fingers stubbed out.

"Come, on," Sten said impatiently. Rykor twisted the
scroll.

The screen furred and then Dynsman was watching two men greet each other in front of the bar.

"Push the sound," Sten snapped.

Alain looked at the man in engineer coveralls, made his assessment, and then said, "Engineer Raschid?"

Sten and Rykor watched the two men go inside, and then flashing shadow hands as Dynsman armed his bomb and waited for the final moments. There was no sound from the bomb's timer, but Dynsman could hear the ticking in his mind. The words "Engineer Raschid" were the key. He had paced out the seconds it would take for them to be greeted by Janiz and then seated in Booth C.

Dynsman beat out the last moment of several people's lives in his mind. Not now... almost now... now... and the brainscan room was filled with muted white light and ear-shattering explosions.

Then the screen became a gurion, pulsing its stomach-mouth toward Dynsman's face. The man that was Dynsman strained against his straps and screamed once again.

Rykor watched him, her eyes filling with tears. "What should I do with him?" she asked.

Sten shrugged. Rykor wiped her eyes. Then she reached out her flipper and pushed the slidepot down the rest of the way. On the table, Dynsman was suddenly very still. He was peaceful then, for the first time in his life.

"Do you believe in ghosts?" Rykor asked.

Sten thought for a minute. "Maybe... but not his."

Rykor considered that, and then pressed the buttons that ordered the chair to deliver her back into her soothing deep-water bath. And just before she disappeared into a explosion of water, Sten heard her say, "You're an optimist, young Sten."

And Sten imagined a hoot of laughter exploding out of the tank. Sten exited the chamber, wondering exactly what she meant.

CHAPTER TWENTY-NINE

STEN SHIFTED THE bulky file from one arm to another, and stood patiently in the doorway to the work area. He watched with no little amazement as the Eternal Emperor bent low over the strange boxlike object held gently in his hands. The curled right fingers of his hand plucked at first cautiously at the strings, and then with more confidence.

He sang in a soft, husky voice:

> *"Now with this loaded*
> *blunderbuss*
> *The truth I will unfold.*
> *He made the mayor to tremble*
> *And he robbed him of his gold . . ."*

One string buzzed against a fret and the Emperor broke off in frustration. "Clot!"

He slammed the instrument down with a loud bang and an echoing of stringed chords. He stared at the thing for a long moment and then kicked it over to a heap of similar objects. Then he spotted Sten. He frowned deeply, and then his face cleared. "Don't *ever* try to build a guitar," he growled.

"I wouldn't dream of it, sir." Sten said as he walked into the work area.

He looked at the pile of discarded instruments and glanced around the room. Hung here and there were other attempts. Some were partially completed. Some consisted of just the cut-out backs. And scattered about were necks in a variety of sizes, drilled for rods. Sten sniffed at the evil-smelling smoke boiling from a pot of goo that was bubbling over an open fire.

"Excuse me, sir, but what's a guitar?"

"A musical instrument," the Emperor said. "Or at least that's what some devil called it when he invented the fretted thing."

Sten nodded thoughtfully. "Oh, that's what you were doing." He picked up one of the discarded guitars. And studied it. He peered past the strings and inside the hole.

"I don't see any circuitry. How do you make it work?"

"With great bleeding difficulty," the Emperor said. He rose and pulled one of the blank backs from its wall hook. Then he sat again and laid it across his knees. "Hand me the sandpaper."

Sten looked around, wondering what his boss meant. Then he connected: Sand. Rough. Some kind of abrasive. He reached down to the litter on the floor and picked up something that he believed would fit the requirements.

"It's all in the inside shape," the Emperor said. "Something to do with how the sound bounces against the box. Trouble is, nobody was very scientific about it back in those days." He took the sandpaper from Sten and began polishing inside the box.

"They did it to taste," the Emperor went on. "So much here..." He rubbed along one curving line. "So much there...." He began sanding at the brace of the strut itself, smoothing and removing spots of what appeared to be glue.

In sudden disgust, the Emperor set the thing down on the floor. Sten saw, however, that this time he was careful to place it on a thick rug. The Emperor noticed where he was looking.

"Lebanese," he said by way of explanation. "Two square yards from said folk. You don't even want to know what it cost."

He looked up at Sten. "Okay," he finally said. "You want a safe place to talk. This is it." He swept his hand around the workshop, crammed with antique tools and materials. "This is the most secure place I know of. I have it swept daily."

Sten smiled thinly. He picked up the thick file folder and slid out a small, slender device. "And I just swept it again, sir," he said, showing him the debugging device.

The Emperor looked at him. "And?"

Sten picked up the guitar that the Emperor had recently dismissed as poor quality. He shook his head.

"Maybe that's what made the, uh, guitar buzz," he said. "Sorry about that, Your Highness."

The Eternal Emperor thought for a moment, considering whether he ought to get mad. After a while, he grinned at Sten. Then he grabbed a pair of tongs, lifted up the pot of evil-smelling goo, and dabbed it on the guitar with a brush.

He looked up at Sten. "Well?"

Sten checked his snooper, and then shook his head. "Clean." Then he opened the remainder of the file and palmed its contents across the desk in a gambler's swirl. "Are you ready, sir," Sten asked.

The Emperor studied him. "You mean am I through clotting around?"

"Yes, sir," Sten said.

The Emperor picked up the unfinished guitar body again and started stroking its sides. "Go."

Sten pulled out a photograph—a still taken from the brainscan room. "That's our boy," he said.

The Emperor studied the picture of Knox. "Mr. Big," he said dryly.

"If by that you mean the main fellow behind this thing, no, sir, I don't think so. He was merely Dynsman's control. Fortunately for us, he wasn't satisfied with just that role." Sten handed over another photo.

The Emperor peered down to see a tight shot of Knox's ring hand. He caught the emblem instantly. "Mercury Corps!"

"Yes, sir. Not only that, we know for a fact that this man—call him Knox for the moment—was a doctor. That means he was probably a Mercury Corps trained medico."

"Former or current?"

"Hopefully, former. We don't know. I've got Lieutenant Haines checking on it."

Sten ran down for a second, watching the Emperor sitting very quietly, rubbing the abrasive against the wood. The Emperor reached into a slit pocket and pulled out a small object. Sten peered forward. The object appeared to be made of metal, and forked. His boss shifted the object around in his hand and then gently tapped it against the side of the instrument. A low, muted tone *thum*ed . . . for many heartbeats. The Emperor pressed it against his cheek, quieting it.

"The harmony," he said, "still isn't right. Go on, Captain."

Sten took a deep breath. What he had to say next was putting him on very dangerous ground. "May I speak freely, sir?" Sten asked, knowing it for a fool question. No one should ever speak freely to a superior. But it was a chance he had to take.

"GA."

"A large piece of this puzzle is missing. Right from the middle."

"What do you need to find it?"

"An honest answer."

"Someone is holding back?"

"Yes, sir."

The Emperor had caught the point long ago. Still, he liked to play things out.

"Would that someone be me?"

"I'm afraid so, sir."

"Ask away," the Emperor said, his face strangely softening.

Sten sighed.

"Thank you, sir. But let me lay the rest of this thing out first. Then I'll ask."

"Okay, we'll do it your way. But hand me the glue."

Sten puzzled at him, and then realized the Emperor was pointing at the evil-smelling pot. Sten picked it up and handed it to the boss.

The Emperor reached over to a dusty shelf and slid out a small wood-handled brush. He let it float on top of the goo pot and reached down between his legs for the top of the guitar. He thumped it with his knuckles. Then he scraped the tuning fork across it, listening intently for the humming sound. He nodded with satisfaction. "This one might be right."

Then he dipped the brush deeply into the hot mixture at his feet and began brushing the goo along the ridges of the guitar's shoe.

"To start with," Sten said, "there was some kind of code phrase that seemed to trigger the bombing. Dynsman's vital functions jumped about twelve beats every time we mind-scrolled it back."

"Which was?"

The Emperor listened closely as he continued working. He fit the top of the guitar to its box and then clamped it into place.

Sten glanced at his notes. "Raschid," he said. "The action was supposed to begin when someone used the name Raschid. To be exact, the phrase was Engineer Raschid."

Sten didn't notice the Emperor's face cloud over in anger. "Go on," he prodded, almost in a whisper.

"Then there was Booth C," Sten said. "Dynsman was supposed to trigger the time bomb when he next heard someone ask for Booth C."

"Stop," the Emperor said. He said it quietly, it was as clear a command as Sten had ever heard. "So I killed her," the Emperor said to himself. "It was me."

"Sir?"

By way of an answer, the Emperor pulled a bottle from underneath his stool. He took a long shuddering drink and then handed it to Sten.

Sten just waited, staring at him. If there was any way of getting through to this man, Eternal Emperor or not, Sten was hoping it was then. "Engineer Raschid?" the Emperor said. "Yeah. That's me. One of my many disguises, Captain. When I like to get down among them."

It all came together for Sten after that admission. "Then, sir, it follows that you were the target. It had nothing to do with Godfrey Alain. Or the emissary who went to meet him in your place."

The Emperor smiled a sad smile. "Yeah. He was supposed to identify himself as Engineer Raschid. Instead of the bar, they were supposed to ask Janiz for Booth C."

"Janiz?" Sten asked. "Who was Janiz?"

The Emperor just waved him on. So Sten continued linking the chain of evidence together.

"Fine. So here was how it was supposed to go. Dynsman had the bomb set up at Booth C. It was shaped to destroy the bar, but only stun its key occupant. Meaning you. The rest is easy. The ambulance was supposed to take you to Dr. Knox."

"And then they figured I'd be in their control," the Emperor said. "Dumb clots. It's been tried."

He started to take a sip from the bottle, then shook his head, corked it, and shoved it under his stool. "Sometimes," he said, "I don't like myself. You ever feel that way?"

Sten figured it was better to ignore this and just press on. "Sir," he said as carefully as possible, "it seems to me that the Tahn have got clot all to do with this. Somebody—probably one of your own people—wants to replace you as Emperor. The Tahn just got dragged into it because of Alain."

He waited for a response, but the Emperor remained silent, thinking his own thoughts. Sten decided that it was time to ask the key question. "Who was she, sir?"

The Emperor raised his old/young eyes. "Janiz," he said. "Just Janiz. We used to be lovers. Quite a few years ago. When I was feeling . . . who the clot cares how I felt.

"I told her a few stories. About what a badass I was. How rich I was gonna be. And she . . . she . . . Hell, son, she listened to me."

"But you were the Emperor," Sten said softly.

The Emperor shook his head, no. "I was Engineer Raschid," he said. "A bully dreamer. A liar. Hell, she believed me. I used to roll into town pretty regular— every year or two. Then I kept promoting myself. And then it was Captain Raschid, ma'am. Captain Raschid."

"But that was a long time ago," Sten guessed.

The Eternal Emperor nodded. "We stopped being lovers. But we stayed friends. I put up the credits for the bar. I was to be a very silent partner. Except for Booth C. I had her keep that just for me, or people I sent there. I had the best antisnooping equipment in my Empire installed.

"Godfrey Alain wasn't the first covert meet I set up there. Strange what you make of old lovers."

He thought for a long moment and then pulled the bottle out from under his feet. He took a small drink to clear his head. "What is your advice, Captain?"

Sten rose to his feet. "We know there's a leak, sir." He began pacing. "We have to shut down everything. Someone, sir, is very definitely trying to kill you."

The Emperor smiled an odd smile. He started to speak but kept it to himself. Sten wished to God he had said what was on his mind. What was he still hiding?

"Okay. You are the target. We don't know how many conspirators there are. So we trust no one. I follow the Knox trail. And, you, sir..."

"Yes, Captain? What exactly do you propose I do?"

Sten caught himself, and wondered if he had gone too far.

The Emperor raised several fingers in a mock salute. "Don't worry about me, Captain," he said. "I'll be perfectly safe. Although sometimes I wish..." The Eternal Emperor picked up his last discarded guitar. He bent low over it and began fingering out a complicated string of chords.

Even to Sten's untrained ear, it sounded pretty good. It also sounded like a final dismissal.

CHAPTER THIRTY

KAI HAKONE GROUND his palms together and the tabac leaves shredded down onto the leaf below. Carefully he sprinkled water onto the leaf, then rolled the leaf around the shreds, folding the ends in on the roll. He finished, inspected the cheroot with satisfaction, then dipped it in the nearly full snifter of Earth cognac before him. Satisfied, he clipped the end and, using a wooden firestick, lit the cheroot and leaned back, looking across the chamber. It was a private room in one of Prime World's most exclusive clubs, where it was very easy for Hakone's fellows to meet, and for Hakone to keep free of monitoring devices.

The other men in the room—perhaps fifty—were Hakone's age or older. Industrialists, retired high-rankers, entrepreneurs with laurels to rest on. To an outsider, they reeked of wealth. To Hakone, they smelled like death.

But to Kai Hakone, that nostril-scorching scent like lamb, like burnt pork, was the smell of his life, and his writing.

Some people are formed by a single experience.

Such was Kai Hakone.

Almost from birth he had wanted to fly. To fly in space. The world he was born on was comfortably settled, as were his parents. His mother had one great idea—that it would be possible to establish a store where persons could walk in, fit themselves into a booth for measurement, then pick a pattern and, within minutes, have a custom-tailored garment. That idea made the Hakones very wealthy and very satisfied.

They had no understanding—but also no disagree-

158

ment—with their son's desire to go out; and so Kai Hak-one ended up commissioned as a lieutenant in command of a probe vessel at the start of the Mueller Wars.

Hakone had taken all the lessons of the Academy to heart and was earnestly trying to lead, inspire, and be an authoritarian friend to the thirty-eight men on the tiny ship. But his probe ship was picked for close-in support of the landing on Saragossa. Five Imperial battlewagons died that day, as did most of the Seventh Guards Division committed on the troopships. Among the million dead, spewed into lung-spilling space or endlessly falling onto a rock-hard planet, were the men and women of Hakone's ship.

His probe ship had died slowly, cut to ribbons by missiles, close-range lasers, and finally projectile-blast guns. Lieutenant Kai Hakone was the only survivor. He'd been dug out of the ruins of the ship and slowly psyched back together.

After the Mueller Wars ground down, the Emperor found it very convenient to allow anyone in the Imperial Service who wanted out, out. Kai Hakone found himself a young civilian, with a more-than-adequate separation allowance, no desire to return to his home world, and the reek of death in his nostrils.

That reek had led him to his current career as a writer.

His first vid-book—a novel on the rites-of-passage-via-slaughter—bombed. His second, a sober analysis of the Mueller Wars, became a best-seller, being published ten years after the war ended, just at the correct time for a revisionist appraisal. Since then, Hakone's works, all grim, all tinged with the skull, were received and reviewed as coming from a major creative artist.

His sixth volume, a return to nonfiction, soberly analyzed what went wrong at the battle of Saragossa, taking the scandalous viewpoint that the young admiral-in-place was a scapegoat for the Emperor's own failings. The work was, of course, cleverly worded to avoid any semblance of political libel.

But that, Hakone realized, was another turning point. That was the reason he was sitting in a rich man's club, smelling rich men's lives and feeling like a spectre at the banquet. But Hakone shut that thought off, much as he closed off the perpetual wonderment of what would have happened to Kai Hakone had the battle of Saragossa been an Imperial triumph.

He clicked fingernails against the table for attention, and the room fell silent.

Again he looked around at the fifty-odd men in the room. If Hakone were brighter, or more analytical, he might have wondered why none of the former military people had rank above one-star, why the industrialists were all people who had inherited their businesses from their forebears, and why the entrepreneurs were those who hustled borderline deals. But the nature of conspiracy is not to question.

"Gentlemen," he began, his quiet voice a contradiction to his bearlike presence. "Before we begin, let me advise you that this room has been proofed against any known electronic eavesdropping, as well as any physical pickups. We are able to speak freely."

A man stood. Hakone identified him as Saw Toyer, who'd increased his riches supplying uniforms for the Guard.

"Time has passed, Sr. Hakone," he accused. "We— and I think I speak for us all—have given more than generously. We expected . . . something to happen following Empire Day. As you promised. Instead, and I am not asking to be privy to the secrets, nothing has occurred. At least nothing which we can see.

"Were I not committed, I might ask if my credits are being poured into a black hole."

"That is the purpose of the meeting," Hakone answered. "To inform you of what has happened."

Hakone could have gone into detail: That the attempt to shock and then kidnap the Emperor had gone awry. That the assassin had successfully fled Prime World. That his control and their operative doctor, Har Stynburn— "Dr. Knox"—had disappeared. But that as far as Hakone knew, the dangling tails of that conspiracy had either been cleaned up—such as the murder of Tac Chief Kreuger—

or had cleaned themselves up. But he knew that the secret to success is never to worry the money-men with minor problems.

"Phase One, as you've said, went awry. But, you'll notice, without any suspicion on the part of the Emperor, other than his assigning one of his personal soldiers to investigate. As guaranteed, we left no traces.

"There is one problem, however. And that is that our normal source of intelligence has gone dry. We no longer have input to the Emperor's next moves."

Hakone swizzled his cheroot in the cognac and relit the cigar, waiting for the buzz of dismay to die. Gutless. Gutless, he thought. These men have never learned that there is always one more kilometer that you must go. So, his optimistic side answered, you learned long ago that you run with what you brought.

Hakone tapped for silence again. The buzz was louder as fear grew in the room. Hakone wetted a finger in the cognac and began moving it around the rim of the glass. The high whine silenced the throng.

"Thank you," Hakone said. "What is past is past. Now for the good news. Our coordinator is most pleased with what is going on."

"Why?" The snarl was unidentifiable.

"Because in spite of our actions, and in spite of Imperial motion, there have been no breaks."

"So what do we do next—find holes and pull 'em in after ourselves?" That came from Ban Lucery, one of the few industrialists Hakone respected.

"That is a firm negative. Our coordinator—and I heartily agree with his decision—has said that we move to Phase Two of what we've dubbed Operation Zaarah Wahrid. Relax, gentlemen. The days of this intolerable Imperial control are numbered. There is no way Phase Two can fail."

CHAPTER THIRTY-ONE

THE LITTLE MEN peaveyed the logs from the pond, hooked them into the chain hoist, and the drunk sat against a pile of peeled logs and cheered. Naik Rai and Subadar-Major Chittahang Limbu watched approvingly.

Sten shut his model box down, and figures disappeared instantly although he was sure that his "drunk" had time to take another swig from the bottle before he vanished.

"This is not good," Haik Rai said. "How will you remember which socks to wear?"

"You are sure this is correct?" Limbu echoed in Gurkhali.

"Goddamn it," Sten swore. "I am not sure of anything, Subadar-Major. All I know is that I am detached on Imperial Service. All I know is that you are to take charge of the Gurkhas.

"And all I know is that if you shame me, on Dashera it shall not be bullocks but ballocks that are cut off. By me, Subadar-Major."

Limbu started to laugh, then saluted. "Captain, I have no idea what is happening. But I do have this feeling that none of us shall meet short of Moksa."

Sten lifted a lip. "Thank you for your confidence, Chittahang. But I wave my private parts at that feeling. That is all. You are dismissed."

The two Gurkhas saluted and were gone. Sten continued packing. Again the door signal buzzed, and Sten palmed it open.

It was Lisa. Sten noticed that she carried a debugging

pouch that was on. The door closed, and he decided the first order of business was to kiss her thoroughly.

Eventually they broke. Lisa smiled up at him. "Everything is ga-ga."

"No drakh," Sten said. "You sound like the Eternal Emperor."

"You're leaving."

"I say again my last. I know I am leaving. For the safe house."

"Nope," Haines said, coming back to the point. "I mean you're *leaving* leaving. You and that tubby thug of yours."

"Uh-oh."

"We've found our famous Dr. Knox." And Haines threw a fiche onto Sten's table.

"Tell me about it."

"Dr. John Knox is actually named Hars Stynburn. Broken out of the Mercury Corps. Court-martial sealed I quote 'for the good of the Service' end quote."

Sten felt a first wave of relief: At least the conspiracy didn't involve the current Imperial military.

"It seems that Dr. Stynburn, who always was fairly militant about his views, was assigned as Med Off to a pacification team. Some world—it's in the fiche—that the Empire had trouble bringing under control.

"The natives on this particular world didn't want much of anything," Lisa said. "Except steel weapons. Dr. Stynburn somehow arranged that the spearheads and so forth were highly radioactive. Is that what you people really do?"

"Knock it off, Lisa."

"Sorry. It's been a long day. Anyway, so the natives kicked—the female ones, since the planet was a matriarchy. Native life span was real short, so by the time Stynburn's team was taken off, the planet was clean for settlement.

"Unfortunately somebody sang like a vulture, and Dr. Stynburn got a court-martial."

By this time, Sten had fed the fiche into his desk viewer, listening to Haines with only a quarter of his attention.

"Busted out. No prison...clot it...should'a spaced him...drifted...no record of employment..." He shut off the viewer and looked at Lisa.

"No record," she said. "But we found him. He's off Prime."

"Where?"

"A little hidey-hole of a planet named Kulak." Haines handed Sten another fiche.

"How'd you find him so fast?"

"Since you pointed out that our Dr. Knox appeared more 'n a bit egocentric, I wondered if he wasn't also dumb enough to keep his career going instead of disappearing as a potwalloper.

"Sure enough. Dr.—his new name's William Block—is the contract medico on Kulak."

Sten fed more fiche into his viewer, scanned the overall description, and was scared several different shades of white. "I should've stayed in Mantis," he said to himself. "All I'd be doing is making a drop into some swamp with no more than ten thousand to one odds. But not dummy me."

"You've heard of Kulak?"

Sten didn't bother with the full explanation, since it was fairly involved. Kulak was a small planetoid with a poisonous atmosphere and a killer environment. Its location was approximately between Galaxy's End and Nowhere. Its only interesting feature was that crystalline metals on the planet had a life of their own, growing like plants. One of those metals was incredibly light, yet far stronger than any conventional metal known to the Empire. Its chemical properties and description were included on the fiche.

But Sten was quite familiar with that substance—he'd "built" the knife hidden in his arm from it, back on Vulcan, in "Hellworld"—the punishment sector for Vulcan's slave laborers. The work area—Area 35—had duplicated Kulak's environment exactly, down to the point of killing over 100 percent of the workers sentenced to it.

And now Sten was required to go back to Area 35. He was as terrified as he'd ever been in his life.

Sten told his swirling stomach to shut up and scanned on. After discovery, Kulak had been abandoned by the discovering company, but it was reopened years later by independent miners, tough men and women who were willing to crapshoot their settlement on Kulak. Since Kulak was not considered a plush assignment, their co-op had jumped at the chance to get a for-real doctor, especially one willing to pact on a two-E-year-contract. Since many of the miners were themselves on the run from Imperial justice, no one was much interested in exactly what Dr. "Block"—Hars Stynburn—had done. On Kulak, Imperial treason rated up there with nonpayment of child support.

Sten corrected his features and yanked the fiche. "Yeah, I've heard of Kulak."

"I have a tacship standing by," Haines said. "Destination sealed, even for the pilot. And I ordered the necessary environmental suits."

None of the replies that occurred immediately to Sten was suitable—and then Kilgour thundered through the entranceway, tapping a fiche angrily.

"Wee Sten," he said. "Y'dinna ken where this daft lass is tryin't to send us noo."

"Yes, I do."

"Sorry, Lieutenant. Ah dinna see you f'r a mo."

"Never mind, Sergeant. Your fearless leader doesn't look as if he's any happier than you are."

"Sten, d'we hae t'do this? Canne we noo con a wee battalion ae Guards to winkle this dog oot?"

"And put him on the run again?"

"Aye, lad. Aye. Ah guess y'hae a point. Nae a good point, but ae point. So where does this leave us?"

"It would appear," Sten said dryly, "that we're doon th' mine."

"Dinna be makit fun ae th' way Ah speakit," Alex said. "Ah'll hae m'mither on y'."

And Sten went back to packing.

CHAPTER THIRTY-TWO

JILL SHERMAN WAS the only law on Kulak. Sherman had been chosen by the Kulak cooperative to provide some species of order in the single-dome village that was home base for the miners. She was at least as mean as any miner on the planetoid, she was generally brighter than the miners, and she had a laissez-faire attitude toward law enforcement. She had only three rules: no weapons that could injure the dome; no crooked gambling; every miner got an honest count on his crystals.

Sherman had found it expedient to take the contract as the only law on Kulak after her previous assignment had become somewhat spectacular. She'd been a police subchief on a world plagued with continual riots—understandable, since that world was *entirely* composed of minorities, each of which put its foot down the throat of the less fortunate after achieving power. Eventually Sherman decided she had seen one too many riots and dropped a mininuke. The explosion had not only blown the current party out of power, but Sherman into flight just ahead of a wave of charges—murder, malfeasance in office, and attempted genocide.

She eyed Sten's credentials, then looked at the two men, who were still recovering from landing sickness.

"Dr. Block's done a fine job here. Why in clot should I help you two Imperials take him out?"

"I won't read the warrant again," Sten said tiredly. "But there's little things like treason, multiple murder, conspiracy, flight to avoid prosecution—you know. The usual stuff."

"This is Kulak, my friend. We don't *care* about what someone did back in civilization."

"Lass," Alex began. "P'raps we could buy you a dram and discuss—"

"That's enough, Sergeant," Sten snapped, perhaps unwisely, but his stomach was still doing ground-loops with the tacship that had fought its way to a landing on Kulak. "You people operate under an Imperial charter. The charter could be lifted with one com message by me, and Imperial support would be on its way. Are you prepared to escalate, Officer Sherman?" If Sten's guts hadn't been sitting in his throat, he probably would have found a different way to go. He had certainly made a mistake, as Alex's near subvocal moan underlined.

"Sorry, uh, Captain it was? Dr. Block can be found in C-Sector, Offices 60."

Sten then made his second mistake. He nodded brusquely, took Alex by the arm, and was on the way out.

Sherman, of course, waited until the double lock on her office cycled closed, and then was on the com.

Even the streets of the domed city were primitive. They were tempcontrolled and oxygenated, but that did not keep the condensation within the dome from continually fogging, raining, and creating much mess underfoot.

"Y'blew it, lad," Kilgour murmured as he and Sten slogged through the mire. "Yon lass wa' admirable. In one wee hour, Ah could'a had her eatin' out'a mah hand."

Sten probably snarled at Alex because he was scared— scared of the world, scared of what it brought up in his past, and scared of the many ways to die slowly that Area 35 had shown him.

He may also have been afraid of the suits they wore. Everyone on Kulak wore suits, even in the dome, unless immediate physical necessities suggested otherwise. The suits were interesting—large, armored, so bulky that even a lithe man like Sten had to waddle in them. One reason they were so bulky is that each limb contained a shut-off element. If a suit limb was holed, the wearer could cut off that segment, instantly amputating and cauterizing the affected limb.

Regardless of the reason, Sten was as afraid as he had been for years.

Dr. Hars Stynburn/Dr. John Knox/Dr. William Block had gotten the tip from Sherman. He hastily finished strapping himself into his suit then armed himself with the usual long, evilly curved near-sword and "harvesting tool."

When a miner harvested a "ripe" chunk of the metal that grew outside the dome, he used a spade-gun, a double-handed, spring-powered rifle that fired a spear about one meter long and faced with a 25-centimeter, razor-edged shovel tip. The spear's velocity approached 500 meters per second, which made it quite a lethal tool.

Stynburn had been expecting an attack—not from Imperial law, but rather from one or another of Hakone's pet thugs. He wasn't angry either way, since he felt it was perfectly legitimate for a covert operation to police up all traces. That was why he'd fled Prime World in the first place.

That was also why his office/quarters had its back wall close against the dome itself, and why Stynburn had set his inner office door as an airseal.

Stynburn closed his faceplate and checked the readout. No leaks. He dumped his office atmosphere back into the dome and kept his hand ready on the button. His eyes were on the vidscreen over the entrance, the vidscreen that showed his outer office.

He did not wait when the door opened and he saw two men enter.

His hand went down on the red switch, and instantly his back wall and the dome's outer seal exploded outward, pinwheeling Stynburn out onto the surface of Kulak.

Even through the chamber, Sten could feel the *chumph* as the inner office decompressed. Reflexively, both he and Alex slammed their faceplates shut. And waited.

The gauges, present in every rooom and every office in the dome, dipped then recovered.

"Th' lad's gone out," Alex said through the suit com.

Sten didn't bother to answer—he was headed back through the entrance, for the nearest dome lock.

But the mucky street outside was filled with miners. Sherman was at their head. Sten stopped and flipped his faceplate open.

"We've decided," Sherman began, sans preamble, "that you have your law, and we have ours. We need a doctor. And we've got one. And we're going to keep him."

Sten couldn't think of a lot of threats that made sense.

"We'll take whatever comes down afterward when it comes down. If it comes down."

"Which means, lass," Alex put in sadly, "y'hae nae intention ah lettin' us gie away?"

Sherman nodded.

Sten's suit roughly duplicated the same type the miners and Sherman wore. But being of Imperial design, there were small changes. Sten hoped desperately that one of them wasn't known.

He took a square container from his belt and twisted the cap open as his faceplate closed. A thin, visible spray hissed out, and Sten tossed the container into the midst of the miners. He flipped his com level button to full and roared "Gas! This is a corrosive gas!" as he began running. For a few seconds the miners were too busy seeking shelter from the squat container as it hissed, buzzed, and danced around the street to worry about where Alex and Sten were headed.

By the time Sherman's outsuit analyzer had figure out that the container was nothing more than an emergency air supply—carried as a liquid for compactness—Sten and Alex were at the dome's outer lock.

"Och," Alex moaned, booting Sten into the inner chamber. "Ah'll be th' wee lad wha' hold 'em a' the bridge."

Before Sten could answer, Alex cycled the lock closed, leaving no option for Sten but to go out after Stynburn.

Alex turned, as the near-mob elephanted up to him. "Aye noo, an' who'll be the first?"

The first was a miner who dwarfed Alex and his fellows. Alex blocked his blow and then swung. The block smashed the man's suit arm, and the punch cartwheeled the monster back through the air into the middle of the crowd. Kulak was a light-gee world—and Kilgour was a heavy-worlder. The mob closed in, and the situation became desperate.

Moderately desperate, since the knives that most of the miners carried were inside their suits, and they didn't have enough room to aim and fire their spade-guns—at least not without taking the chance of sending their bolts through the nearby dome wall.

So Alex-at-the-lock deteriorated into a vulgar brawl. In any other society, it would have been called a massacre, but on Kulak it was merely a fight that would be told about for a few years until the people involved struck it rich and moved off or died.

And there was nothing that Kilgour enjoyed more than a vulgar brawl. In motion, he looked like a heavily armored ball that ricocheted away from the lock entrance to connect with a target and then spun back to position, an armored ball confusedly quoting half-remembered and terrible poetry.

> "Tha' oot spake braw Horatius.
> Th' cap' ae th' gate:
> T' every man upon the airt,
> A fat lip cometh soon or late.'

The fat lip was a miner's smashed faceplate and a near-fatal concussion. Alex was too busy to see the man fall as he grabbed a swinging, grab-iron-wielding arm and shoved the grab iron into a third miner's gut, exploding the pressurized suit.

> "Ae Astur's throat Horatius
> Right firmly pressed his heel . . ."

That miner gurgled into oblivion.

> *"An' thrice an four times tugged amain..."*
> *Sorry lad for the poetic license.*
> *"Ere he wrenched out the steel."*

The miners pulled back to regroup. Alex turned his suit oxy supply to full and waited.

The mob—only half of it was still interested in fighting—grew hesitant.

> *"Wae none who would be foremost*
> *To lead such dire attack;*
> *But those behind criet 'forrard.'*
> *An' thae before cried for their wee mums."*

That was too much, and the miners phalanxed forward. A phalanx works very well, so long as nobody takes out the front rank. Alex went flat in the dome's muck and rolled toward the onrushing miners. The front rank stumbled and went down, effectively blocking the airlock. And Alex was running amok in their rear. The ram of his helmet was as effective as his feet and fists, and then the mob was hesitating, turning, and running down the narrow passageways, away from Alex.

He collected himself, chopped his suit's air supply, and opened his faceplate, breathing deeply to let the euphoria and adrenaline ebb somewhat.

> *"It stands some'eres or other*
> *Plain for all to see.*
> *Wee Alex in his kilt an' socks*
> *Dronk upon one knee*
> *An' underneath is written*
> *In letters ae of mold*
> *How valiantly he kept th' bridge*
> *Ee the braw days ae old."*

Alex looked around, hoping for an appreciative audience. There was none—the battle casualties were either terminal, moaning for a medico, or crawling away at speed. But Alex wasn't bothered.

"Tha," he went on, "wa a poem Ah learn't a' m' mither's knee an' other low joints." He looked worriedly at the lock behind him. "Now, wee Sten, if y'll be snaggi't th' doc so we can be away afore thae dolts realize Ah'm guardin't a lock 'stead of a bridge..."

The dust was metal filings, quickly being blown into the yellow fog that clouded the outside of the dome. Sten briefly looked at the exploded walls that had been Stynburn's chambers, then went after the footsteps in the dust.

They sprang, one every ten meters, up into what might have been called—had they not been swelling constantly, pulsating, then collapsing into ruin—hills.

The trail led around a boulder. Intent on the ground, Sten almost died, jerking aside only as the growth on the boulder matured, blossomed, and explosively "spored."

The trail led along the edge of those hills, then down into a widening valley past a river of liquid metal.

Too easy, Sten's mind warned him. Sten fought to see through the yellow haze, trying to track the quickly vanishing prints as they led up from the valley, then disappeared on a germinating pool of rock. Sten used his hand to sweep in a circle around the last truck, his arm-stretch a rough indicator of a man's tracks.

He looked up. Below the rock bed was a small grotto. The winds hadn't yet brushed the metal dust on the floor, and Sten could see footprints leading out of the cleft, headed down toward the river.

He was in the grotto, pacing carefully. Three steps in, and all systems went to red with an old joke: How can you tell a Mercury Corps man. By his tracks. He always walks backward. Sten rolled awkwardly in the suit as Stynburn dove at him from ambush at the edge of the grotto.

Stynburn's clubbed spade-gun went for Sten's faceplate, but Sten's smashing feet sent Stynburn sailing over his head to roll in the dust.

Sten righted himself just as Stynburn came up firing the spade-gun. Having seen the spade-gun, Sten was turning, to offer as small a target as possible; by chance his suited arm intersected the spear's trajectory, deflecting the projectile harmlessly.

Two men, wearing suits that turned them into blobbed caricatures of humans, faced each other in an arena of metal dust that whirled and dissolved in the yellow wind.

Stynburn turned on his com. "Who are you? Who am I facing?"

Stan was not a man for dramatics. "Captain Sten. On His Imperial Majesty's Service. I have a warrant, Dr. Stynburn."

"You have a warrant," Stynburn said. "I have a death."

"We all do, sooner or later," Sten said, looking for a strike point.

"I will tell you one thing, Captain—Sten it was?"

"Doctor, you sound like a man who wants to die. I want to keep you alive."

"Alive," Stynburn mused. "Why? Evidently it's all failed. Or perhaps it has not."

Sten's eyes widened. This wasn't the first time he had faced someone who appeared mad, and Stynburn's words were proclaiming just that.

"Failed? What's failed?"

"You want me to talk, don't you?"

"Of course."

"Captain, you must know what I was."

"Mercury Corps. So was I," Sten offered, maneuvering toward the man's left.

"In another world, another time, we could have been friends."

Sten deliberately stood straight, as if considering. "Yeah," he said slowly, musingly. "Maybe we could have. Clot, I always wanted to be a doctor."

"But that would have been another time," Stynburn said. Sten realized the man was playing games.

"I have two deaths is what I should have said. Yours and mine."

"Then it's your move, Doctor." Sten braced in suit close-combat position.

"Not that way, Captain. You shall die. Here and now. But I shall give you this. No man should die in ignorance. I shall give you an explanation. That is Zaarah Wahrid."

Sten keyed his mike then realized that the two words were explanation enough for Stynburn. He saw the man contort in his suit.

Years of Mantis training had taught Sten the various ways an agent could kill himself, and he knew full well that the contortions were Stynburn's attempts to cramp his shoulders back. Sten was in motion, diving and rolling behind a growing/shrinking rock, hoping that the living mineral would stand as—

The first crash was not that loud. The bomb that had been implanted between Stynburn's shoulder blades wasn't very effective. The most powerful explosion was the oxy-atmosphere in Stynburn's suit fireballing across the grotto.

And then there was nothing except the gale's howl in Sten's outer pickups as he lifted himself over the rock and stared at the few tatters of suit that were scattered across the dusty floor.

Zaarah Wahrid, Sten thought as he picked himself up. One lead. Sten had a fairly good idea that one clue would not be enough.

He headed back down the trail, checking his helmet compass for bearings back to the dome.

The first job was to rescue Alex. If he was still alive, that'd be easy.

Because the next job was to face the Emperor with almost nothing.

BOOK FOUR

DECLIC

CHAPTER THIRTY-THREE

THE BLUE BHOR was a two-story, rambling building that sprawled along the banks of the River Wye. Built nearly a century before, it was an inn that catered to the local fisherfolk and small farmers on the Valley Wye. The valley was gentle, with rolling, rocky hills that climbed up into low, gray-blue mountains—a place where someone could make a passable living fishing or a grumbling living digging out rocks from ground that sprouted stones faster than potatoes. Still, it could be a pleasant life in a place that was good to raise a family.

Then the sportspeople of Prime World discovered it. And fishing season after fishing season, people streamed into the valley to catch the elusive golden fish that darted along the river. New roads were built. Many, many businesses sprouted up, and even a town—the Township of Ashley-on-Wye—was created where only farms had existed before.

As the valley boomed, so did the Blue Bhor. It began as a single, not very comfortable bar with a rent-a-room above. Owner after owner expanded the inn to handle the growing business and then sold out. Eventually the Blue Bhor boasted two bars, a ramshackle kitchen the size of a house, and more than a dozen rooms, each with a wood-burning fireplace of a different design. Since every new owner of the Blue Bhor had added a room, a patio, or a fireplace, there was nothing unusual about the Blue Bhor this particular day as the construction sleds hovered up and unloaded materials and workers.

There were greeted and guided by the newest owner, one Chris Frye, Prop. He was a tall, rangy man with little use for any Bee Ess except his own. Frye had purchased the place with his pension monies, and things had not really been progressing very well. His biggest problems were that he was exceedingly generous and had a tendency to pick up the tab for people he liked; he mostly preferred to close up the joint and just go fishing; and the only people he really got on with were fisherfolk—serious fisherfolk like himself who rarely had money and were always putting their bills on the tab.

Frye had just about been ready to toss the whole business over, sell out, and then spend the rest of his life fishing, when Sten showed up. Sten and Frye only knew of each other by reputation. They formed an instant liking for each other on first meeting, as only two old hands from Mantis Section can.

Frye had spent the last years of his military career in Mantis Section overseeing the transition of Lupus Cluster from a fanatic religious culture to a trading system loosely ruled by the shaggy Bhor. He'd spent many cycles drinking Stregg with the shaggy Bhor, toasting mother's beards and father's frozen buttocks. He had also heard a thousand different stories about how the Bhor had come to rule the Lupus Cluster. Mostly, the stories were not to be believed. They all came down to a single root: a young man named Sten. Sten, they all agreed, was the greatest fighter, lover, and drinker in Bhor history. Besides, they liked the little clot, even if he was human.

"In the whole time I was there," Sten confessed to Frye, "I only got laid twice, and I lost almost every battle except the last."

"The one that counts," Frye said.

"Maybe so," Sten said, "but my ass was seriously in a sling the whole time I was there. Clot! You can't drink with the Bhor! Unless you sneak some sober pills, and even then I was flat on my back after almost every party."

Frye decided that Sten was a pretty nice fellow. Of course he was a clotting liar from Mantis, taking on the persona of the *real* Sten. He had long ago decided that the Sten of legend would have been a royal pain. Who the clot would ever want to drink with the perfect being the Bhor were always going on about? So Frye just smiled when Sten introduced himself, and accepted without a giggle the cover name he was using. Frye figured the name Sten was about fifty different people. Mantis did things like that.

Over one long night of hospitality Blue Bhor–style— which meant groaning platters of fresh fish, game, and side dishes, all from the Valley Wye—they struck a bargain. The Blue Bhor was to be Sten and Haines's safe house. Since it was off-season in the Valley Wye, the cover was near perfect. Frye would close for remodeling, just like every other new owner of the inn. To cut the cost of the extensive repairs, he would house and feed the construction crew.

It was a great bargain on both sides. To make the cover work, they *really* would have to remodel the old place. Not only that, but the bill for the rooms and the food would have to be paid, in case there was a smart bookkeeper snooping around. This allowed Haines to bring in a fairly large crew of experts to work on the case. It also allowed her to haul in as much sophisticated equipment as she needed, hidden between the stacks of construction materials.

The deal would make Frye's best year ever—especially coming during the off-season. He was even thinking about maybe staying on a few years longer; on the kind of credits Sten was stuffing into his account, Frye would be able to entertain fisherfolk for eons to come.

Haines stumped into the main bar and slid onto a stool. Behind her the last group of workpeople were unloading the last gravsled of equipment. She sniffed at her foreman's coveralls and wrinkled her nose. "I smell like I been dead for two weeks."

Frye gave one more swipe with his rag at the gleaming wood bartop, grabbed a tall glass, and frothed out a beer. He slid it in front of her, then leaned over and gave an ostentatious sniff. "Smells better to me," he grinned. "Less constable and more good, honest sweat."

Haines gave him a hard look and slugged down a healthy

portion of beer. This put her in a better mood, especially since Frye topped it up again. "You don't like cops, huh?"

Frye shook his head. "Does any sensible person?"

Haines considered this for a moment. Then she gave a short laugh.

"No," she said. "Even cops don't like cops. That's why I got into homicide. When you're really doing your job, other people don't like to associate with you."

Frye's retort was interrupted by the sound of footsteps, and they turned to see a grizzled man, in battered clothing and old-fashioned waders. He was lugging what appeared to be archaic fishing equipment.

"Bar's closed," Frye sang out.

The man just stood, peering into the place, as if letting his eyes adjust from the bright, clear Valley Wye sun outside.

"I said the bar's closed," Frye repeated.

"Remodeling," Haines threw in.

The man shook his head, and then shuffled slowly over to the bar and sat down on a stool. "Worst fishing I seen in years. I need a beer."

He clinked some credits on the bartop. "A tall cool one. No. Give me a whole damned pitcher."

Frye shoved the credits back. "You haven't been listening, mister. I told you, the bar is closed. For remodeling."

The man wrinkled his brow in a frown. "Well, I'm not walking to Ashley for a beer." He glanced over at Haines' frosty mug. "She got one, so you must be serving. So gimme one. I'll pay double! Tap's working. What the hell do you care?"

Haines felt her neck prickle. Something wasn't quite right here. She slid a hand into a coverall pocket and touched the small weapon nestled there. Then she slid off her stool and stepped a few paces to the side, covering both the man and the door. "Listen when you're being spoken to, mister," she said. She nodded at his gear by the side of the stool. "Now, the place is closed. Pick up your things and go."

She noticed that Frye was reaching under the bar for something.

"So," the grizzled man said. "What if I don't?"

Then he casually reached across the bartop, grabbed Haines' beer, and calmly chugged it down. He slapped the glass down and looked up at them. Haines had her gun out.

"Lieutenant!" a voice barked behind her.

Hearing Sten's voice, she partially turned, keeping the grizzled man in view. He grinned broadly, and then Sten was plucking the weapon from her hand.

Haines was ready to roundhouse Sten. She gaped as Sten stepped past her and came to attention in front of the beat-up old fisherman.

"I'm sorry, Your Highness," Sten said. "We weren't expecting you until tomorrow."

Haines chin started to fall toward the swell where her breasts began.

"No problem," the man said. "Thought I'd stop by a little early. Get in a little fishing. Check things out."

Sten stepped behind the bar and drew the man a beer. He slid it over and the fisherman took it in one long shallow. He turned to Haines and gave her a little wink.

"Lieutenant Haines," Sten began, "allow me to introduce you to—"

"It's the Emperor," Haines croaked. "The clotting Eternal Emperor."

The Emperor bowed low over the stool. "At your service, ma'am."

Sten had to grab for Haines's elbow as the hard-bitten lieutenant of homicide felt her knees buckle.

"Zaarah Wahrid." The Emperor rolled the phrase over on his tongue, puzzling at it, searching his memory. He shook his head. "Doesn't mean a thing to me. That's all he said?"

Sten sighed. "I'm afraid so, sir. I'm sorry, but the whole thing has been nothing but a mess from the moment you put me on it."

He drew his beer toward him, and then pushed it away. "Sir, I really think I ought to—"

"*Quit*?" the Emperor thundered. "No clotting way! I'm up to my neck in drakh and you want me to relieve you?"

"With all due respect, sir," Sten pushed on, "I *have* failed to carry out every portion of this assignment to any kind of satisfaction."

The Emperor started to jump in, but Sten raised his hand, calling on his rights as a free individual to quit a job if he wanted. "I've done nothing but spend a shipload of credits for zed information. All we've still really got are much supposition and too many rumors.

"Beautiful. I hit Stynburn. Raise a whole lot of hell. Probably take you two years to settle those miners down. And all I come back with is a phrase nobody's ever heard. If this were a Mantis operation you or Mahoney would have had my head and sent me to deep freeze as well."

The Eternal Emperor thought for a moment. Whether it was for effect, or whether he was indeed considering an evil future for Sten, the young captain would never know. Finally, he gave a loud snort. Then he held out his glass for Sten to fill with some of Chris Frye's finest.

"I am *where* I am," he said, "because I make quick decisions and then follow them through, no matter how lousy the robe of many colors turns out to be in reality. I've blown it once in a while. But mostly I win. Check the history archives and see if I'm not borne out by this little flight of ego I'm allowing myself."

Sten decided it would be far from politic to comment on the "little ego" remark. Instead, he drained his beer, took a deep breath, and then leaned forward across the table. "Very well. Orders, sir, if you please."

The Emperor hesitated for a nanosecond, considering how much he should really tell the young man in front of him. And then he caught Sten watching and knowing the hesitation for what it was, and just plunged on.

"It works like this," he said. "The Tahn are all over my royal behind for some kind of a meet. My advisors argue that no one of any real diplomatic stature has even recognized their odious system, much less sat down and talked to them."

"But," Sten said, "I get the idea you agree there ought to be some kind of meet."

The Emperor sighed. "Has to be. I've been trying to stall. If they want to talk to my exalted self, maybe I'll do it, or maybe I won't. That would be the ultimate recognition of those warlords. Cause me no end of problems with the rest of the Empire. For clot's sake, the Eternal Emperor can't just be at the beck and call of every Tom, Dick, and ET.

"Fouls up the whole system. There is my Imperial mystique to be considered. And that, Captain, is not ego, it's the glue that keeps this whole mess together."

"So you're stalling them," Sten said.

The Emperor smiled. "Isn't that what diplomacy is all about? It's either stall or war." He shrugged. "A couple of my high-priced lawyers might disagree, but I've always found 'going to court' cheaper than a war."

He finished his beer and rose. "And I don't think a war with the Tahn will be a little one."

The Eternal Emperor turned to go. Then he stopped and gave Sten one of his most charming grins. "I sure could use a good barely-living guilty party to throw off the sleigh right now."

"How long can you keep stalling?" Sten asked.

"Less and less," the Emperor said. "I want you to grind it until the last minute."

Sten nodded. "I'll find your boy, sir."

"Yeah. You will."

And then the Eternal Emperor picked up his fishing gear and shambled out the door. Sten watched him go. For just a second, he wondered what would happen to young Captain Sten if he failed.

Even if it had been a Mantis operation, the safe-house system Sten, Alex, and Lieutenant Haines had worked out at the Blue Bhor would have been a wondrous thing. Just to begin with, it involved several different departments, a task usually impossible under almost any circumstances. Even cynical Alex was impressed about how well everyone blended in.

To begin with, security was an absolute must. Sten and Alex needed some definite thugs to keep trigger watch on anyone who might show an interest in the old inn.

So they carefully felt out old Mantis Section buddies who were either on I&I or using up sick leave. There were never any snarls from these people. They either smiled and kissed you or smiled and cut your throat.

Next, there were the police/Imperial people. Haines had carefully selected known trustworthy police people.

The way the safe house worked was that the security people patrolled the outside and Haines's group ruled inside, with occasional bursts of temper when Alex or Sten put in their two credits. The talents inside unfortunately guaranteed that everyone was potentially at the other person's neck. They were all mostly cops. But they were all super-specialists. The talents ranged from hackers to real computer techs to archivists to com-line snoopers. All were very bright, trustworthy, and friends of Haines.

One thing Sten had to give them—they were damned good. They were the beings who had tracked down Dynsman and finally located Stynburn.

And the way they had gone about it had been something to behold. In a similar operation, if Mantis had been assigned, the most sophisticated, high-powered computer would have trashed through millions of files in the search. The big problem with Prime World was that anything of even medium industrial power sent out red signals in all directions. Prime World was also the capital of all spydom, including the fortunes that were spent on industrial snooping.

So Liz Collins, the head cop computer tech, had proposed that they supply themselves with fifty or so tiny computers, each with the IQ of a five-year-old. Then she and her aides had strung them all together, resulting in a system as sophisticated as anything on the planet. More important, because of the way they were linked, they could dive in and out of information systems without being detected and usually without leaving a trace. As a side benefit, Liz had set the system up so that it could steal power. A constant monitor/feeder slipped in and out of power sources like a burglar, stealing just enough to keep the entire system operational, but not enough to show up significantly on individual power bills.

Alex also decided that Liz Collins was a woman he might want to get close to. She was slightly taller than he, and was built with all the proper and more than ample curves that Alex liked, plus many rippling muscles. Alex had been in ecstasy when he met her while setting up shop at the Blue Bhor. A gravsled had got itself mired near the riverbank. Before he could respond, Liz had leaned down and, with some crackling of bones, had lifted the sled from the muck then patted it on its now friction-less way. Alex could imagine those shapely, powerful arms around his heavyworlder body. It had been a long time, he realized, since he had felt himself *really* hugged.

The main readout Collins had set up in the computer linkage system was in the largest room of the Blue Bhor—King Gilly's Suite. Alex walked into the room and tried desperately not to be a beast and to keep his eyes off her muscular apple-shaped behind. Her structure narrowed then, he thought. licking dry lips, to proper lady's pro-portions before blooming to the most wonderful set of shoulders, and frontal mammary structure. It was the kind of sight that made a Scotsman *know* what he had under his kilt. She was the most beautiful woman Alex had ever seen.

She turned away from the screen and gave Alex a look that melted his heart, as well as a few other areas. "Could we hold on that drink a bit? I should be getting something from the linkup soon."

Alex would have given her anything in the world. "Nae too thirsty mysel', lass," he cracked. "Now, wha' be we s' far?"

Liz turned back to the computer, all business again. "We're running two main search patterns right now. The first is the most difficult."

"Zaarah Wahrid?"

"Stynburn's last words. And so far they don't mean a thing anyplace we're checking. And I mean *any*place. We've gone through a couple of thousand languages. Every encyclopedia. Religious tracts. All of it."

"Could it be—"

"Don't even bother. We're covering all possibilities. Trouble is, 'all possibilities' means a hell of a lot of time, even with this setup." She smiled fondly at the main terminal of her elaborate computer linkup system.

Alex warmed, wishing he were the computer. "Lass," he said. "dinna y' think it's aboot time y' rested y'r wee mind wi' a bit ae th' hops?"

He leaned casually on the table supporting the computer readout screen, carefully keeping himself from encircling her rounded waist. Liz smiled over her shoulder at him, and Alex thought it lit up the room. His heart always thumped on her rare smile, and he beamed a cherub grin from his own round, red face.

"I think we're coming in on something now," she said.

Alex peered at the words and figures bubbling up on the screen. He had to free his mind for the high-speed scrolling, and then he had it.

"Appears you have the late Doc Stynburn in th' crosshairs."

Liz nodded enthusiastically. Alex loved her even more when she was on the hunt.

"Do we! Look at this. He set up about a half dozen cutout corporations. Based in frontier banking planets. Each time he took a new job or consultancy, he ran it through one of the corporations."

"A wee tax scam," Alex said.

"You got it. Foolproof one, as well. Leave it to a doctor."

He cleared his throat loudly, bringing himself back to some sort of reality. "An' th' second search," he said. "Stynburn, Ah s'pose?"

Liz nodded. "That's killing time for opposite reasons. Instead of too much, we've got too little. The guy knew every Mercury Corps trick in the book."

"Then you thought of the corporate cutout business," Alex said admiringly.

Liz blushed. "I thought it was a small stroke of genius."

Alex could barely keep himself from patting her. What if she took it wrong? Or right? Or . . . He tried to pull his mind away from the swirl of figures on the screen. He cleared his throat again. "Anything else, lass?"

Liz handed him a thin sheaf of printout. "I'm not sure, but since I picked these up my cop brain's been sneezing."

Alex scanned them—very dry police-jargonese reports of four deaths. All had two things in common: They were accidental, bizarrely so; and they had all occurred within the vicinity of the palace. Alex rechecked the first death: Female victim. High blood alcohol. Strangled on own vomit. Slight bruise on throat. He buzzed past the name to the woman's history. Deserter from the Praetorian Guard. Alex felt a small mental tingle. He quickly thumbed through the other reports and the answer glared up at him. "You were right, lass, police officer tha' y' be."

Then he showed her the common thread.

"Every swinging Richard is a former government," Collins realized. "Ex-clerk. Ex-tech. Ex-museum security. And all with—"

"—palace connections," Alex finished for her.

Liz slumped into her chair and gave a long exasperating sigh. "Murder. Murder, murder, murder. Aw clot."

Then, just as deep depression was about to fog the entire room, the vid-screen began blinking red. Liz leaped to her feet and studied the screen. After thousands of computer hours, the first major break in the case was staring her in the face. They had finally broken through Stynburn's elaborate corporate cutouts.

"Sweet Laird," Alex whispered. "Th' clot worked for Kai Hakone."

CHAPTER THIRTY-FOUR

"I HAVE NEVER seen one of these before," Kai Hakone said. "May I examine it more closely?"

Sten handed him the Imperial Service card. The Imperial emblem on the card, keyed to Sten's own pore and pulse pattern, blinked as Hakone took it, held it for a moment, then passed it back to Sten.

"Actually, Captain, while I've no idea what you need, your appearance is fortunate."

"Ah?"

Hakone was about to explain, but his words were cut by the loud whine of a ship lifting on Yukawa drive barely half a kilometer overhead.

Hakone's mansion was located on the largest hill overlooking Soward, Prime World's biggest port. It had been built as an off-voyage hobby by the captain of a tramp freighter, who intended it to be his retirement home.

That trader's retirement never came about, since he made the tactical error of offering play-pretty beads to a primitive culture more interested in sharp-pointed and deadly objects. But since most people, let alone those who could afford the price of a Prime World mansion, weren't fascinated with the sound and bustle of a spaceport, Hakone had been able to lease the sprawling house cheaply. Since then, he'd finished the interior and added his own concepts, which included the hemispherical battle chamber in its rear.

The Yukawa-drive cut off, and, in the utter silence of AM2 drive, the ship disappeared. "I like to hear what I write about," Hakone half explained as he led Sten into the house. "Is it too early for a tod, Captain?"

"The sun's up, isn't it?"

Hakone smiled and led Sten through the large reception area, the even larger living room, and into his own den.

Hakone's "den"—office and writing area—was styled after an Old Earth library, with innovations. Vid-tapes, reports, even bound antique books lined the twenty-meter-high walls. The center of the room was a long, flat table. But from there, the resemblance to eighteenth-century Earth was gone, since the table was lined with computer terminals, and the laddered access to the shelves was automated.

At one end of the room was Hakone's bar, and it extended across the width. Sten scanned the bottles as Hakone motioned for him to make his choice.

"You happen to have any, uh, Scotch?"

Hakone was up to it. "You have adopted the Emperor's tastes!" he said, reaching down a bottle and pouring two half-full glasses of the liquor.

Sten touched the glass to his lips, then lowered it. Hakone, too, had barely drunk. "You said fortunate, Sr. Hakone?"

"Yes. I was planning to contact you, Captain." Hakone waved Sten toward a wide couch nearby. "Did you happen to see my masque? The one which was performed prior to Empire Day?"

"Sorry, I was on duty."

"From what the critics say, perhaps you were lucky. At any rate, I now find myself between projects. And then I discovered something most fascinating. Are you aware that no one has ever done a history of the Imperial palace?"

Sten pretended ignorance, shook his head, and sipped.

"Not only the building, but the people who are assigned to it," Hakone went on, with what seemed to be a writer's enthusiasm.

"An interesting idea."

"I thought so. As did my publisher. Especially if the

tape deals with the people who are assigned to it. I want to tell a history of people, not of stone and technocracy."

Sten waited.

"As you know," Hakone continued, "I am primarily a military historian. I have, frankly, my own sources. So when I conceptualized this project, the first thing I began investigating was the people assigned to that palace.

"That is, by the way, why I made such a point of wanting to meet you at Marv and Senn's party. You are a peculiar man, Captain Sten."

Sten looked solemnly interested.

"Are you aware that you are the youngest man ever assigned to head the Imperial bodyguard?"

"Admiral Ledoh told me that."

"That interests me. Which is why I availed myself of your military record. Wondering, quite frankly, why you had been chosen."

Sten didn't bother smiling—he knew that his phony. file was intrusion-proof. Only Mantis headquarters, the Emperor himself, and General Ian Mahoney knew what Sten's real military history was.

"You have a perfect record. *No* demerits at OCS. Commissioned on such-and-so a date, all qualifications reports rated excellent, all commanding officers recommending you most highly, the appropriate number of hero-moves for the appropriate awards."

"Some people are lucky."

"If I may be honest, Captain, perhaps too lucky."

Sten finished his drink.

"Captain Sten, what would you say if I told you I suspected your whole military background was a tissue?"

"If I were not on Imperial business, Sr. Hakone, and depending on the circumstances, I would either buy you a drink or a nose transplant."

"I did not mean to be insulting, Captain. I am merely suggesting that you have been assigned to your present post because of previous performance in either Mercury Corps or Mantis Section."

Sten pretended stupidity. "Mercury Corps? Sorry,

Hakone. I was never in Intelligence, and I've never heard of Mantis."

"The response I expected. And I appear to have offended. Change the subject. What brings you here?"

Hakone replenished the drinks.

"You once employed a Dr. Hars Stynburn," Sten said, trying the sudden-shock approach. Hakone reacted, indeed, but quite obviously, sending the top of the liquor decanter spinning to the floor.

"Clot! What's the imbecile done now?"

"Now? Sr. Hakone, I must advise you that this conversation is being recorded. You have a right to counsel, legal advice, and medico-watch to ensure you are not under any influence, physical or pharmacological."

"Thank you for the warning, Captain. But I don't need that. Dr. Hars Stynburn did indeed work for me. For a period of four months—Prime months. At the end of that time I discharged him, without, I might add, benefit of recommendation."

"Continue, Sr. Hakone."

"My household normally consists of between fifty and three hundred individuals. I find it convenient to employ an in-house medico. That was one reason I initially employed Dr. Stynburn."

"One reason?"

"The second reason was that he was, like myself, a veteran. He served in the Mueller Wars, the battle of Saragossa."

"As did you."

"Ah, you've scanned my tapes."

"On précis. Why did you dismiss him?"

"Because . . . not because he was inefficient or incompetent. He was an extremely good doctor. But because he was a man locked into the past."

"Would you explain?"

"All he wished to talk about was his time in the service. And about how he felt he had been betrayed."

"Betrayed?"

"You're aware he was cashiered from the service? Well, he felt that he was fulfilling the exact requirements of the

Empire, and that he was used as a Judas goat after those requirements were fulfilled."

"The Empire generally doesn't practice genocide, Sr. Hakone."

"Stynburn believed it did. At any rate, his obsession became nerve-wracking to me. And so I found it easier to release him at the expiration of his initial contract."

Sten was about to ask another question, then broke off. Hakone's eyes were hooded.

"Locked into the past, I said, didn't I?" Hakone drained his drink. "That must sound odd to you, Captain, since you've reviewed my tapes. Don't I sound the same way?"

"I'm not a historian, Seigneur."

"What do you think of war, Captain?"

Sten's first answer—blatant stupidity—was something he somehow felt Hakone didn't want to hear. He held his silence.

"Someone once wrote," Hakone went on, "that war is the axle life revolves around. I think that is the truth. And for some of us, one war is that axle. For Dr. Stynburn— and to be honest, Captain, for myself—that was Saragossa."

"As I said, I'm not a historian."

Hakone picked up the two glasses, fielded the decanter from the bar, and started toward a nearby door.

"I could tell you, Captain. But I'd rather show you." And he led Sten through the door, into his battle chamber.

The Mueller Wars, fought almost a century before Sten's birth, were a classic proof of Sten's definition of war. The Mueller Cluster had been settled too quickly and was too far from the Empire. The result was a lack of Imperial support, improperly defined and supplied trade routes, and arrant ignorance on the part of the Imperial bureaucracy administering those worlds.

And then war, war by the various worlds, fighting under a banner that might have been headed "Anything but the damned Empire." By the time the Emperor realized that the Mueller Cluster was a snowball rolling downhill, it was too late for any response except the Guard.

But Imperial overexpansion had reached into the military as well. The battles that were fought were, for the most part, on the wrong ground, with the wrong opponent, and at the wrong time.

The Emperor still, when he began feeling self-confident, had only to scroll his own private log of the Mueller Wars to deflate himself to the proper level of humanity. Of all the disasters, before the Mueller Cluster was battered into semi-quiescence, the worst was Saragossa.

Saragossa should never have been invaded. Its isolationist culture should have been ignored until the Saragossans asked to rejoin the Empire. Instead a full Grand Fleet and the Seventh Guards Division were committed. The invasion should have been easy, since it involved landing on a single world, which had only a few low-tech satellite worlds for support.

Instead the operation became a nightmare.

The grand admirals who ordered the assault might have wondered why initial intelligence reported some seven moonlets around Saragossa, and the landing surveys reported only one. But no one wondered, and so nearly a million men died.

The landing plan was total insertion, so the Guards' transports were committed, and the heavy support—five Imperial battleships—were moving toward the ionosphere when the question of the missing moonlets was solved.

They'd been exploded, quite carefully, so the fragments maintained planetary orbit. And then any fragment larger than a baseball had been manned with Saragossans who were less interested in living than keeping the Empire away. Imagine trying to push a landing force through an asteroid belt that is shooting back.

The first battleship was holed and helpless more than three planetary units offworld. The admiral in charge of the landing—Fleet Admiral Rob Gades—transhipped with what remained of his staff to a command ship in time to see his other four battleships explode into shards.

At that point it was too late to recall the troopships. Even before the ships split into capsules, most of them were destroyed. The landing caps that entered atmosphere without support lasted bare seconds under the ravening fire from the surface.

That, Hakone explained to Sten as he swung ships through the battle chamber, was when his own probeship was destroyed. He never saw the end of the battle. What ended it was Admiral Gade's order—*sauve qui peut*, save what you can. One third of the assault fleet was able to pull off Saragossa.

"One third, Captain," Hakone said, as he shut down the battle chamber. "Over one million men lost. Isn't that enough of an axle?"

Sten flashed briefly to the livie he'd undergone before basic training—experiencing the heroic death of one Guardsman Jaime Shavala—and his subsequent decision that he had less than no desire to see what a major battle felt like, ignored his gut agreement, and used the safe answer of stupidity. "I don't know, Sr. Hakone."

"Perhaps you wouldn't. But now do you understand why I hired Stynburn? He went through the same hell I did."

Sten noticed with interest that Hakone, while he'd been sitting behind the control chair of the chamber, had gone through half the decanter of Scotch.

"By the way, Captain, do you know what happened to Admiral Gades?"

"Negative."

"For his—and I quote from the court's charge—retreat in the face of the enemy, he was relieved of command and forcibly retired. Do you think that was fair?"

"Fair? I don't know what is fair, Sr. Hakone." Sten brought himself to attention. "Thank you for your information, Seigneur. Should we have any other questions, may I assume your further cooperation?"

"You may," Hakone said flatly.

Sten was about to try a wild card and ask if the phrase Zaarah Wahrid meant anything to Hakone. Instead, he shut off his recorder, nodded, and headed for the exit.

If he had left a few seconds earlier, he might have

caught one of Hakone's men clipping a tiny plas box to the underside of Sten's gravsled.

Hakone walked out of the battle chamber, back into his library. Colonel Fohlee was waiting, and looking distinctly displeased.

"You think I erred," Hakone said.

"Why were you giving him all that, dammit! He's the Emperor's investigator."

"I was fishing, Colonel."

"For what?"

"If he'd shown one iota of understanding—one flicker of what is important—we might have been able to make him one of us."

"Instead you ran your mouth and got nothing."

"Colonel! You are overstepping."

"Sorry, sir."

"As a result, I found that this Captain Sten is unreachable. I have a tracer attached to his gravsled. Put a team of the deserters after him. Track the sled until we have the location of the safe house he's using for his investigation. Then kill this Captain Sten. That is all!"

Fohlee found himself saluting, pivoting, and exiting, and never wondered why he had that response to the command voice of a man who had not worn a uniform for almost a hundred years.

CHAPTER THIRTY-FIVE

THE VID-SCREEN GLOWED in the darkened room. In one corner, the computer held its target: the phrase ZAARAH WAHRID. The rest of the screen was filled with line after constantly changing line of information. At the moment, the computer was postulating that the phrase meant some kind of commercial product. It was searching the Imperial patent office for everything registered since the department was founded.

Liz Collins, the hunter, tried to keep her eyes glued to the screen, looking for some kind of connection or vague reference. As each line rolled up the screen, her eyes followed, and then automatically clicked down a stop for the next. At the moment, she was scanning a catalogue of household bots, almost all of them a century or more out of date.

She had to fight to keep her brain on her job. Steady on, woman, she thought to herself. If you think this is boring, guess what comes next. Then she groaned as the finis asterisks rolled up and the next and a worse category came up: Defense.

The air stirred behind her and then she heard the door open and soft footsteps pad in. She turned to see Alex standing behind her, two mugs of frothy beer in his hands.

"'Bout that drink, lass?" he said softly. "Ah whidny be disturbin' y' noo, would Ah?"

"Oh, my god, yes," she said, meaning the drink. Then she caught Alex's crestfallen face and corrected herself. "I mean, no. No, I mean . . . right, I could use a drink."

She palmed the computer to automatic, setting up the

search alarms, and then rose to take a glass out of Alex's hand. She took a small sip and gave a bit of a start. "This isn't just beer!" She grinned. And then she noticed the shot glass sitting in the bottom of the mug.

"A wee boilermaker," Alex explained. "Beer and a good single-malt Scotch that'll oil th' bubbles."

Liz took a long, slow swallow. "Mmmm, I don't mind this at all."

She crossed over to the fur-covered couch and sat down, crossed her legs, then started to tug her uniform skirt down over her knees. She stopped when she saw the wistful look in Alex's eyes as the slight flash of thigh started to disappear. "What the clot." She patted the place next to her. As if almost suddenly coming awake, Alex shook his head then took the few steps required to reach the couch and sank hesitatingly down beside her. He carefully studied the wall opposite them, afraid to meet her eyes.

"So," he finally said, "do y' think we'll be finding this Zaarah whatever it is?"

Liz remained absolutely silent. She just took another sip of her drink.

"Ah mean, y' been workin't your pretty, beg your pardon, y' been workin't hard, lo these many—"

"Alex," Liz whispered, breaking in.

He turned and looked directly at her for the first time since he entered the room. "Yes, lass."

"Do we have to talk?"

"No, lass."

"Well, then..."

Alex finally got the point. He reached out his arms to enfold her, and he felt the muscular but somehow so soft arms go around him. Slowly they sank down into the couch.

Once again, Liz didn't bother about the flash of thigh as the uniform skirt rose higher and higher and...

Unnoticed by them, the computer screen began winking red. It sat patiently, pulsing that it had found it... found it... found it...

The screen read:

ENT: JANES, Historic Records. BATTLESHIP: ZAARAD WAHRID (Flower class—14 constructed).

The entry went on, covering the ship's dimensions, crew, armament, launching date, and history, ending with the information that *Zaarah Wahrid* had finished her illustrious career as flagship on the Saragossa invasion during the Mueller Wars. The ship was totally destroyed, with a loss of 90 percent of its crew...

Fortunately for the lovers, it would be many hours before they read the entry. Because once again the case had come full circle. *Zaarah Wahrid* was a ship that no longer existed.

CHAPTER THIRTY-SIX

STEN LIFTED THE gravsled away from Hakone's mansion and set his course directly from Soward across the city of Fowler toward the Imperial palace.

Once past the city limits he dropped the sled's height to 50 meters. Thus far, he was doing exactly what Hakone had predicted, and would next set his course for the safe house in Ashley-on-Wye.

But several hundred people, were they not deceased, might have advised Kai Hakone never to predict Sten's actions.

The gravsled may have appeared standard Imperial issue, but it was not. The man who planted the tracer on the sled should have noticed its fairly elaborate com gear. But he didn't.

So while Sten put the sled's controls on auto, and hung the aircar in a slow orbit over the trees, he checked himself and his vehicle for bugs. At 22.3 Hz, his detector sounded off like a banth in heat. Sten unhooked the directional transponder from the board and went over the sled. It took only a few seconds to find the tracer unit.

Sten went back to the controls and considered the various possibilities. He decided, turned the sled onto manual, and lifted it to 1000 meters. Then he set a new course, directly for the Great South Sea. This was, on compass, 80-plus degrees, magnetic, away from his proper destination, the Blue Bhor. Sten had no idea what the tracer was intended for, but he had decided to play the hand, at least for a few thousand kilometers.

It didn't take that long.

Sten's prox-radar blipped at him and advised that an object was rapidly approaching from his rear. He turned and scanned through the sled's binocs.

Ignoring the modifications, Sten's gravsled was a standard combat car: McLean-generator-powered, ten meters by five meters in dimension, seating four people in the open. The object coming toward him was also a standard Imperial combat vehicle, about twice the size of Sten's gravsled, and intended for a combat platoon of twelve or so beings.

Sten counted six men in the sled, which was closing on him at a rate of about 60 kph. He decided to make their job a little easier, and slowed his own sled. The sled behind also slowed.

Tacmind thinking, Sten automated: They are trying to track me. Given mission: Find the safe house and ... six men in that sled ... take me out.

Sten *tsk*ed to himself and snapped the double safety harness around him.

He shoved the control stick forward for full-speed and snapped the built-in dopplering radar off. On normal combat cars, this was permanently on, insuring that no matter how much an idiot the pilot was, he could not run into something in fog, smoke, rain, or drunkenness. But Sten's car *was* a modified one.

Another modification went on, a second, also doppler-stupid radar. It fixed on the platoon gravsled coming up on Sten, giving a closing speed of nearly 80 kph. Very slow reactions, Sten decided.

Before the pilot of the sled realized what was intended, Sten chopped the control stick, then lifted the stick into control attitude and yanked it back again, almost into his lap. Standard combat cars—gravsleds—had no such capability. Which may have been the reason that the pursuing pilot gaped as Sten's sled curved straight up and around in a perfect Immelman, then dropped directly toward the pursuers.

Sten saw fear, panic, and motion as he dove straight for the other sled. The platoon sled's pilot cut power and sank, barely in time to avoid Sten's seemingly kamikaze dive.

It banked and recovered. Doors on the smooth side of the vehicle opened, and missile banks whirred into sight. Fire, smoke, and four air-to-air (atmo) missiles blasted out.

Sten already had his combat car on its back. As G-forces yanked at his face, his hands clawed for the distress flare button.

The flares bloomed out, multicolored phosphorus fires. And, obediently, the pursuers' heat-seeking missiles homed on the flares. Four missiles impacting at the same time made a helluva bang, enough to send the platoon sled skidding out of control momentarily, the five passengers grabbing for handholds. And then out of the smoke dove Sten's combat car. The platoon sled's pilot panicked and pirouetted his sled on its own axis. Again late, since Sten's car was now just above him.

And then the last thing the six thugs in the sled might have expected happened. Sten flipped his combat car to orbit, unsnapped his safety harness, and jumped straight over the side, into the other gravsled.

He twisted in midair, his clawed hand bringing out his knife, while his mind looked for a soft landing.

The landing was on the first man, Sten's heels crushing his rib cage and Sten going down to his knees—under the clubbed willygun swing of the second man—and then straight up, spread fingers going into eyeballs and brain.

Sten whirled as the second corpse fell. His knife swung across the wrist of the third man, whose hand fell away, blood hosing across the sled. He gaped at the spouting blood, stumbled, and fell away into nothingness.

Sten never saw that he was on automatic pilot, realizing a man was swinging a long, issue Guards combat knife at him. Sten blocked with his own crystal blade—and sheared through the alloy steel. The fourth man didn't even have time to react before Sten's steel bootheel slammed up, crushing his skull.

Air ionized, and Sten went flat, skidding across the checkered metal of the aircar's deck, the willygun projectile sizzling overhead, and Sten was diving forward, and his foot went out from under him as he skidded on a patch of blood.

Sten took the fall, but his knife hand lashed out, braced at the wrist. The speared knife caught the fifth man just below the belt, then slashed through his spinal cord. The living corpse spasmed backward over the sled's pilot, who was trying to unbuckle himself.

Sten slammed into the copilot's seat, then tucked his feet under him and snapped up.

The sled's pilot had fought his way free of the body and was standing. Sten came in on the man. His intentions were to take one prisoner and ask very serious questions.

But the pilot took one look at the gory Sten and that small sliver of metal that was death itself, screamed, and hurled himself over the side of the combat car.

Sten grabbed for the man, but too late. He watched the screaming form pinwheel down toward the parkland far below.

Collect . . . collect . . . and no-mind died, combat madness went away, and Sten swore to himself. Breathe . . . breathe . . . and he sat down, not noticing the blood that swirled and trickled across the gravsled's deck.

Rationality returned, and Sten looked at the five dead men in the sled. Haines can find something out about them, one part of his mind decided. Less important, another told him. You don't believe in coincidence. You went to Hakone. You were given a song-and-dance. On your leaving, someone attempted to kill you.

Considering the Imperial warrant he had been given, Sten had enough to arrest Hakone and use any means necessary, including brainscan, to find out how Hakone tied into the conspiracy to assassinate the Emperor.

But that was too easy a solution.

Somehow Sten had the idea that no one as highly visible and vocal as Kai Hakone would be the mastermind behind the attempt.

CHAPTER THIRTY-SEVEN

FOG SWIRLED OVER the long, brilliant-black ship that sat on a landing field barely longer than itself. Lights haloed around the loading ports as men and women loaded equipment and themselves on board.

The landing field was carried on Prime World's books as an Imperial Fleet tacship/emergency field, but it was actually used only by the Emperor for arrivals and departures he did not want to see blazoned on the vid-screen.

The ship itself was equally obscure. According to the record books, it had been constructed as the Imperial Merchant Ship (Passenger) *Normandie*. A luxury, superspeed liner that had been mothballed after its third voyage.

The *Normandie* did appear, from the outside, to be a conventional liner, but it had been built for one purpose only—to be the Emperor's vehicle, whether for secret missions or for vacations. It had the armament of a fleet destroyer and the power drive of a fleet cruiser.

It took less than a hundred men to run the *Normandie*,

which was state-of-the-art automated. That did not mean the ship was cramped, since the largest percentage of the *Normandie* was taken up with Imperial accommodations. Movable bulkheads and decking insured that the Emperor could hold anything from a private party for himself and a lady to an Imperial summit meeting.

Since the ship officially did not exist, it did not have to worry about proper clearances. When necessary, it was easy for the *Normandie* to assume one or another of the identities of its supposed sister ships.

It may have been the biggest cloak-plus-dagger ever built.

"Marr, you are being a daffodil. There is no possible pollution here."

"You talk and talk," Marr sniffed, "but I tell you, I can *smell* the fumes from the drive."

Marr and Senn were possibly the only caterers in history given an EYES-ONLY security clearance.

They stood near the waist of the *Normandie*, watching as their supplies rolled up the conveyor into the guts of the ship.

"All right, so there is pollution. I touch your delicate nostrils. But what will that matter to the fish? They are in tanks, not standing out here in the murk catching their death.

"I am merely concerned that these Tahn beings will find our food offensive," Marr said. "How would you like to be responsible for this conference's falling apart because of indigestion?"

Their predawn bickering was broken off as Subadar-Major Limbu strolled up. The Gurkha officer was in full combat gear, including willygun and kukri, hung in its sheath in the middle of his back. He saluted. "These fish," he indicated. "They are not for my men?"

"They are not, Chittahang. I have enough dahl, rice, and soyasteak to turn every one of your naiks into balloons such as the one you are starting to resemble."

Chattahang glanced at his stomach reflexively, then recovered. "Ah. Very good. But I shall tell you a secret.

That bulge is not from my stomach. I find it necessary to coil some of my other organs above my belt." He grinned, winked, and went back to supervising the loading of his men.

"Marr, do you ever think we shall get the better of these small brown ones?"

"Probably not." Marr turned and reacted. "Our fearless leader has arrived."

Five large flitters settled beside the *Normandie*, and people unloaded.

"See, it's that glut Sullamora with the Emperor," Senn hissed. "Why was he invited?"

"I am not the Emperor, darling, but I assume that, since he is an Imperial trader there must be something involving trading rights with these Tahn—Senn, are you *sure* we are prepared?"

Marr and Senn had been alerted to provide rations shortly after the Emperor-Tahn meeting had been set. They had immediately researched the tastes of the Tahn, particularly of their Lords. Fortunately, vid-tapes on exotic cooking were still popular in the fortieth century. They had provided everything from live brine shrimp to starch to still-growing vegetables. Plus some surprises of their own, since every chef feels he can improve on anyone's diet.

Bootheels thudded on the tarmac, and the contingent of Praetorians doubled in from the security perimeter. They were ordered and counted by Colonel Den Fohlee, and paraded on board.

"Do we have enough?" Marr worried.

"We have enough! One hundred fifty Praetorians, and we have enough starch and raw protein to keep them happy for a millennium. Thirty Gurkhas. The crew, with its own rations. The Emperor—who knows what he'll want—Sullamora . . . I procured his favorite recipes from his cook. Extras enough for these Tahn, even if they feed their starving hordes. We are *ready*, my love."

"Yes, but what are *we*—you and I—going to eat?"

Just as Senn's membranes wrinkled in alarm, the boarding alarm gonged.

The last of the rations went on board, and the ship's ports swung shut. The flitters cleared the field, and then the *Normandie*'s Yukawa-drive hissed more loudly, and she lifted away.

Offworld, *Normandie* would rendezvous with a destroyer squadron and a cruiser element. Those Imperial sailors had been told only that they were to escort a ship to a location, prevent anything from happening to that ship, and then return it to its base. They had no idea that the Eternal Emperor was on board, nor that the meeting with the Tahn lords was the only chance of avoiding an eventual intergalactic war.

CHAPTER THIRTY-EIGHT

THE GROUP SAT silently around the huge table that was Frye's main groaning board. Solid depression had set in. At the far end of the table Haines was idly doodling on her miniscreen. At the other end sat a strangely quiet Alex. He gloomed across the table at Liz, who was punching in a few last commands at her ever-present control unit.

Sten entered, a sheaf of print-outs under his arm, and saw the expectant looks come suddenly up at him. "No," he said, "I don't have a thing . . . but maybe I've got some kind of weird map we can all jump off from."

People came alive again. Sten began handling out the sheafs of paper. "One thing I learned as a crunchie—when you're stuck in it, make a list of what you know. And what you don't know."

He gave them all a sickly grin and shrugged. "Keeps you looking busy and important, anyway."

They began going over Sten's list. The facts had been boiled down:

1. The original plot was to assassinate the Emperor. All information indicates a wide-ranging conspiracy.
2. The plot is continuing. Otherwise, why the mysterious deaths near Soward—all former Praetorians or palace employees? Also, why the attack on Sten? By former Praetorians—mostly deserters. Subfact: At least forty Praetorians disappeared in the last E-year.
3. The plot seems to involve someone in the palace itself. Consider the multitude of computer taps and scans on the outside that lead, and then disappear, in there.
4. To repeat, the plot is continuing, and the Emperor logically is still the ultimate target.

"As a cop," Haines broke in, "it sure would make me feel better if I knew the target was out of the way."

"At least that has been solved," Sten said. "The Emperor has left Prime World. I can't tell you for where, but he is absolutely safe and surrounded by trusted advisors and security."

Alex breathed a sigh of relief. "Thank th' lord," he said. "No clottin' Romans."

"Has the Emperor been informed how deep in the drahk we are?" Liz asked.

"Negative," Sten answered. "We've agreed on absolute com silence. I can only reach him in an emergency. There is a line established at the palace."

They waited for him to say more, and then when he didn't, continued reading.

5. Kai Hakone is obviously one of the main conspirators. Key indicators here are Stynburn and the many other connections to the Battle of Saragossa. Also, Sten was attacked immediately after interviewing the suspect.
6. *Zaarah Wahrid* is another connection to the Battle of Saragossa. Question: What does a destroyed ship have to do with the conspiracy?
7. Complicating factor: Hakone had no connection with the palace. He is a known adversary of the Emperor and is not welcome.

"When do we arrest this clot, lad? Ah'll twist his guts into a winding sheet an' find out what we mus' ken."

"Not a chance, Alex," Sten said. "To defuse this thing we've got to pick up everybody at the same time. Especially the inside man at the palace."

"Take Hakone now and we blow it," Haines agreed. They bent their heads to read the rest.

8. Should we be checking the archives for more on Saragossa? Could other connections be hidden?

"Have you got a year?" Liz said dryly. "I don't know a computer in the Empire that could run that scan sooner."

"Forget it, then," Sten said.

"Is that all?" Haines asked.

"Yeah," Sten answered. "Except Hakone."

"I'm running him now," Liz said, pointing at her monitor screen.

"A stupid suggestion to the expert," Sten said to Liz.

Liz gave a low chuckle. "When all else fails," she said, "stupid works with a computer."

"He's got to have a headquarters somewhere," Sten said. "Hakone can't be running plotters in and out of his home, or meeting them on street corners or some such rot."

"A vacation home?" Haines postulated.

"Someplace remote?" Liz said.

Collins was already keying in an ownership search. She used the same program she had jury-rigged to break through Stynburn's corporate maze.

"Th' mon's a military fanatic," Alex said. "There's where we'll upend him. Certain a' he wrote his bloody great work on the Mueller Wars—"

Before he could finish, the answer swarmed up and curled into place on the screen. Alex's guess had hit close.

"*Zaarah Wahrid*," the screen entry began. "Register No. KH173. Berth 82. DO YOU REQUIRE DESCRIPTION?"

"Clotting yes," Sten shouted as Liz typed in the orders. Kai Hakone was the owner of the tiny and well-worn space yacht *Zaarah Wahrid*, which was berthed in a private port only a hundred or so kilometers away.

"Get the ship's computer on the line," Haines snapped.

"Not so fast, Lieutenant," Liz said. "What if the onboard's been rigged?"

"She's right," Sten said. "We've gone too far to get in a hurry now."

"I'll ask the computer if the ship needs servicing," Liz said. "Real routine." The answer came back negative.

"Okay, now something official but innocuous."

"When's the last time the ship left port?" Sten suggested.

Liz tapped her keys. "Not for more than a year. But that's fine. I can do a log search. Nothing pushy. Just the surface info. That'll keep *Zaarah Wahrid* on the line." The little boat began running through its log as Liz gently inserted a few of her probes—always keeping just out of the way, hovering and buzzing like an electronic fly.

"Will you look at this?"

Liz had run an IQ scan on the onboard.

"This little putt-putt has a computer big enough to run a liner!"

"Why would a little yacht need something that size?" Haines asked.

"Ah—ah, ah, no you don't, *Zaarah* clotting *Wahrid*." Liz shut down fast. "She's also got more booby traps then you can drink beer," she said to Alex. "I hang on anymore, and the least she'll do is wipe."

Sten slumped down, exasperated. "Is that all you could get, Liz?"

"No, I tricked it into giving me its key." She scribbled it down.

Sten climbed to his feet. "Come on, Alex. I think we better do a little lightweight breaking and entering."

They headed for the door.

"Oh, Captain?" Liz said.

"Yeah."

"You probably ought to know something else."

"Go."

Apparently *Zaarah Wahrid*'s got a bomb on board. Seems like a pretty big one."

"Thanks."

"Don't mention it."

Sten and Alex slouched out.

CHAPTER THIRTY-NINE

IT WAS A tiny main cabin aboard an equally tiny speedster. Although the speedster was only of moderate value, at one time someone had put a great deal of care and work into it, maintaining the plaswood floor and walls and deep ebony fittings and cabinetry. But it had become a mess. Clothing was littered about, and it was cluttered with dirty food containers that the current occupant hadn't even bothered to dump into the waste system.

Tarpy was sprawled across a bunk, his eyes closed and a small smile on his face. He was swarming with cats. In another age they might have been called alley cats. Certainly their pedigree would have been questioned. Tarpy called them spaceport cats, and they were every size and color imaginable. He was stroking the furry bodies that threatened to bury him, and idly monitoring the goings on of the *Zaarah Wahrid,* a rust bucket berthed about half a klick away.

Somebody *urr*ed beneath his left shoulder, and Tarpy lifted it enough for a kitten to escape. The kitten joined several others nursing at Momma's teats. Momma was permanently enthroned on Tarpy's stomach.

The cats were the only thing keeping Tarpy sane. Nothing, absolutely nothing had happened around the *Zaarah Wahrid* since he had taken up post. He had backup muscle stashed just on the other side of the *Zaarah Wahrid*, but Tarpy had kept contact with them to the absolute minimum. He considered them all dim-witted clots, whose only value was a willingness to die in place.

For company, on the long watch, Tarpy preferred his pussycats.

He felt a slight tingle at his left ear and heard a faint *beep-beep-beep*. Tarpy's heart raced and he ordered his pulse to slow. Finally something was happening!

He gently disentangled himself from the cats and sat up in the bunk. He punched in the visual monitor and began sweeping the area around the ship's berth.

The space-yacht port was fairly easy to survey. It looked like a two-kilometer-high metal tree with many branches. The trunk of the tree was devoted to shops, restaurants, maintenance and fueling. The branches were divided into private registry berths housing everything from yachts of near-liner size to little put-abouts.

Just to the side of the *Zaarah Wahrid* Tarpy saw something move. He scoped in on the movement as Sten and Alex walked out of the shadow of an overhanging ship and sauntered vaguely toward the craft. Tarpy grinned in recognition and hit the alarm buzzer to alert his muscle.

He rose from the bunk and slipped on his weapon harness. He strolled toward the door then paused for a moment. Tarpy looked at the open containers of food on the floor. It was more than enough to keep his friends happy until the job was done.

The door hissed open and Tarpy disappeared.

Alex gave the berth area one more quick visual check. No one. Not even a tech around. "Gie it a go, lad, we're clean as the queen's scantlings."

Sten walked straight to the lock panel near the ship's entrance, flipped it open, and began punching in the lock code Liz had given him. He entered the first three numbers and then waited for the computer to check them and give him the go-ahead for the next group. "Get ready to jump, Alex. Can't tell what's on the other side of the door."

Alex nodded and made his visual sweep again. Almost before he spotted the muscle, the heavyworlder felt his muscles bunch and a cold chill beneath his spine. "A wee lot a' comp'ny," he hissed to Sten, and stepped quickly away from the ship's lock.

Sten whirled in time to see a figure dash from one conex to another. Alex and Sten gave it one heartbeat, then two, then three, swiftly looking for and finding cover and quietly slipping willyguns from tunic holsters and palming them.

"There!" Alex said.

Sten slowly turned his head as Tarpy stepped out alone.

"Help you, bud?" Tarpy drawled, moving toward them. Sten noticed that the casualness masked a professional and subtle half-circle. He wasn't coming directly at them, but moving to one side.

"The fuel tank," Sten whispered to Alex.

Alex nodded, catching the fact that Tarpy was putting a huge supply container within range of an easy belly dive. They heard the rustle of footsteps to either side as Tarpy's thugs moved into position.

"A few wee rats," Alex said.

"How many?"

"Four. Maybe five."

Sten forced a grin at the approaching enemy. "You have a name, friend?"

"Tarpy, if anyone cares."

Sten just nodded, keeping the stupid grin going. "You got something to do with this rustbucket?"

"Might," Tarpy said. "That is, if you have business with it, I do."

"I could," Sten said. "Me and my partner have been looking for something cheap. Something we could fix up."

Tarpy smiled a lazy smile back. "She's a fixer-upper, all right," he agreed. "But whatcha gotta do is talk to the owner. Get permission and all that."

"Now!" Alex shouted.

Sten brought his willygun up and snap-fired at Tarpy as he dropped to the ground in a shoulder roll and came up behind a tumble of ship iron. A round spattered against the hull behind him and almost simultaneously he heard a shriek of pain.

"Ah was right, lad," Alex called from the other side. "'Twere definitely five wee rats. Four noo."

Tarpy had easily made it to cover. Sten chalked up another mark under the professional column and began checking the area for the others.

There was a clatter of footsteps on plating beneath him, and Sten glanced down through the gap between the *Zaarah Wahrid* and gravslip. Right beneath was a large and very expensive yacht. One of Tarpy's yahoos was stalking him below. It was like playing three-dimensional chess. The enemy could come from every side as well as down and up. Sten signaled to Alex. He had the left flank and Sten the right. They would take care of the bullyboys first and *then* worry about Tarpy.

He heard a heavy thud as Alex dropped ten meters down to the next berthing slip. Above Sten was a ladder leading to the next deck, half shielded from prevailing winds by a curving metal reef. Sten took two steps to one side to draw fire and then leaped for the ladder and began clambering upward. He was hoping to hell no one was in position, and his back crawled under imaginary sights as he monkey-sprinted up the rungs.

Sten spotted the first man's buttocks almost immediately as they slowly disappeared across the hull of a moored gravflit. The man *was* trying to find the high ground. Sten shot him through the bowels.

Then he stalked on, looking for one more, and knowing that he was still probably following Tarpy's plan. It was obvious from their clumsy creeping that Tarpy's backup troops were unskilled grunts. If Sten were Tarpy, he'd use them as a screen: gun-fodder for him and Alex. That would leave Tarpy in complete control. *He* would then set up the killing ground.

Sten heard a whisper just above him. He glanced up at the overhead catwalk, running out to a slip. Tarpy? Sten didn't think so. He waited until the footsteps stopped. Whoever it was, he was next to a fuel conex. A tube led from the conex to the berthed craft, and Sten could just make out the square edges of a robofueler manipulating the tube. The footsteps moved a pace or two more as the man above took up position.

Port regulations forbade on-board presence during refueling. Sten took careful aim at the conex and hoped that whoever owned the boat was a law-abiding citizen. He squeezed the trigger.

Flames exploded in all directions. Sten took one step to the side and dropped back down to the *Zaarah Wahrid*. Instinctively, he rolled as he hit, expecting return fire. As he came to his feet, something black and charred and vaguely human dropped past him with no sound, just a black thing with a gaping red hole where a mouth should be.

A little shaken from the drop, Sten paced forward along the slip, back toward the front of the *Zaarah Wahrid*. He peered cautiously out and saw Alex moving between a jumble of tie-up cables. Alex spotted him and gave a thumbs-up sign. The other two wee rats had been taken care of. Sten felt an itching in his right hand and looked down to see a slight coil of blood oozing out. Sometime during the fight someone had pinked him. Remarkable how you don't feel things on an adrenaline rush, Sten half thought. He switched the willygun from one hand to the other and raised his hand to suck on the sore spot.

All the while he was thinking of Tarpy. Somehow, he was sure, they were still playing the pro's game. Sten was positive Tarpy was just out of sight, waiting for the perfect shot. Was he stalking Alex?

Then Sten saw his friend's expression change, and at almost the same moment sensed someone just behind him. He spun, trying to bring up the willygun, but knowing the gun was in the wrong hand. He curled his fingers as he pivoted and tried desperately to drop...

Tarpy had him. He saw the man called Sten just in front of him. The huge man, Alex, was in a direct line. It was a perfect chess move, Tarpy thought as he pulled the trigger. The first shot would take out Sten, and then all he had to do was keep squeezing and the big man would fall less than a heartbeat later.

Then Tarpy felt himself suddenly go cold. It was a desperately weakening kind of cold that seemed to start at the shoulder and move quickly down the body. His knees buckled under him and he fought to keep his mind from blacking out.

Tarpy looked down and saw his own gun lying beside Sten. A hand was clutching the gun, and its fingers reflexed on the trigger and the gun fired.

Tarpy wondered *whose* hand was holding the gun. He heard the sound of flies and felt buzzing around his face. Tarpy reached up to brush the flies away. And then he saw his own arm, spouting bright red arterial blood.

Oh, Tarpy thought as he fell. It's *my* hand holding the gun.

Sten stared at the sudden corpse that had been Tarpy. He double-reflexed his fingers and the knife shot back into its sinew sheath. He felt Alex's heavy presence move up behind him, and let his friend help him to his feet.

Sten looked at Alex. "He had us both. You know that, don't you?"

Alex gave him a slight squeeze and then pushed him forward to the *Zaarah Wahrid*'s lock panel. "So he did, laddie. But then, someone hae t' sometime, dinnae they?"

With a loud creak of old, unused metal, the yacht's door groaned slowly open. Sten barely waited for room to spare and dived inside. Alex turned back to stand guard.

The interior was a gutted hulk, a jumble of valueless machinery and dangling wires that led nowhere. Sten cautiously edged his way through what had been the main cabin toward the pilot's cubbyhole. Though he encountered no booby traps, Sten realized that no one had ever intended to use the craft.

He checked the doorway to the pilot's center. Nothing of danger that he could spot. He peered around the corner and his eyes widened in amazement.

Someone had laser-torched away the entire control board. Sitting in its place was an enormous computer. Unlike everything else aboard the ship, it was gleaming spotlessly. Even as he watched, a tiny duster bot hummed out and made its mindless little trek across the main board. It shot out a thin polarized mist in front of it and then efficiently sucked up the motes of dust.

Sten stepped up to the board. He still had no idea what would trigger the bomb. All he was really concerned about was when. Sten was betting that the thing was set up on some sort of a timer. That was logical, if for no other reason than to prevent an accident that would also wipe out the computer's files.

His fingers ran across the keys: ATTENTION! ZAARAH WAHRID! The vid screen lit up. IDENTITY? Sten hesitated, and then made a fast guess: HAKONE. More digestion followed then: HAKONE, G.A.

Sten sighed in relief. So far, so . . . and he continued tapping on the keys without hesitation. There was always a chance that a lack of instant response from the operator was the trigger. REVIEW FILES. The computer went at its task, calling up endless data. At first Sten couldn't figure out what he was seeing, and then he realized it was a list of main subheadings, hundreds of them, and they were repeating themselves, scrolling up the screen and then off. Sten tried to focus on the headings. Finally one scroll up: WAHRID COMMITTEE, DETAILS OF.

Sten cranked the cursor up and froze the heading. REQUEST DETAILS, he punched in.

The screen blinked twice, and then names and figures began sliding up the screen. Something else also appeared. Five overly large letters, forming a word or a name, began flashing urgently in the right-hand corner of the vid-screen. GADES! GADES! GADES! Over and over again, it repeated itself: GADES! GADES! GADES!

Sten's insides went frigid. The bomb had been triggered. Obviously, he was required to punch in a code response to shut it off. He had no idea where to begin. Therefore, he did the most logical thing. Logical, if you are not particularly worried about living.

He stared at the screen, concentrating as hard as he could on the blur of names and numbers and other details.

A warning horn began to hoot. The bomb was moments away from going off. But still Sten remained there, frozen—taking in all his mind could hold. The hooting dimmed. It became only a minor annoyance in the back of his brain. He read on, and on.

He heard an odd growling sound behind him. And then an enormous hand encircled his body and Sten felt himself being lifted up from the floor. All he could see was the swirl of data, and he realized that someone was carrying him through the ship at a dead run.

An explosion of light burst into his face as they cleared the door.

Alex stopped for a microbeat just short of a large loading container. Then he hurled Sten fifteen feet through the air. Sten felt himself soaring over the top and then saw the ground rushing up at him on the other side.

An enormous explosion shook the area, deafening him.

He came woozily back to reality, shaken by the blast. Somehow Alex was lying beside him.

His friend stood up slowly and dusted himself off. Sounds of sirens wailed in the distance. Alex helped Sten to his feet. "Ah mu' talk to y', lad," the Scotsman said, "aboot th' nasty habit y' hae a' nearly killin' us."

CHAPTER FORTY

THE GROUNDS AROUND Hakone's mansion looked like a military base as uniformed men loaded weaponry into gravsleds, boarded, and the sleds sidled around, like so many dogs ready for a nap, into combat formation.

The uniformed men were not *ex*-soldiers, since they were still carried on the roles of the Imperial military. They were deserters from the Praetorians who had been seduced or subverted into disappearing and used for long months for the conspiracy's dirty jobs.

They were gleefully back in uniform, and in motion. After all those years Hakone should have been delighted; it was finally happening!

But, like most things in life, it was happening at the wrong time. Even though Haines and Collins had thought every link to *Zaarah Wahrid* had been cut, one alarm link had remained. When the ship exploded, Hakone knew immediately.

Kai Hakone, not unsane, prided himself on his ability to instantly scope a situation. *Zaarah Wahrid*, both the computer files and the ship itself, were gone. He was under orders from the conspiracy's coordinator to wait until a certain signal was received from the *Normandie* before he moved. But things had changed, and he had no way to consult the coordinator, then aboard the *Normandie*.

Hakone took command responsibility and put his people into motion. After all, the Emperor's death was a certainty, and the worst thing that might happen was that his people might have to hold in place for a limited amount of time.

Hakone forced himself into cheeriness—he'd long recognized a tendency to brood—and bounded down the steps as his own personal combat car slid up to them and grounded.

"You know the route, Sergeant."

"Damn well better after all these years," the grizzled ex-Praetorian said. The car lifted off. The assembled gravsleds followed, tucking themselves into an assault diamond as the sleds hissed over the port of Soward.

CHAPTER FORTY-ONE

THE PILOT CHECKED his proximity screen and radar, then grunted to himself in satisfaction. He touched controls, and the crane-mounted pilot's chair swung back and around from the banked array and deposited him at ground level. He unbuckled, and then decided his honor deserved a display. As he stood, his fingers brushed a control that turned the huge main screen to visual.

Light-years away from the pulsar was a glare, visually and on all instruments. The Tahn pilot heard a murmur of discomfort from the Lords standing before him, then he blanked the screen and bowed. "Our coordinates are those ordered. We have the Imperial ships onscreen, and rendezvous is expected within ten ship-hours."

Lord Kirghiz returned the pilot's bow before he and the other leaders of the Tahn system solemnly filed out of the control room.

The pulsar—NG 467H in the star catalogs—was the third option given to the Emperor by the Tahn for the meeting. It had been the only one approved. The Emperor realized that the pulsar insured total radio silence from all parties. So unless an ambush was already set—and the Empire had more than enough confidence in the superiority of Imperial sensors to eliminate that possiblity—no surprises would await, beyond whatever the Tahn dignitaries might want.

Also the Emperor had a hole card. Imperial science being a notch ahead of the Tahn, the Emperor had a complex com-line out, all the way to the palace. The Emperor was desperately hoping that the line would be used during the summit. Not by him, but by Sten. If Sten managed to produce the main conspirator who had inadvertently caused Alain's death, negotiations would proceed far more smoothly.

The *Normandie* and its flanking ships had picked up the incoming Tahn fleet hours before. An Imperial supersecret was responsible for that. Not only was the fuel AM2 solely controlled by the Emperor, but before it was sold the fuel was "coded." Only Imperial ships ran pure fuel. All others ran modified AM2. Imperial scoutships could pick up and identify at many light-years' distance the existence and rough identity of any non-Imperial ship.

On the screens, the Tahn ships pushed a violet haze behind them as they moved toward the rendezvous.

The Emperor shut down the monitor screen in his quarters, looked at Ledoh, and took several deep breaths. "And so now it begins."

CHAPTER FORTY-TWO

"ARE Y' FINISHED, wee Sten," Alex inquired gently. Sten coughed and straightened from the commode. Too quickly; his guts spasmed and he heaved again.

"Advice, lad," Kilgour went on. "When y' feel a wee furry ring comin't up on y', swallow fast, since it's y'r bung."

Sten recovered. Everything seemed stable. He rinsed his mouth at the sink then glared at Kilgour. "Your sympathies are gonna be remembered, Sergeant Major. On your next fitness report."

He wobbled into the large central room of the Blue

Bhor, then dropped into the nearest chair as the world swam about him again.

Across the room Haines looked at him in concern, as did Rykor, her thick, whiskered face staring over the top of her tank.

"Bein't brainscanned is aye no a pleasure. Ah know y'll nae be wishin' naught." Alex poured drinks for Collins, Haines, and himself and extended the jug toward Rykor, who shook her head.

"What did we get?" Sten managed. Less than two hours after the *Zaarah Wahrid* had blown, Sten had reluctantly put himself under Rykor's brainscan—as, earlier, he had done for Dynsman.

"We have a complete list," Rykor began, "of all conspirators."

Sten groaned in relief.

"I amend that. We have a list of all sub-conspirators."

Haines swore. "The little guys. Who's at the top?"

"We already know that," Sten said. He was very, very tired. "Kai Hakone."

Rykor whuffled through her whiskers. Somehow she'd gotten the idea that the salt-spray might be taken as an expression of condolence. "You are incorrect."

Alex broke the silence. "Clottin' Romans!"

Sten suddenly felt much better—or much worse. He fielded the decanter and poured about three shots straight down. His stomach immediately came back up on him, and Sten let his brain concentrate on not being sick for a moment.

Haines muttered and stared at her carefully drawn conspiracy chart.

"There was a link from the ship directly to the palace, just as there was a feeler into your files, Lieutenant," Rykor went on. "Unfortunately the palace end was not an information link, as you thought. It was a command input terminal."

Sten started to blurt something, then caught himself. "Rykor, logic control."

"As you wish."

Sten forced his mind to reason clearly. "If Rykor's

right, then our 'inside man' is actually the one we've got to take before we can nail all these little guys."

"Correct."

"And we have zed clues at present. Therefore, we need to snatch Hakone and drain him."

"Error," Rykor said. "There is one possible clue. Also, since Hakone is near the top, should we not assume that any attempt on Hakone would immediately send all our conspirators to flight, leaving the dry rot still in place within the palace?"

"Correction," Sten said, and then reacted. "Rykor, what's the clue, dammit?"

"The computer bomb."

"Gades," Sten remembered, pronouncing it as it appeared flashing on the *Zaarah Wahrid*'s screen.

"Try the same word with the accent on the first syllable," Rykor went on. Haines, Collins, and Alex were puzzling—and Sten was the only one who knew that Hakone, when he was describing the battle of Saragossa to him, had used the name.

Rykor allowed herself the pleasure of submerging while Sten reacted, but she surfaced and continued before Sten could explain. "Second point. The conspirators are entirely too—cute, I believe was the word you used. They insisted on giving meaningful names to their scurryings.

"Third. Somehow, the battle of Saragossa links all these beings together."

"Collins," Sten barked. "The name is Gades. He was some kind of admiral at Saragossa. I want his file. Everything. Hell, is the clot alive? Is this the clown we're looking for?"

Collins was headed for the nearest terminal.

"Watch the references, Sergeant," Haines said, going after her. "The file might be booby-trapped."

Since his stomach wasn't actively coming up on him anymore, Sten felt he deserved another drink.

Alex went to Rykor's tank and looked properly respectful. "Lass, since y' no drinkit, Ah dinnae ken wha' y' should have as ae reward. Perhaps a wee fish?"

Rykor heaved, flippers coming out of the tank and

smashing down, salt water cascading over the room. For a moment Sten thought she was in convulsions.

"Sergeant Kilgour!" Rykor finally managed as the waves subsided, "and for all these years I felt you humans lacked humor. You are a good man."

"Alex," Sten crooned as he walked over and draped an arm around his sergeant. "At last we've found someone who understands your jokes.

"Your next assignment will be as a walrus."

Unfortunately Sten's hopeful easy solution was not to be.

Admiral Rob Gades was very, very dead, by his own hand, three years after being relieved by an Imperial court after the debacle at Saragossa.

Despite testimony that Gades's order for retreat had salvaged a full third of the invading force, the Imperial Navy was in no more mood than was the Empire itself to listen to a loser's explanations. Though the testimony was enough to keep the man from being stripped of his rank and awards and sentenced to a penal battalion, it was insufficient to keep him on active service.

He'd used his retirement money to purchase a small planetoid in a frontier system and outfit it rather luxuriously. Then he'd disappeared. The mail ship that toured the planetoids three times a year had discovered the body, six months after Gades had put his parade sword against his chest and leaned forward.

The Saragossa episode was his only black mark. He had been one of the youngest officers to reach flag rank, even allowing for the service-expansion the Mueller Wars had brought.

Son of an Imperial Navy officer ... superior records in crèche ... admitted to a service academy at the minimum allowable age ... fourth in his graduating class ... commissioned and served on tacships, fleet destroyers, aide to a prominent admiral, exec officer on a cruiser, commander of a destroyer flotilla, Command and General Staff school, military liaison on three important diplomatic missions, commander of a newly commissioned battleship, and then flag rank.

"Th' lad hae luck, until th' last min," Alex considered.

Sten nodded.

Rykor *tsk*ed. Given the otarine structure of her head, it came out more like a Bronx cheer, but the proper intention was obvious.

"You two disappoint me. Mahoney told me that you—" Rykor was about to say Mantis soldiers, but reconsidered, unsure whether Haines and Collins knew. "—people don't believe in luck."

Sten looked at Alex.

"We're missing something."

"Aye. The wee crab-eater hae somethin'. Gie her th' moment a' triumph."

Rykor savored it a minute before continuing. "Who recommended Gades to that exclusive military school? Who suggested to a certain admiral that Lieutenant Gades would make an excellent aide? Who boarded him for the flotilla command? Who got him those—I think you would use the phrase 'fat'—diplomatic assignments?...

"One person—and one person only."

Sten scrolled Gades' record and read the signatures at the bottom of those glowing recommendations and requests.

"Oh Lord," he whispered softly.

The rank and even the signature changed over the years. But the name was the same. Mik Ledoh. Imperial Chamberlain and the man closest to the Emperor!

"And now we know who is at the peak of the conspiracy, do we not?"

"But why Ledoh? What in blazes did he have to do with Gades?"

Rykor flipped her own computer terminal open. ORDER: COMPARE LEDOH AND GADES, ALL CATEGORIES. REPORT ALL SIMILARITIES.

And eventually the computer found it.

In the gene pattern...

* * *

Regicide sometimes springs from very small begin-
nings—small, at least, to those not immediately involved.
Philip of Macedon died because he chose public instead
of nonobjectionable private sodomy; Charles I could possibly have saved his head if he'd been more polite to a
few small business people; Trotsky could have been less
vitriolic in his writings; Mao III of the Pan-Asian Empire
might have survived longer had he not preferred the
daughters of his high-ranking officials for bedmates. And
so forth.

Admiral Mik Ledoh's attempt to kill the Eternal
Emperor was rooted in equally minuscule events. Ledoh's
first assignment in logistics was as supply officer on a
remote Imperial Navy Base.

The base sat outside even what were then the Empire's
frontier worlds. Though a long way from nowhere, the
base was positioned on an idyllic planet, a world of trop-
ical islands, sun, and very easy living. Since the base's
function was merely to support patrol units, dependents
were encouraged to join wives or husbands on that assignment.

Understaffed, the patrols and patrol-support missions
were long. A probe ship would be out for four months or
more before returning to duty. Compensation was provided by an equivalent time on leave.

There was not much for those soldiers and sailors
assigned to this tropic world, beyond fueling and maintaining the probe fleet. Bored men and women can find
wondrous ways of getting into trouble. Ledoh, a hand-
some lieutenant, found one of the classics—falling in love
with the wife of a superior officer.

The woman was an odd mixture of thrill-seeker, roman-
tic, and realist. Two months into their affair, one week
before her husband returned from long patrol and subsequent transfer, she told Ledoh that she had chosen to
become pregnant. While the young officer gaped, she listed
her other decisions—she would have the child; she loved
Ledoh and would always remember him; under no circumstances would she leave her upward-bound husband
for a young supply officer.

First real love affairs are always gut-churners. But that woman managed to make the memories even worse for Ledoh. He never saw her again, but he managed to keep track of her—and his son.

The woman's husband burnt out young, and became just another alky probe-ship cowboy. Ledoh had hopes that . . . but she never left the man. The best that Ledoh could do was to shepherd his son's career. He was delighted to find that, from an early age, the boy wanted to follow in his "father's" footsteps. Ledoh made the necessary recommendations.

When Rob Gades graduated from his military academy, a very proud Mik Ledoh watched from the audience. But he was never able to approach Gades, even later in the man's career.

Someday, he promised himself. Someday there'll be a way I can explain.

Someday, he felt, was shortly after Gades was promoted to admiral.

But the Mueller Wars happened, and Ledoh found himself organizing and leading the Crais System landings. He succeeded brilliantly—unlike his son, who was relieved of command after Saragossa.

Ledoh protested the board's decision, but uselessly. At that point he wanted to go to his son and tell him what would happen—that sooner or later sanity would return.

But he couldn't find the words.

Before he did, his son died, a suicide.

Two weeks after hearing of the death, Ledoh applied for retirement, to the shock of the Imperial Navy. Since the Crais landings were one of the few bright spots of the Mueller Wars, there was an excellent possibility that Mik Ledoh was in the running for Grand Admiral.

The conspiracy might even then have been avoided if anyone had known of Ledoh's ties to Gades. But Mik Ledoh hewed close to the old and stupid military adage: "Never explain, never complain."

Men who have spent most of their lives in company do not handle the solitude of retirement well, and Ledoh was no different. Retirement only gave him the chance to brood at leisure, and brooding led him to the conclusion that the reason for his son's death, the reason for the deterioration he had come to see in the Empire since the Mueller Wars, and the reason for his own unhappiness was the Eternal Emperor himself.

Kai Hakone's sixth vid-tape, built around the premise that Admiral Rob Gades had been a true hero and a scapegoat, provided the spark.

The rest, from his use of the old-boy's network to return from retirement for a position in the Imperial household to his subversion of bright Colonel Fohlee to his friendship with Hakone to the building of the conspiracy's octopus-links made perfect sense.

Or would have, if any historian had been permitted to dig into what happened that year on Prime World.

Instead, two policemen, two soldiers, and one walrus-like psychologist sat in a room over a rural pub, staring at two displays on a computer screen: father and son.

In an age when limb transplants were as commonplace as transfusions, and a medico needed to know the proper factors to prevent rejection, gene patterns were automatically recorded for any member of the Imperial military, just as blood type had been recorded a thousand years before.

Sten finally got to his feet, blanked the screen, considered a drink, and regretfully decided against it.

"Orders group," he said. "Haines, I want a full strike force available. Kai Hakone is to be secured immediately. Imperial warrant. When you have him in custody, all other conspirators on Rykor's list are to be taken and held incommunicado.

"Sergeant Kilgour."

"Sir!"

"We're to the palace."

And Sten and Alex were in motion, headed for the only com-link to the Emperor.

CHAPTER FORTY-THREE

STEN'S ALARM SHOULD have gone off when he and Alex doubled into Arundel's gates. But the fact that the two Praetorians on duty were in parade battle dress instead of their normal monkey suits just did not register. Nothing else would have given away the revolt. Clerks scurried about, dignitaries mumbled in corners, and the palace was normal.

Normal, until Sten and Alex came out of the lift on the Emperor's private level. And then it was Alex who realized something was wrong.

"Captain," he said. "Wha' be y'r Gurkhas?"

And Sten came back to immediacy. Those Gurkhas the Emperor hadn't taken with him on the *Normandie* should have been patrolling the corridors. Instead there were Praetorians, all in full Guards combat dress.

The realization was very late, as four of the Praetorians snapped out of an alcove, willyguns leveled.

"Lads," Alex started. "Ye're makin't a wee mistake."

And then Kai Hakone, in uniform, stepped out of the chamberlain's office. He nodded politely to the two. "Captain Sten, you are under arrest."

CHAPTER FORTY-FOUR

NG 467H WAS a maelstrom of blinding light and howling interference that blanked the two fleets hanging in the white shadow of the spinning neutron star.

The *Normandie* and the Tahn battleships were motionless in their orbits, support and escort ships patterning around them. Since the pulsar eliminated conventional navigational methods, the ships maneuvered using computer-probability screens, computers that were normally used only for navigational instruction and simulated battles. Communication between ships were either by probe ship or by unmanned message-carrying torpedoes.

Pilots, whether Tahn or Imperial, were of course well-skilled in instruments-only conditions, but so near NG 467H, most instruments were equally useless. So, using known (by computer projection) locations, cruisers eased around the bloated hulks of the *Normandie* and the Tahn ship, hoping none of the Big Ugly Clots had altered their orbits, and the destroyers and probe ships ran infinitely variable patrols using a central plotting point cross-triangulated from the three nearest stars, and crossed fingers.

The vicinity of NG 467H was the ultimate whiteout, and the two leviathans and their pilot fish and remoras were as blind as if at the bottom of a deep.

BOOK FIVE

THE RED MASS

CHAPTER FORTY-FIVE

STEN LAY ON his bunk, running progs.

After their arrest, Alex had been frog-marched away to join the Gurkhas in their dungeon. However, to his initial surprise, Sten was merely ordered to his quarters. But after analysis, the move seemed to make sense—at least sense from Hakone's point of view.

Hakone was obviously thinking beyond the obvious next moves.

Nevertheless, having been involved in more than a few coups d'etat, Sten thought Hakone had his head up. If *he* were Kai Hakone, he would have ordered Sten, Kilgour, and the Gurkhas shot instantly, and worried about explanations later.

Sten may have been sent to his quarters, like any officer ordered under Imperial hack, but Sten's room had been fine-combed for weaponry and three armed former Praetorians had been stationed outside. Sten's only real weapon was the knife in his arm, which had gone undiscovered.

Sten was somewhat uncomfortably coming to the conclusion that he was gong to die rather quickly. He'd already checked his layered maps of the castle, but the nearest chamber that accessed the wall passages and tunnels was some fifty meters away.

Sten didn't even consider the window, assuming that Hakone would have a couple of hidden sharpshooters on the ground below ready for Sten to try that exit.

Keep thinking, Sten. Assume, for the sake of stupidity,

231

that you can go out the door, immobilize three guards, and then get into the palace's guts.

Ho-kay.

Then you head for the radio room, the room with the sole link to the *Normandie*. Further assume that you have time to broadcast a warning to the Emperor; that your broadcast gets through to the ship; and that the call isn't fielded by Ledoh.

Clottin' unlikely again.

But assume it, lad. Assume it. Then what happens?

What happens then is Hakone kills you. Then the Emperor comes back (hopefully), retakes his own palace, and, if that happens, gives you some sort of medal.

A very big medal.

Sten had never wanted the Galactic Cross. Especially posthumously.

He dragged his mind back. Hell with it, man. You can't even get out of your room yet.

A fist thundered against his door, and Sten rolled to his feet.

"Back against the far wall, directly in line with the doorway."

Sten obeyed.

"Are you against the wall?"

"I am."

"This door is opening. If you are not immediately visible, I have an unpinned grenade ready."

The door opened, and there stood a man he was already considering his chief warden, grenade ready. The other two guards stood slightly behind him, willyguns up.

And behind them was Kai Hakone.

Sten stayed motionless as the guards came in and flanked him, carefully staying meters to either side, as Hakone paced into the room.

"Captain Sten, a word?"

Sten grinned—a lot he had to say in the matter.

"Outside. As an officer in the Guard, will you give me your parole?"

Sten considered lying, then discarded it. He still had

a job, and being inside the palace made its accomplishment slightly more possible. "No."

"I thought not." Hakone beckoned, and four other guards came into the room. "But I still would like to discuss matters with you."

Sten had a fairly good idea that, if the Emperor survived and returned, he would have a major case of the hips. His gardens were being busily dug up and entrenched or sited for ground-to-air missile launchers by Praetorians. Hakone seemed to notice none of the activity as he walked beside Sten.

The seven Praetorians held diamond-formation around Sten, their weapons leveled and aimed.

These also Hakone ignored. He was, like any thinker-turned-activist, in the middle of a near-compulsive explanation. "It would have been simpler if Phase One had been successful."

Sten, equally compulsive an intelligence officer, wanted more information.

"Phase One, Sr. Hakone? I don't have all the pieces. You were intending the bomb to stun the Emperor, correct? He was then to be hustled to Soward Hospital, where Knox would take over the case.

"What would that have given you?"

"The Emperor traditionally withdraws from the public after Empire Day for a rest. One, perhaps two weeks. During that time he would have been reconditioned."

"To follow whose orders?"

"Ledoh and others of us who recognize that the Empire must be redirected to its proper course."

"But now you're going to kill him."

"Necessity is a harsh master."

Sten mentally winced—Hakone couldn't *really* think in those clichés.

"So he dies. Why did you take over the palace?"

"Once the Emperor is dead, and with us holding the center of all Imperial communications, no false information will be broadcast."

"Like who really did it?"

Hakone smiled and didn't bother answering.

"By the way, Hakone, if you don't mind my saying, who *is* going to be your judas goat?"

"The Tahn, of course."

"Don't you think that those delegates might have their own story? And be listened to?"

"Not if they're equally deceased."

Sten's poker face melted. "You're talking war."

"Exactly, Captain. With a war starting, who will be interested in a postmortem? And a war is what this Empire needs to melt the fat away. That would also settle the Tahn question."

"When is this going to happen?"

"We have no exact timetable. The Praetorians and I were supposed to take the palace three days from now. Your discovery of the *Zaarah Wahrid* forced us into premature motion. The actual termination of the Emperor will be decided by Admiral Ledoh."

"You really think this committee, or whatever you're calling it, *could* run the Empire?"

"Why not? Twenty minds are obviously superior to one, aren't they?" Sten could have answered by stating the obvious—no, because any junta becomes an exercise in backstabbing as each leader tries to take out the others. Instead he went in another way.

"Twenty minds don't know the secret of AM2."

"Captain, you really believe that drivel?"

Drivel, hell—Sten had spent enough time around the Emperor to realize the man *had* that ace up his sleeve.

"There is no way I can believe that one man—one mortal man—controls AM2. That the answer is nowhere in his files."

They continued to walk, Sten maintaining silence, waiting for the offer.

It came.

"The reason I wanted to talk to you privately," Hakone finally continued, "is that after the . . . event, there will probably be a certain amount of resettlement. You could be of service."

"To you personally, or to your committee?"

"Well, of course, for us all. But I would want you to report to me."

Sten didn't let himself smile. Already Hakone was figuring on having his own people to guard his back. The man didn't even believe his own theories. "What would be my new job description?"

"You would be allowed to maintain your present position. But I—I mean we—would have you detached for special assignments in the intelligence area."

"You're forgetting I swore an oath. To the Emperor."

"If the Emperor no longer existed, would that oath be valid?"

"Suppose I say no?"

Hakone started to beam, then studied Sten closely. "Are you lying to me, Captain?"

"Of course."

Hakone's smile was subtly different as he beckoned to the guards.

"You are a careful man, Captain. Let us leave things as they are. You are restricted to your room until notified otherwise. After the Emperor's death, perhaps we should rehold this conversation."

Sten bowed politely, then followed the guards back toward his quarters. He was not interested in Hakone at the moment; he'd figured a way out of his confinement—and a way that gave him almost a 10 percent chance of surviving the ensuing debacle.

That was better odds than was normal for Mantis.

CHAPTER FORTY-SIX

LORD KIRGHIZ IGNORED the grumblings of his fellow Tahn lords, fitted himself into the lighter's bare-frame jumpseat, and buckled in. After getting Kirghiz's curt nod, the co-pilot hissed orders to the pilot, and the lighter broke lock with the Tahn battleship and arched toward the *Normandie*.

Kirghiz was showing less the stoicism required of a man worthy of ruling the warrior Tahn than that of a man with worries far more serious than the indignity of being chauffeured in a troop transport. To begin with, less than one third of the Tahn council had agreed to the summit meeting, and those who had deserted him were the most adamantly anti-Empire, prowar faction of the Tahn lords.

Kirghiz's control of the Tahn council was very tenuous, based on an uneasy agreement among a majority of the various Tahn factions. In his absence, he knew that the ruling council might very well change its entire structure.

Still worse were the demands he was required to make on this, the first day of the summit. Several were deal-killers, conditions which Kirghiz knew, from his decades as a diplomat and power broker, the Emperor could not agree to.

In fact, if he were the Emperor, Kirghiz would consider breaking off the meeting moments after hearing those demands.

He prayed, to whatever gods he disbelieved in, that the Emperor was the consummate politician he should be, and would recognize the demands as nothing more than cheap grandstanding for the Tahn peasants and the peas-

236

ant-mentality of those lords who proposed them. Because, if the talks broke down, Kirghiz saw no other alternative than war between the Tahn worlds and the Empire.

No computer he'd used could predict the outcome of such a war, but all of them showed one thing: Defeated or victorious, the Tahn worlds would be in economic ruin at the war's end.

Kirghiz being a Tahn, a Tahn warrior, and a Tahn lord, he did not even think about the other result to the talk's breaking down—the certainty of his own trial for treason and execution if he returned without a treaty.

CHAPTER FORTY-SEVEN

IF HE SURVIVED the breakout attempt, which was very unlikely, Sten made a note to put the cost of replacing his miniholoprocessor on somebody's expense account. Because sure as death and dishonesty, Sten's hobby machine was ruined.

The holoprocessor was intended to create the illusion of very small—no more than 100-centimeters-high—figures, machines, or dioramas.

Cursing his ineptness at electronics, Sten had replaced all of the holoprocessors's fuses with heavy-duty wiring stripped from a shaving light and cut the safety circuits out. He had searched through the holoprocessor's memory looking for some sort of horrible beastie to use, then laughed and input the description and behavior of the wonderful gurions he and Alex had met shortly before.

That complete, the miniprocessor was pushed to a few meters from the door. Its actuating switch was boogered out to a remote, under Sten's foot.

Sten took the required position, directly across from the door opening, and then considered cheap lies. Sick? Nobody's that dumb, not even a Praetorian. Hungry? Still worse. Then Sten was struck by inspiration. He tossed a vid-tape at the door and got an appropriate clunk.

"What is it?" came the guard's suspicious voice.

"I'm ready now."

"For clottin' what?"

Sten allowed puzzlement to enter his voice. "For Sr. Hakone."

"We have no orders on that."

"Hakone—you must have heard—told me to contact him immediately after our meeting."

"He didn't tell us that."

Sten let silence work for him.

"Besides, he's given orders that no one is to see him until further notice."

"Kai Hakone," Sten said, "is in the Imperial com bunker. I think he would like to speak to me."

Any sergeant can fox a grunt, just as any captain can fox a sergeant. Or at least that's the way it had worked when Sten was on duty in the field. He hoped things hadn't changed much.

"I'll have to check with the sergeant of the guard," came the self-doubting voice.

"As you wish. Sr. Hakone told me that he wanted nobody to know."

There was an inaudible mutter, which Sten's hopeful mind translated as a conference, consisting of yeah, Hakone works things like that, nobody told us nothin', that figures, what'th'clot we got to worry about if we just take him to a com center. And then the louder voice: "Are you back against the wall?"

Sten held out his hands. Indeed, he was standing, obviously unarmed, against the far wall. The guard eyed him through the freshly drilled peephole, then unbolted and opened the door. He was three steps inside, his back-ups flanking him, when the two-meters-high image of the gurion rose from the holoprocessor and walked toward the guards.

The reaction was instant—the guards' guns came up, blasting reflexively and tearing hell out of the ceiling.

Sten's reaction was equally fast: He flat-rolled, hit, half rose over the self-destructing holoprocessor, his knife lanced before him, and then buried it in the chest of the lead guard.

Sten used the inertia of the guard to stop himself, and the knife came out, splashing blood across the room, through the rapidly fading gurion. And Sten was pivoting, his left, knuckled hand smashing sideways, well inside the second guard's rifle reach, into the man's temple, while his right arm launched the knife into—and through— guard number three. Cartilage and bone cracked and broke in guard number two, and Sten recovered into attack position before any of the three corpses slumped to the floor.

Wasting no time in self-congratulation, Sten catted down the corridor, heading for the palace's catacombs.

Kilgour, too, was trying moves.

"Clottin' Romans," he bellowed down the corridor. "y'r mither did it wi' sheep. Wi' goats! Wi' dogs! Clottin' hell, wi' Campbells!" No response came from the guards outside the cell.

He stepped back from the window and looked apologetically at the 120 Gurkhas sharing the huge holding cell with him.

"Tha' dinnae ken."

Kilgour's plan, for want of a weaker word, was to somehow anger the guards so much they'd come into the cell to bust kneecaps. Alex hoped that, regardless of weapons, he and the 120 stocky brown men in the cell could somehow break out.

Havildar-Major Lalbahadur Thapa leaned against the wall beside him. "In Gurhali," he offered helpfully, "you might try one pubic hair."

Alex laughed. "Now that's the stupidest insult Ah've heard in years."

"Stupider, Sergeant Major, than calling someone a Campbell—whatever that is?"

Without warning a section of seemingly solid stone in

one wall slid open, and Sten was suddenly leaning non-chalantly against the far wall. "Sergeant-Major, I could hear your big mouth all the way down the corridor. Now if you'd knock off the slanging and follow me.

"The arms room," Sten continued, as the Gurkhas recovered from their astonishment and bustled into the low tunnel Sten had emerged from, "is three levels up and one corridor across."

"Ah'm thinkit Ah owe y' a pint," Alex managed, as he forced his bulk after the Gurkhas. Sten looked very knowing as he palmed the rock wall shut.

CHAPTER FORTY-EIGHT

YEARS LATER, STEN and Alex would have a favorite pondering point. They could understand why the Emperor built Arundel. They could also understand why a man who believed in romance required a castle to have secret passages.

The problem was the *why* for some of those passages. Both men thought it very logical that a backstairs went from the Imperior chambers to feed into the various bedchambers. Sten could even understand why the Emperor wanted a tunnel that provided secret egress from cells in the dungeon far below.

They were never able to explain to everyone's satisfaction why a few of the tunnels opened into a main passageway.

Some of the former Praetorians involved in the revolt might have wondered, too, if they had survived. Most did not.

A Praetorian paced down a seemingly doorless corridor

then a panel swung noiselessly open and a small grinning man swung a large knife that looked to be a cross between a machete and a small cutlass.

There were only a little over a thousand Praetorians, facing 120 wall-slinking Gurkhas. The battle was completely one-sided.

The reoccupation of the palace went quickly, silently, and very, very bloodily, as Sten deployed his troops in a slow circle, closing on the Imperial chambers, the communication center, and that one room with the com-link to the Emperor.

The armored door to the com center was sealed, which offered no potential problem to the Gurkha squad deployed around it. The lance-naik already had his bunker-buster loaded and the rocket aimed at the door's hinges when Sten kicked him aside. "Yak-pubes," he snarled in Gurhali, "do you know what would happen if you discharged that rocket in this passageway?"

The lance-naik didn't seem worried. Kilgour was already slapping together a shaped charge from the demopack he'd secured from the armory.

"Best w' be all hangin't on th' sides ae the corridor," he muttered, and yanked the detonator. Sten had barely time to follow the suggestion before the charge blew the door in. The Gurkhas, kukris ready, leaped in the wreckage but could find nothing to savage. The Praetorians inside had been reduced to a thin paste plastered across the room's far wall. Kukri in hand, Sten ran past them, leapt, and his foot snapped into the thin door leading to the com room itself. He recovered and rolled in, low, to find himself looking at a shambles of crushed circuitry, looped power cables, and spaghetti-strung wires.

And Kai Hakone, standing in an alcove away from the doorway, mini-willygun leveled at Sten.

"You're somewhat late, Captain." Hakone motioned with his free hand, eyes and gun never moving away from Sten.

"You have the palace, but we have the Emperor. The com-link is destroyed. Before it can be rebuilt..." and Hakone gestured theatrically. His eyes flickered away as he scanned for Sten's accomplices—enough time for Sten to grab the end of a severed power cable and throw it into Hakone's face.

Hakone fried, and in his convulsions the willygun went off, its projectile whining away harmlessly as his flesh blackened then sizzled before the circuit-breakers popped and the body collapsed, leaving Sten in the ruins of the com room.

"'Twould appear th' only hope our Emp hae is us bairns doin't o'er th' hills t' far away."

Sten nodded agreement, and then he and Alex were moving, headed for the palace's command center.

CHAPTER FORTY-NINE

"... AND LASTLY, THE Aggrieved Party solemnly petitions His Imperial Majesty to publicly display his historic sense of justice, and deep feelings for individual tragedy, by recognizing the heroic and tragic death of Godfrey Alain. Alain was a man respected by..."

Admiral Ledoh droned on and on, reviewing once again the demands of the Tahn. His audience consisted of two very bored men: the Eternal Emperor and Tanz Sullamora. Sullamora was fighting to stay awake, and doing his best to remain attentive. He kept watching the Emperor for a signal of his feelings. It was an impossible task. The Eternal Emperor's face was a complete stone.

"... and, by an agreed time, the Emperor will read, or have read, an agreed-upon message to his subjects, whose basic points should consist of—"

"Enough," the Emperor said. "Clotting *enough*. I got their point. Now, the question is, what is our response?"

Admiral Ledoh raised an eyebrow. "I was about to suggest that if we agree that we are completely familiar with their demands, we should have them analyzed by the diplomatic computer."

The Emperor laughed. "Relax, Ledoh. You're starting to sound like the damned Tahn." He picked up a pot of tea and refilled three cups. "As for the diplomatic computer, forget it. I can run it down faster and more accurately. I've been doing this kind of thing for more centuries than I've got stars."

Sullamora nodded. "I was waiting for you to say just that, sir. And I hope that you don't think me immodest to point out that I have had many years of experience with these people."

"That's why I brought you along. They trust you about as much as they can trust any non-Tahn."

Sullamora smiled. "It isn't trust, sir. On their part it is pure greed. After all, I am the only person you have sanctioned to trade with them."

"That's why you're my ace in the hole," the Emperor said. "Because you are gonna be my well-baited hook."

Sullamora hadn't the faintest idea what the Emperor meant, but he reconized praise when he heard it, and smiled back graciously.

"Now," the Emperor said, "let's translate some of this into plain talk. They have five basic demands, and I believe all of them are negotiable.

"Starting with number one: They want my Imperial contract to administer the Fringe Worlds. Translation: They want a gift of all those systems."

"You'll say no, of course, sir," Sullamora puffed.

"Sort of, but not quite."

Sullamora started to protest, but the Emperor held up a hand. The Emperor barely noticed that Ledoh had been strangely noncommittal.

"Let me boil the rest down, and then I'll tell you how we probably ought to play it.

"Second demand: Open immigration. My objection: They can pack the system with their own people. That's a double giveaway.

"Third: unconditional amnesty for Godfrey Alain's people. No problem. Granted. I can always round up the real hard-core types later, on the quiet.

"Fourth—and here's another sticking point—They want to set up a free port in the Fringe Worlds."

"That has a lot of commercial possibilities," Sullamora said.

"Sure. But it also means I'm supposed to increase their AM2 quota. Which means they can stockpile even more and give me much bloody grief down the line.

"Last of all, they want me to publicly apologize for Godfrey Alain's death."

Ledoh raised his head and gave the Emperor a thin smile. "You never apologize, do you, sir?" he said bitterly. No one noticed his tone.

"Clotting right. Once I start apologizing I might as well start looking around for someone to take my place.

"Last time I admitted I was wrong, it cost me half my treasury."

"A firm no, sir," Sullamora advised. "Frankly, I don't see a single point we can give on. My vote is to send them packing."

"On the surface, I would agree with you, Tanz. But let me run back what I propose. Then see what you think."

Sullamora was suddenly very interested. He could sniff a profit.

"To start with, I flip their last point to my first."

"You mean the apology?" Sullamora was aghast.

"Sure. Except I do it this way. I propose that we build a memorial to Godfrey Alain. To commemorate his death and the many deaths on both sides of this whole mess.

"Instead of an apology, I put it to them that all peace-loving peoples are responsible for this ongoing tragedy.

"For frosting on the cake, I fund the whole clotting shebang. I build a memorial city on the Tahn capital world. A sort of Imperial trade center."

Sullamora grinned wolfishly.

"In other words, you get to put a garrison on their home planet."

The Eternal Emperor laughed loudly. "Good man! Not

only that, but I guaran-clotting-tee you that every man and woman will be from my elite troops."

"Excellent! And if I know my Tahn, they'll swallow the whole thing," Sullamora said.

"Next: Instead of letting them administer the Fringe Worlds, I propose a peacekeeping force. Manned fifty-fifty."

Sullamora shook his head.

"Not so fast, Tanz. I let them appoint the commander."

Sullamora considered. "But that would be the same as handing it over to them."

"It would appear that way. Except, since I provide the ships, and those ships would be commanded by my people, their top guy would be helpless when it came to any action.

"And to copper my bet, I double the basic pay of my troops."

Sullamora especially liked this. "Meaning, compared to the Tahn, they'd be relatively rich. Also meaning, you'd be undermining the morale of the common Tahn soldiers."

He made a mental note to try this tactic in some of the more difficult trading posts under his corporate command.

The Eternal Emperor continued. "Open immigration, fine.

"Now, for the free port concept. I'll agree. With the proviso that I get to appoint the man in charge."

"They'd have to go for that," Sullamora said. "After you let them pick the chief of the peacekeeping force. But who would you propose?"

"You," the Emperor said.

That rocked Sullamora back. The profits he had been sniffing were soaring to the sky.

"Why me?"

"You understand them, but your loyalties are to me. Therefore, I keep complete control of the AM2 supply. Through you, of course."

"Of course." Sullamora knew better than to cook his books as far as energy supplies were concerned.

"Finally," the Emperor said, "I have a magnanimous

proposal. It'll really sound that way when the diplomatic fools get through flowering it up.

"The Tahn's main problem, besides being plain fascist clots, is they're under heavy population pressure. That's why we're knocking heads in the Fringe Worlds."

Sullamora nodded.

"Therefore, to take the pressure off, I agree to fund an exploration force. I will bankroll the entire thing and provide the ships and crews."

Even the silent chamberlain came forward for that one. "But what advantage—"

"The ships will be ordered to explore away from the Fringe Worlds. If we find anything..."

If there was to be any further expansion, the Tahn would be moving the other way. With luck, that pioneer rush to other systems would bleed some of the tension out of their military culture.

"Well?" The Eternal Emperor leaned back in his seat, looking for comments from his two key men.

"It seems fine to me," the chamberlain said quickly.

Sullamora, however, thought for a very long time. Then he slowly nodded. "It should work."

"I sure as clot hope so," the Eternal Emperor said. "Because if it doesn't—"

The light next to the hatchway blinked on-off-on.

Ledoh frowned annoyance and touched the annunciator key.

"Communication officer, sir."

"This conference was not to be—"

"Admiral," the Emperor interrupted. "This may be what I'm expecting."

Ledoh palmed the door to open.

The watch comofficer didn't know whether to salute or bow to the Emperor, so he compromised ridiculously.

The Emperor didn't notice—he was hoping that the signal was from Sten, announcing that he had the conspirators nailed, on toast, and ready for delivery to the Tahn.

"Uh ... sir," the officer said, finding it easier to deliver his message to Admiral Ledoh. "This signal isn't from the source we expected. It's a distress signal. Standard sweep-band broadcast. Our satellite just happened to pick it up."

"Clot," Ledoh swore, and took the printout. "We didn't need this. No response."

"Hang on. Let me look at it." Ledoh passed the sheet to the Emperor. According to the burst-broadcast signal, the merchant ship *Montebello* was in a desperate situation, number of light-years, estimated, off the radio pulsar NG 467H. Fuel explosion on-board ship, all officers injured, most crewmembers severely burned, request immediate assistance from any receiving ship.

"Jerks!" the Emperor said. "Cheapjack shippers, trying some kind of econo slingshot orbit, and they're not capable of finding their way out of a closet with a torch."

"Your Highness," Sullamora said. "Admiral Ledoh is correct. There are far more important things happening than a few dozen burnt spacebums."

The Emperor would probably have made the same decision. But, characteristically, Sullamora put it wrong, and the Emperor flashed back more than a thousand years to when he himself hadn't been much more than a space-bum.

"Lieutenant," he said to the com officer. "Transfer this message to the ComDesRon. Order him to dispatch one destroyer immediately."

The officer only saluted this time, then scurried out of the Imperial presence.

The Emperor turned back to business. "Now, Admiral, would you please put all of our common-sense into the appropriate diplomatic drakh, so Lord Kirghiz won't think that we've gone insane?"

CHAPTER FIFTY

"THANK YOU, MR. Jenkins. I have the con."

The hell I do, Commander Lavonne considered as his deck officer saluted and stepped back. That lousy game machine we're using to keep us off the BUCs is telling me what to do.

He rechecked the computer-prob screen that was giving him his course. "Nav-point zeroed?"

"Zeroed, sir," his executive officer said.

"From zero...course left thirty-five degrees, down fourteen degrees."

"Course left thirty-five, down fourteen."

"Secondary drive...quarter-speed."

"Secondary drive at quarter-speed."

Lavonne mentally crossed his fingers and hoped the next few seconds didn't produce anything unusual, such as an intersection orbit with another destroyer. "Engage drive."

"Drive engaged." The Imperial Destroyer *San Jacinto* hummed slightly as the ship's gyro clutched in, turning the ship into the correct direction, and Yukawa drive shoved the *San Jacinto* away from the thronged fleet.

Lavonne let thirty seconds elapse. "Increase secondary drive to half-speed."

"Secondary drive at half-speed," came the toneless echo from his quartermaster.

"Mr. Collins...from the count...now! Five minutes to main drive."

"Five minutes until main drive, Captain, and counting."

Five minutes gave the skipper of the *San Jacinto* brooding time. He considered slumping into his command chair, then brought himself up. We are all getting a little sloppy out here, he reminded himself. He then concentrated on his brooding.

Under normal circumstances Commander Lavonne would have been biting handrails in half when he'd gotten his assignment. He had spent entirely too many years pulling tramp steamers' tubes out of cracks to enjoy another rescue. As far as he was concerned all merchant fleets should be under military control. Lavonne was not at all a fascist—he'd just seen too many freighters permitted to offplanet with out-of-date or nonexistent safety sections, red-lined emergency gear, and officers who weren't competent to command a gravsled.

But the new assignment would give the commander and the men and women of the *San Jacinto* something to do.

Basically Commander Lavonne was ticked. Originally he and his ship had been pulled from their DesRon and ordered to rendezvous and escort a liner to its destination.

Initially Lavonne felt very proud. Somebody Up There—Up There with Stars—felt that the *San Jacinto* was as good a ship as the commander and his crew knew it to be. Lavonne, in his few selfish moments, also recognized that the whole enterprise, whatever it was, would probably look very good in his record jacket when it came time for promotion.

Ship's scuttlebutt soared when they reached the destination—off NG 467H—and then peaked when the incoming Tahn ships were identified. Lavonne figured out that he and his men were participating in something Terribly Significant and Probably Historic. The question was, what? Lavonne had a mental image of himself as a frizzly old admiral taping his memoirs and saying: "And then I was permitted to participate in the Empire-shaking (whatsit) located off a distant radio star, in which (nobody ever told me) happened."

What made it worse was the radiation from NG 467H.

Since all vid-ports and com-screens were sealed, the sailors felt even more than usual like sardines in a tin.

Orders from the squadron commander arrived in the messenger torps but were less than helpful: Patrol from such a point to such a point, then return exactly on orbit.

It's a sailor's right to piss and moan, but not within earshot of his division commander. Sailors went on report. Several paired sailors requested permission to join the general mess decks, breaking up long-standing relationships. Lavonne's most trusted bosun's mate, who only got busted when the *San Jacinto* berthed in a liberty port, was reduced to the ranks after he modified one of the ship's water purifiers to produce something that, when drunk, hit with the potency of AM2 fuel.

The *San Jacinto* was not a happy ship, so Lavonne was actually grateful when he got the orders to break from the fleet, operate under independent command, and relieve the disaster-stricken MS *Montebello*.

"Four minutes, thirty seconds."

Lavonne brought himself back to the ship's bridge. "At fifteen, give me a tick count."

"At fifteen, aye, sir. Coming to fifteen...fifteen, mark! Twelve...eleven...ten...nine...eight...seven ...six..."

"On order, engage main drive."

"Standing by."

"Two...one..."

"Mark!"

And the *San Jacinto* shimmered as the AM2 drive smashed the ship into the orbit that would arc it very close "over" the pulsar toward the nearest intersection point with the *Montebello*.

"Ah, lad," Alex mused. "Th' remind me ae m' ancestor."

Though it appeared to be a tramp steamer that had far more owners than semiannuals, the ship was really a Mantis Q-ship, an intelligence ship mounting as much power as an Imperial destroyer and far better electronics. In addition to the normal four-men crew, Sten, Alex, and forty Gurkhas were crammed into it.

Before he punched the panic button that had alerted the fleet, Sten had prepositioned several remote satellites outside NG 467H, satellites that hopefully would report the drive-flare of any ship headed in his general direction. Then he'd sent the distress signal, knowing that the satellite originally intended to field the tight beam from the palace would respond and communicate with the fleet itself, even though the ships were inside NG 467H's interference blanket.

"I did not know, Sergeant Major Yeti, you were aware of just who your ancestors were," Naik Gunju Lama said in seeming innocence.

Kilgour sneered at him. "Frae off'cers Ah hae t'take drakh like tha', but no frae a wee private who hae to gie back to Katmandu to have his pubes pulled.

"As ae was sayin't, Captain. One ae m'ancestors went on th' dole, an'—"

"What the hell's a dole?" Sten asked. There'd been no signals from his remotes, and so they had time to kill. Listening to another of Kilgour's absurd stories seemed as good a way to pass the time as anything.

"A wee fruit, shaped like a pineapple. Now dinna be interruptin' me, lad. So it's necessary tha' m' ancestor sees a quack, to certify he's nae able to ply his trade.

"The doc looks a' m' ancestor, one Alex Selkirk Kilgour, an' blanches. 'Lad,' he says. 'Y' be missin't parts!'

"'M' ancestor says, 'Aye.'

"'Why'd y' nae hae transplants?'

"'It was nae possible,' Selkirk explains. 'Y' see, till recent, Ah was a pirate.'

"The doc thinkit tha' makit sense, an proceeds wi' th' exam. Whae he's done, he says, 'Sir, y'be't healthy aye a MacDonald.'

"'Exceptin' tha' missin't parts.'

"So Selkirk, he explainit: 'Y'see't tha' missin't leg? Wi' the peg? Ah was boardin't a richun's yacht, an' th' lock door caught me.'

"Th' medico listen't, mos' fascinated.

"'Th' hook?' Selkirk gie on, 'Tha' be from't ae laser blast. Took m' paw off clean't ae whistle.'

"'An' the eye?' the doc asks.

"Selkirk, e' fingers th' patch. 'Th' eye? Tha's frae seagull crap.'

"Th' wee surgeon's a' puzzled an' all.

"'Seagull crap?'

"'Aye. Ah was dockyard, starin't up ae a crane, an a gull go't o'er an' deposits.'

"'But how can seagull crap...'

"'Ah, doctor, y'see, Ah'd only had the hook twa days.'"

Sten sought for the proper response and then found it. "Clottin' Romans!" And then he focused his attention back on the warning screens.

The *San Jacinto*, keeping itself sunward of the tumbling tramp freighter, matched orbits with the pinwheeling ship and nudged closer. Then a volunteer officer, his suit visor at maximum opacity, jetted a line across to one of the *Montebello*'s tie-down pads. Then the destroyer's winches, at their lowest gearing, drew the two ships together.

Lavonne had assumed that the *Montebello*'s lock system would not match his, in spite of Imperial design regulations, so he had the accordion tube ready. It inflated and spread out, fitting and sealing over the *Montebello*'s lock.

Lavonne, an officer who believed in leading from the front, was suited and waiting inside the *San Jacinto*'s lock. Behind him twenty sailors were suited up. The lock, one passageway, and a room were set up for the anticipated burnt crewmembers of the *Montebello*.

"Ten kilos, sir."

"All hands, seal suits." He, his twenty sailors, and the rest of the crew of the ship snapped their faceplates closed.

"Open the outer lock."

"Outer lock door opening, sir."

Air whooshed from the lock chamber into the accordion tube as the atmospheric pressures equalized. Lavonne grabbed the line running down the center of the tube and hand-over-handed to the *Montebello*'s lock.

He keyed it open then he and his chief medical officer stepped inside. Lavonne punched the emergency code that allowed both lock doors to open simultaneously, and waited as atmosphere reequalized. He was braced for almost anything—null-atmosphere with exploded bodies; fire-blackened men and women; mutiny; chaos. *Almost* anything.

What he saw was three men. All wore Imperial uniforms. The slender man in front had the rank tabs of a captain in the Imperial Guard. All three men had willyguns aimed at his chest.

Lavonne gaped, but before he could recover, the captain said, "Imperial Service, Commander. I am commandeering your ship!"

CHAPTER FIFTY-ONE

THE MEETING ROOM was a hush of diplomats. It was packed with the Tahn contingent and the Emperor's aides. In the far corner of the room the Emperor himself huddled in conference with Lord Kirghiz and Tanz Sullamora. Underlings on both sides were waiting for the final word. Was there to be an agreement or were they about to go to war?

If they had been inside the Emperor's head when the Tahn delegation arrived for the final meeting, there would have been no question. He had noted that everyone, from the lowest-ranking Tahn lord to Lord Kirghiz himself, was dressed in formal uniform. They were decked out in emerald green cloaks, red tunics, and green trousers. The tunics were covered with a rainbow of ribbons and dangling medals.

The Eternal Emperor covered a smile when he saw them; people put on their best for a party, not a declaration of war. He himself was dressed in his most simple uniform: It was a rich, light gray. And he wore only one decoration: his rank as head of state—a small gold button with the letters AM2 over a background of the null-element's atomic structure. The Eternal Emperor had pointed out to Mahoney once that the way to stand out in a crowd of gold braid was to upstage with simplicity. "When you're the ultimate boss," he once observed, "you don't have to announce it."

The Emperor rose to his feet and extended a hand to Kirghiz. "Then we're agreed?"

Lord Kirghiz fought to maintain a dignified face. But he couldn't help his smile of victory. "Agreed."

"Then let's leave the details to our staffs," the Emperor said. "We can dot our i's and cross our t's on a mutually beneficial date.

"Now, I have taken the liberty of anticipating our peaceful solution to the late difficulties. Gentlemen. Ladies. If I may invite you to a small dinner of appreciation."

He waved his hand and huge doors hissed open behind him. The Tahn craned their necks to see a richness of food and drink yawning out behind the Emperor. There were loud cheers, much laughter, and the Eternal Emperor led his guests into the banquet room.

The banquet was the highlight of Marr and Senn's long career. They had spared nothing to lay out one of the most exotic official dinners in Imperial history.

To begin with, they had been faced with the task of making the enormous ship's banquet hall feel cozy. So they'd ordered the bulkheads moved in, and then draped them in soft colors to warm the atmosphere. The tables were artfully placed so that no one felt cut off from the main attraction, the Emperor and Kirghiz, who were seated across from one another at the head table. They had also gutted the lighting system and installed indirect illumination that picked out the gleam of silver and polish of plate and highlighted the appetizing dishes being served.

The greatest miracle was the food itself. Naturally, since the Emperor was the host, the menu consisted of Tahn dishes, offering condiments and spices that the caterers knew would compliment and entice the Tahn palate.

As for service, they went one step further. The ultimate in luxury was to be served by a person, rather than a machine or even a high-priced waiter bot. Therefore, Marr and Senn had pressed the Praetorian Guards into service. Behind each diner was a Guardsman in full dress who, at the slightest gesture, would pour wine, change a dish, or sweep something out of the way.

The man most pleased with the arrangement was Admiral Ledoh. He couldn't have planned it better himself. He picked up his wine goblet and took a small sip. He had to admit that Marr and Senn were a very talented pair. It was unfortunate that their greatest banquet was to be their last.

Ledoh glanced over to Colonel Fohlee, who was seated at the far end of the table. Ledoh raised his glass to Fohlee in a silent toast. Fohlee returned the salute.

CHAPTER FIFTY-TWO

IN A TIME when subspace communication was nearly perfect, the ship-to-ship wire-line was as archaic as a speaking tube. But not off NG 467H. And so the bot jetted out toward the *Normandie* on peroxide rockets, trailing wire behind.

Its circuitry may have been thirty years old and out of use, but it still told the bot to home . . . home *there* . . . on that ring of sensitive metal . . . closing . . . reverse . . . jets . . . and the com-line clicked home and the line was open to the *Normandie*.

"This is Dr. Shapiro," came the voice from the *Normandie*. "How many casualties do you have?"

"This is Commander Lavonne. Thirty-five. My med officer says twelve are critical, third-degree flash burns, unstable. All others second- or third-degree burns, semi-stable."

"Stand-by."

Half-moon clamps slid out from the *Normandie*, locked onto the *San Jacinto* and pulled the two ships' cargo doors into proximity mating, and the doors opened.

Sten's forty Gurkhas spilled out into the *Normandie*'s hold firing. Each carried not only his kukris and willygun, but a stungun hung on a retracting combat sling around his neck.

Sten's orders had been simple: 1. anyone you see is to be taken out; 2. if they are unarmed, stun them—if they are armed or violent, kill them; 3. find the Emperor and secure him; 4. no one, emphasis *no one*, is to approach the Emperor under any circumstances—anyone, no matter what explanation or rank, who tries is to be killed.

Gurkhas being Gurkhas, and appreciating simple orders, every person in the hold was down and unconscious in five seconds. Even the "talker," linked to the *Normandie*'s command center, had no time to report that the ship was being attacked.

On command, as if it were a drill, Corporal Luç Kesare stepped forward with a napkin-covered platter. Kirghiz turned and smiled, awaiting the new dish, as Kesare's left hand retained the platter and his dagger-holding right shot out, the blade going through Kirghiz's smiling mouth, through his palate, and into his brain.

And so the slaughter started...

CHAPTER FIFTY-THREE

THE COLUMN OF Gurkhas, Sten at its head, was doubling silently through the crew quarters central corridor when the ship's PA system blared: "All hands...the banquet room...somebody...they're trying to kill the Emperor—" The voice stopped and confused sounds chaosed for a moment before the system went dead.

Crewmen stumbled out into the corridor and went down as the Gurkhas stunned them.

At a lift tube Sten raised a hand and the forty men were motionless. He issued orders sending half his men, under Havildar-Major Harkaman Limby, up through officers' territory with orders to secure the *Normandie*'s com center and control room. The other twenty followed Sten toward the banquet room.

The huge main doors to the banquet room were yawning open when Sten and Alex sprinted up. Sounds of fighting raged somewhere deep inside the room. At Sten's signal, Alex and the Gurkhas cautiously edged their way inside.

The work of art that Marr and Senn had created was gone. Tables were overturned and smoking. The room was ankle-deep in smashed plates and smeared food. Horribly mutilated corpses grinned up at the Gurkhas.

Sten and the others crept through a long, twisting aisle of gore. It was hard for them to keep their footing in the nightmare mess. Sten noted the many dead Praetorians and Tahn. Sprinkled here and there were the bodies of Gurkhas who had died fighting for their Emperor.

Alex viewed the massacre, his eyes hard and cold. "Aye," he said. "Tha be ae betrayal worthy a' th' Campbells."

Sten noted with relief that the Emperor's body was not among the carnage.

Just past the end of the head table was a circle of perhaps fifteen Praetorian traitors, all dead, and all with gaping wounds. In the center of the circle was a Gurkha who had been shot through the throat. Sten recognized him as Jemedar Kulbir. He had died on his oath to protect the Eternal Emperor.

"Yon lies a hero, lad," Alex whispered reverently.

Before Sten could answer, a sudden blaze of fire erupted from a corridor off the banquet area.

"Go!" Sten shouted, and they hurdled the remaining bodies and charged across the room.

As they turned the corner, they found a squad of Praetorians mopping up the last of a three-man team of Gurkhas. Sten had just enough time to see Subadar-Major Limbu draw his kukri and suicide-charge the knot of men. Two Praetorians died before they even had time to open fire, and then Limbu fell.

Sten's Gurkhas sprayed the Praetorians from behind.

In a blink, fifteen more were dead, and Sten's people were sprinting past on the trail of the Emperor.

CHAPTER FIFTY-FOUR

THE EMPEROR BOOTED Tanz Sullamora's chubby body down the companionway, then turned, willygun in hand, and went down the ladder after him. As his feet went off the risers onto the handrails, braking his sliding descent, part of his mind was mildly amused that his body still remembered how to move in an emergency.

The Emperor hit the gun-deck plates and threw himself to one side as an AM2 round exploded where he should have been standing. Four rounds went back up the companionway before the Praetorian's chest exploded. The Emperor kept his finger twitching on the trigger, and hosed the gunblast across the top of the companionway. The antimatter rounds ripped the top of the ladder away, and the Emperor shoulder-blocked it down.

"That'll give 'em a minute, figuring how to get down," he said.

The Emperor took half of that minute considering his position. When the Praetorian had killed Kirghiz, the Emperor had frozen momentarily. A tiny segment of his mind snarled at him: Maybe it's time to get in a couple of bar brawls and get the moves back.

The Gurkhas had saved his life during that blur of death, as short brown men swarmed the central table. Naik Thaman Gurung had wrapped the Emperor in his arms and brought him to the floor, taking a willygun blast in his own body. Subadar-Major Chittahang Limbu had a willygun on full auto, spraying rounds into the banquet room.

The Emperor had rolled out from under Thaman's corpse, grabbed the Gurkha's weapon, and put his troops into motion. Find a barricade, he kept thinking, as his group fought their way toward the exit. The Emperor might have chosen to retreat toward his own quarters, but the ex-engineer part of his mind propelled him toward the ship's stern, toward the *Normandie*'s engine spaces.

He realized the handful of Gurkhas under Subadar-Major Limbu, who set up the rear guard, could only hold for a few moments. But those few moments would give him a start toward the engine room. Once there, the Emperor knew, he could run any number of assassins round and round into oblivion.

The Emperor surveyed the gun deck. Except for the missile launchers, gun racks, and gun positions studding the passage that curled from near the ship's nose back to end before the fuel/engine areas, the *Normandie*'s gun deck would have looked like any conventional liner's promenade deck. Not here, he decided. This isn't a place for even a moment's stand.

Ledoh was already waiting at the next hatchway that led down toward the kitchen areas.

The Emperor motioned, and his men moved. He was mildly startled to realize that he had only Sullamora, Ledoh, and two Gurkhas left.

And even more surprised when he caught himself enjoying what was going on.

Sten, Alex, and the Gurkhas dropped down to the gun deck through an overhead shell hoist. Fifty meters away a knot of Praetorians was crowding a down-passage.

Twenty of them—and Sten's eyes registered that one of the Praetorians had seen him and was shouting an alarm.

As Sten went down, his hand slapped a red switch on the wall. The switch read LOAD.

A Goblin missile sitting on the overhead of the gun deck slid smoothly down track toward a launcher on the far side of the Praetorians.

The system could launch one missile per launcher every six seconds, so the missile moved very, very rapidly down the loading track, approaching a speed of nearly 60 kilometers per hour when it intersected the Praetorians. One thousand kilos of steel contacting a few hundred kilos of flesh at that speed produces casualties.

By Kilgour's count five Praetorians were down before the remaining fifteen found shelter behind launchers, gun tubes, and such, and opened up.

"Ah hae quite enow a' this drakh," he muttered and took action.

The *Normandie*'s armament was intended not only for deep space but also for planetary action. Of course atmospheric weapons such as chain guns were normally maglocked in place behind the sealed ports they fired through. An assortment of weapons was racked on the bulkhead, but all were intended for firing from a mount, and—of course—out-ship. One of those devices was a flare projector which, under normal circumstances, took four men to wrestle to the firing port.

Sergeant Major Alex Kilgour, heavy-worlder, was not normal under any circumstances. He had the projector off the wall, loaded, aimed, and the firing switch keyed before anyone could react.

The flare burst down the long corridor, hit the far bulkhead, ricocheted, and ... flared.

A signal flare that is intended to be seen for about half a light-second makes quite an explosion when it goes off in a ten-meter-by-ten-meter passageway. The Gurkhas and Sten had barely enough time to flatten ahead of the oncoming fireball before the *Normandie*'s automatic extinguishing system *yeek*ed and dumped several tons of retardant on what it perceived as a fire.

Too late for the fifteen little mounds of charcoal that had been Praetorians.

Sten and his troopies hot-footed down that melted companionway to find their Emperor.

CHAPTER FIFTY-FIVE

MARR AND SENN had taken refuge inside an enormous sonic oven. They were in the vast stainless-steel kitchen of the liner when the massacre began. When they heard the hysterical shouts on the PA system, they had wisely decided to stay put.

Senn hugged Marr close. "When they're done," Senn said with a shiver, "they'll hunt us down and kill us, too." He stroked the fur of his lifelong companion. "Oh, well. It's been a good love, hasn't it?"

Marr suddenly rose to his full height. "Bugger them," he said.

"Do we have to?" Senn asked.

"One thing we know, dear," Marr said, "is kitchens. And if those brutes invade *my* kitchen they are going to be a sorry set of humans."

He began bustling about, getting himself ready for the final confrontation. Senn saw what he was doing and leaped up, all thoughts of a tender death swept from his mind.

They started with the sonar oven. It was about three meters high and as many wide. Inside were many cooking racks and a retractable spit that could hold an entire bullock. The cooking source was a wide-beam sound projector, which looked somewhat like a large camera, mounted on hydraulic lifts. When the oven was operated, thick protective safety doors automatically locked, and the projector swept across the food, spitting bursts of ultrasound to cook whatever was inside.

The first thing Marr did was smash the safety lock. Then the two of them muscled at the sonar cooker.

Many boots thundered just outside the kitchen, and the two turned to see the Eternal Emperor back into the huge room. He was dragging Tanz Sullamora with him, and firing back through the doorway. A split second later they saw first the chamberlain and then the two remaining Gurkhas follow. Naiks Ram Sing Rana and Agansing Rai shouted defiance at their pursuers and sprayed them with their willyguns.

They ducked as the Praetorians returned fire. Behind them, the stainless steel walls of the kitchen hissed and bubbled and turned to molten metal.

"This way," the Emperor shouted, and he led his tiny group toward the kitchen's emergency exit. Just beyond that was a tunnel leading to the main storehouse area and then the engine rooms.

A thunder of Praetorians followed them. Ram gave a soft cry and dropped as a willygun round sizzled into his abdomen. The rest of the Praetorians crowded toward the Emperor's group, who were just disappearing through the emergency-exit door.

Without hesitating, Senn turned his body into a furry ball and rolled out of the oven they'd retreated to. He palmed the KITCHEN STEAM-CLEAN button and then dove back into the oven.

Steam hissed from nozzles in the walls. Sanitation sniffers instantly analyzed the area for foreign—meaning biological—objects and then directed the huge volumes of steam on the invading organisms.

Eleven Praetorians opened their mouths as one to scream. Their lungs filled with intensely hot steam and were parboiled before sound could reach their lips. Their flesh swelled and blistered, then the blisters broke and ran.

The cleaning process took only thirty seconds—just as the instruction manual predicted!—before shutting off. By then, all eleven Praetorians were dead. Or dying. The human body is tough.

More bootheels, more firing, and another group exploded through the doorway, Fohlee at the head. He saw Senn's small face peering from the oven. "Kill them!"

Fohlee shouted. A squad leapt forward as Marr and Senn rolled out of the oven. Fohlee and four of his Praetorians ran for the emergency exit the Emperor had taken. But the door was momentarily blocked.

Meanwhile the flying squad of Praetorians was pounding toward Marr and Senn.

"Help me!" squeaked Marr, and Senn slid his tiny shoulders under the sonar cooker and strained upward.

Slowly . . . slowly . . . it came up.

"*Now!*" Marr shouted, and the two of them jumped through a rain of willygun fire. Marr just had time to hit the cooker button before they were safe behind a steel food bin.

The lens of the sonar cooker blinked and then glowed full on. The invisible but deadly beam coned outward as the squad of Praetorians charged directly into it.

Marr and Senn huddled behind the bin, listening to the terrible sounds of the Praetorians dying. Within seconds every member of the squad had been cooked. The high-frequency waves heated from the inside out, and so, even before the flesh began to curl and smoke and brown, their internal organs exploded outward, spattering fifty meters of kitchen wall with gobs of flesh.

Marr peered out at the gore and shuddered. Senn tried to peek out after him, but Marr pushed his lover back, saving him from what he knew would be a lifetime trauma. Marr felt a small place of beauty shrivel inside him.

Many shouts and thundering. Marr looked up at the main entrance to the kitchen and repositioned himself at the cooker control button again. Whoever came through the door would die like the squad of men before. His finger was almost hitting the button when he saw the slim figure crash into the room.

In one heartbeat he recognized Sten and his finger brushed past the button. Marr didn't even wait to see what happened next. He dropped back behind the bin, beside Senn.

Marr looked at the large luminous eyes of his friend. "I almost killed our young captain!"

He buried his face in Senn's soft fur and wept.

* * *

Sten and Alex back-shot the four Praetorians who were straining at the emergency-exit door. Fohlee had just enough time to spot them, and crammed his body behind the butchering machine, a free-standing bot of red-enameled steel. Its three-by-five-meter bulk stood motionless, razor-sharp knives and meat-gripping claws still and lifeless.

Sten dropped to his knees and edged his slender body into the gap between the machine and the walls. He pushed slowly down the dark tunnel. Would Fohlee keep moving, or was he waiting just around the turn? There was almost no room to maneuver, and Sten had to shift his gun to his left hand to move forward.

There! He saw the black snout of Fohlee's weapon, and Sten struck out at it, losing his balance and falling to the floor. But his knuckles hit cold metal, and he felt the weapon rip from Fohlee's grip then heard the gun clatter to the kitchen floor. Sten kick-rolled out of the narrow tunnel and started to his feet. A heavy blow sent him down again, and he twisted his body clumsily as he fell, just avoiding Fohlee's dagger. He saw the shadow of a boot flashing down at him, but he managed to get three fingers on a heel and twist. Fohlee staggered backward, slamming against the bot.

Machinery came to life with a shriek, and the bot's upper body whirled, meat-grabbing claws searching for flesh. Before Sten could recover, Fohlee dodged the claws and picked up his gun. The two brought their weapons up at the same time. But a meat hook on a chain swung out of the bot and caught Fohlee in the throat. He screamed in agony as the hook dragged him into the butcher bot's claws.

Sten found himself watching in awful fascination as the machine skillfully dealt with Fohlee. Within seconds, many knives had skinned him while still alive. Tiny hoses snaked out to suck up the blood. Saws whirred in to cut the joints, and boning knives flicked in and out to separate the flesh.

Fohlee's final scream was still echoing through the

kitchen when the last of him had been carved, packaged, and shipped into cold storage.

Absently, Sten reached out and shut off the machine. Then he walked heavily around the butcher bot to find Alex.

CHAPTER FIFTY-SIX

POWER SOURCES AND engines may have changed immensely, but any twenty-first-century deep-space blackganger would have been at home in the *Normandie*'s engine room. The chambers were the same huge echoing metal rooms, throbbing with unseen power. The gleaming AM2 drive units could have been diesel-electric or nuclear, and the same walkways spidered up, around, and over bewildering machinery and arcane gauges.

Since the *Normandie* wasn't under drive, only one watch officer and a wiper had been on shift, and they lay in pools of blood.

The Emperor spotted the two Praetorians one level up, crouched behind an AM2 feedway. He considered, then aimed carefully and fired four times. The four rounds hit on either side of the spiderwalk and cut it free, and the Praetorians dropped. Just like skeet, the Emperor thought as he snap-shot both men before they crashed to the deck.

"Come on, Admiral. CYA," he shouted, and Ledoh and the last remaining Gurkha helped him weasel a portable welding rig to the emergency door. The Emperor was slightly proud of himself as his body-memory adjusted the oxy-gas mix, fired the torch, and spot-welded the emergency hatchway they'd come through shut.

"That'll give us some more time, Mik."

Ledoh was glaring at him, and another part of the Emperor's brain wondered what the hell was going on with the man. When the shooting had started, Ledoh'd been one of the first to pull out a service pistol, but it had been knocked from his hand by what the Emperor considered an overly protective Gurkha. The man couldn't be scared, the Emperor thought. But maybe he is, he went on, as he led the three men up catwalks. Maybe it's been too long since he'd had somebody shooting directly at his tail.

Maybe he's as scared as Tanz Sullamora, who was wheezing up behind the Emperor, his face near-coronary flushed.

Ledoh waited until all four men were on the next platform. Now, he decided. Now. That damned Gurkha had spoiled his first chance. Now was the time, and his ceremonial sword was in his hand and he was lunging, the blade aimed for the middle of the Emperor's back.

But just as the conspirators had underestimated the lethality of the Gurkhas, so did Ledoh underestimate the reaction time of Naik Agansing Rai.

Rai—Sten's ex-batman—somehow leaped between the Emperor and the blade—and was spitted neatly through the lungs. He sagged down, almost dragging the blade from Ledoh's hands.

Ledoh stepped in, pulled the blade from the man's chest, and came back for a swing—and then Tanz Sullamora became a hero.

The fat man somehow managed to wildly swing his willygun—the willygun he had no idea how to fire—into Ledoh's ribs, staggering him into the platform's side railing. Sullamora was still reacting to his own bravery as Ledoh pivoted back and slammed the sword's pommel into his neck. Gasping for air, Sullamora went down, and Ledoh was in lunging position...

To find the Emperor standing four meters away, at the end of the platform. He was empty-handed, his willygun still slung across his back.

"That figures," the Emperor said. "Do I get to know why?"

Ledoh could barely speak—all those years, all the plans, all the hatred. But he managed, "Rob Gades was my son."

And then he was attacking.

Again the bystanding part of the Emperor's mind was wondering who in hell Gades was as he pulled a breaker bar from the emergency fire kit on the bulkhead behind him, held it two-handed in front of him, and parried Ledoh's blade clear.

Ledoh's eyes glittered as he stop-stanced closer and slashed at the Emperor's waist, a cut that was again deflected, and then the Emperor was in motion, left foot kicking out into Ledoh's chest.

A sword against a crowbar appears an unequal fight— which it is, as several people who'd pulled blades on the Emperor during his ship engineer days had found to their considerable surprise.

As Ledoh tried to recover, the Emperor slid one hand down the bar and swung, two-handed. The steel crashed against Ledoh's sword, snapping the blade just above the hilt, before the Emperor changed his swing and the bar smashed back against Ledoh's forearm.

The bone snapped loudly and Ledoh screamed in pain. Clutching his arm, white bone protruding through his tunic sleeve, he went to his knees.

The Emperor studied him. "You poor bastard," he said, not unsympathetically. "You poor, sorry bastard." He stepped back, to the emergency com next to the fire kit, and considered the next step.

Kilgour was wrenching mightily at the welded-shut hatch into the engine spaces when Sten elbowed him aside.

The knife popped from its sheath into his hand, and he held his wrist in a brace then forced the knife through the hatchway itself. The crystal blade sliced through the steel as if it were plas. Sten made two cuts around the blackened areas that marked the weld, then shoulder-blocked the hatch open and was into the engine room, kukri in one hand, his own knife in the other.

Four bodies... no Emperor. He scanned above him, then was up the ladders, moving like a stalking cat.

Levels overhead he could see two more sprawled bodies and two men.

Emperor. Still alive. Praise a few dozen gods. Around the walkway. Other man... on his knees. Ledoh.

Neither the Emperor nor Ledoh heard Sten.

Sten was on the catwalk just below the two when he saw Ledoh force himself out of his pain. His unbroken hand went back into his waistband and emerged with a tiny Mantis willygun, and Sten was only halfway up the ladder as Ledoh aimed the pistol.

A kukri cannot be thrown. It's single-edged, and its bulbous-ended off-balance blade guarantees that, once thrown, the knife will spin wildly.

It is, however, almost a full kilo of steel.

Sten overhanded the long knife at Ledoh, in a desperate last chance to save the Emperor's life.

At best the blade should have clubbed Ledoh down. But the whirling blade sank point first into the back of Grand Chamberlain Mik Ledoh, severing his spine.

Ledoh, dead before his finger could touch the willygun's trigger, spasmed through the guardrails to thump finally, soggily, on the deck plates many meters below.

Sten came up the last few steps and stood looking at the Emperor. One or the other of them should probably have said something terribly dramatic. But dramatic gestures happen, most often, during the retelling. The two bloodstained men just stared at each other in silence and relief.

CHAPTER FIFTY-SEVEN

NAKED UNDER A bright summer sun, Haines considered perfection. The drink comfortably close at hand was icy; the sun was hot; a cool breeze from the forest below kept her houseboat comfortable.

Almost perfect, she corrected herself.

One thing missing, and one problem.

The last months, after the Emperor had returned to Prime World, had been very long indeed, and the attempts to clean up the mess had begun.

Haines was fairly grateful that she'd only been witness to part of them; Sten had told her about the rest.

Evidently, after the last Praetorian had been hunted down on the *Normandie*, the Imperial fleet had immediately scudded since even the Eternal Emperor couldn't cobble together any believable explanation that the Tahn would accept for the deaths of their chief lord and his retinue.

Kirghiz or one of his underlings must have been under orders to report regularly, because barely two days out, the fleet found itself pursued. One Tahn battleship and cruiser and destroyer escorts should have been an over-match for the *Normandie* and its escorts. But the Emperor had already called in reinforcements and two full battleship squadrons rendezvoused with the *Normandie*.

The Tahn fought bravely and in ignorance. Despite all attempts to communicate, they fought to the last man under complete radio silence. Sten never knew if they thought they were rescuing Kirghiz or revenging him.

On return to Prime, the Emperor immediately attempted

to explain to the Tahn, but diplomatic relations were severed and all Tahn personnel were withdrawn.

Haines had barely noticed, since she'd been too busy rounding up the surviving conspirators. She'd never arrested so many wealthy, high-ranking people in her life.

Then there was a show trial because the Emperor was hoping that somehow the Tahn would listen to the truth. Of course they wouldn't—any good totalitarian knows he can always find somebody to pin a crime on. Even attempts to convince the Tahn of the truth by neutral diplomats from cultures constitutionally incapable of dishonesty were ignored.

The series of trials was mind-numbing. At least Haines had the opportunity to testify in open court. Sten, under Imperial orders, gave his testimony from a sealed chamber, his voice electronically altered to prevent any possibility of identification.

In spite of the defense counsels' howls about star chambers, ninety-five percent of the conspirators were found guilty—and treason and attempted regicide were still capital crimes.

Even the acquitted five percent weren't free of the Emperor's vengeance. Just the day before a small item on the vid reported that a recently freed industrialist's yacht had exploded with him aboard... Haines closed down that line of thought. She was contemplating perfection, and to her even Imperially ordered assassination was still murder.

The sun was slowly moving her toward sleep, and she was musing on casually lustful thoughts when a flit hummed nearby. She forced herself awake and up, reaching for a wrap. Then she recognized Sten in the flit and lay back, her thoughts becoming somewhat less casual.

Sten tied up to the houseboat, wandered through the kitchen, fielded a beer, and joined her on the deck.

"How'd it go?" she asked.

"Hell if I know," Sten said. "Better and worse."

"Shed and tell, Captain."

"Uh... well, that's part of the good news. I just got promoted."

"Well pour the bubbly and get naked, Commander."

Sten followed orders, stripped, and lay down beside her. He grunted in animal satisfaction. Haines waited as long as she could.

"Come on, Sten. Talk to me!"

The day had, indeed, been better and worse than Sten expected.

After the *Normandie* returned to Prime, while Sten had been retained as commander of the Gurkhas, he'd actually been detached for special duties, which included the endless appearances in court.

The Gurkhas had been built back up to the strength and were headed by Subadar-Major Chittahang Limbu, even though he was still technically recuperating from his wounds.

Sten had only been in the palace to eat and sleep, and the few hallway encounters he'd had with the Emperor had been worrisomely formal and brief.

Until the day's Imperial summons.

When Sten entered, saluted, and reported, the Emperor had been sitting, completely still, behind his desk.

Long moments passed before he spoke.

Sten had been expecting several things to be said. None of them were right.

"Captain, are you ready to go to war?"

Sten blinked, found that all his potential responses sounded dumb, and stayed silent.

"I will make a prediction, Captain. Ex Cathedra Eyes Only. Within five E-years we will be fighting the Tahn."

The Emperor took slight pity. "At ease, Captain Sten. Sit down."

Sten was somewhat relieved. He didn't figure that the Emperor ever busted somebody out of the service if he allowed the clot to be seated first.

"Well, Captain? Your thoughts?"

Sten was perplexed. Like any professional military man, he truly believed the somewhat contradictory line that a soldier's job is to avoid war.

The Emperor seemed to be slightly prescient. "It's gonna be a bitch when it comes.

"By the way. No way am I wrong. Intelligence says that every Tahn shipyard has converted to warship construction. The Tahn are buying up every particle of AM2 they can get, no matter what the price.

"Also—and I'm keeping this off the vid—there've been a whole clottin' group of skirmishes with my normal patrol ships around the Tahn worlds. Aw hell. Why am I lying to you? Every spy ship I send in they send back full of holes."

The Emperor then took out a flask from his desk. Sten felt slightly more relieved—first sit down and then maybe a drink. Maybe he would keep his captain's bars. "The reason I have been avoiding you, Captain, is that this whole sorry-ass mess is something I've been trying not to think about.

"So anybody who had anything to do with it was on my drakh list, frankly. Being an Emperor means never having to say you're wrong if you want things that way."

He poured into two small metal cups, and Sten recognized the smell of Stregg.

"This stuff gets to you after a while," the Emperor said, but he made no move to offer a cup to Sten. "Remember when we got loaded on Empire Day?"

Sten did.

"Remember what I told you?"

Sten remembered.'

"Well, I took the next step *for* you." The Emperor took from his desk drawer a set of orders and tossed them on his desk.

"Don't bother reading them now. You're reassigned. Flight school. Oh yeah. By the way. That chubby thug of yours?"

"Sergeant Major Kilgour?"

"Him. You wonder where he is?"

Sten had. Alex had disappeared most mysteriously a month or two earlier.

"Yeah. I lifted him because he was actually applying through channels to get married. To some cop or other.

Clottin' idiot. Neckbreakers like him shouldn't ever get married. Anyway, he's now learning how to make like a big bird, too.

"Also he ain't a sergeant major anymore. I kicked him up to warrant officer. If he's gonna be in the clottin' navy, at least he won't have to put up with their silly class system."

The Emperor picked up and fingered his cup. "Captain, you might want to return to some kind of position of attention."

Sten was standing, locked and rigid in an instant.

"The other thing"—and the Emperor reached into his desk yet again and took out a small blue box—"is you're now a commander. Here's your insignia." He shoved the box across to Sten. "Now, pick up that cup."

Sten obeyed.

"I'm gonna call the toast—it's to you, Commander. Because no way I'll ever see you again."

The Emperor stood. "To your health, Commander Sten!"

To Sten, the Stregg tasted very odd indeed.

Haines was running all this input—less the Emperor's certainty of imminent war, which Sten had not mentioned—as Sten finished his beer, went back into the boat, and got another.

"Another thing I picked up," he went on after he sat. "You're going to get some kind of promotion, too."

But Haines was considering something else. "So you're going to go off and become a junior birdman. When?"

"That's the rest of the good news," Sten said. "It seems, uh, I've come into some money." Ida's illicitly acquired and invested funds had finally caught up with him, and Sten was sitting on more credits than he believed existed.

"Also me and you're on long leave before we report to our new duty stations."

Haines smiled, took a sip of her drink, and then winked. "Hey sailor. You want to fool around?"

Sten started laughing and knelt beside her. She pulled him down, and he felt her breasts and her lips, and then there was nothing but the blinding warmth of the sun itself.

About the Authors

CHRIS BUNCH is a Ranger—an airborne-qualified Vietnam vet—who's written about phenomena as varied as the Hell's Angels, the Rolling Stones, and Ronald Reagan.
ALLAN COLE grew up in the CIA in odd spots like Okinawa, Cyprus, and Taiwan. He's been a professional chef, investigative reporter, and national news editor of a major West Coast daily newspaper. He's won half a dozen writing awards in the process.

BUNCH AND COLE, friends since high school, have collaborated on everything from the world's worst pornographic novel to over seventy-five television scripts, as well as a feature movie. In addition to their *Sten* novels, they are the authors of the Pulitzer Prize nominee, *A Reckoning for Kings*, a novel about the Vietnam war. Most recently they were story execs on Fox-TV's *Werewolf*.

Allan Cole and Chris Bunch

present imaginative,

suspenseful adventures

for die hard science-fiction fans